everything
grows

HIGH PRAISE FOR

everything grows

BY AIMEE HERMAN

A SWEET AND moving read about a young person growing up, coming out, and trying to find the right words to speak their truth. The awesome soundtrack is a bonus.
  EASY VEGAN

EVERYTHING GROWS WILL grow inside you like a revelation, slowly unfolding to a shape that is vulnerable, raw and beautifully alive. . . . There's tender wisdom and a wonderfully rendered young voice that anyone can recognize as human and real—all against a backdrop of riot grrrl rebellion. Herman writes a real story, teaching everyone a little about life as lived— genuinely and in discovery.
  MAX WOLF VALERIO, author, *The Testosterone Files; The Criminal: The Invisibility of Parallel Forces*

EVERYTHING GROWS IS haunting. It touches the darkness of bullying and suicide, yet brims with hope. Aimee Herman's tender debut novel is an achingly real exploration of grief, self-discovery, forgiveness, and love.
  MEAGAN BROTHERS, author, *Weird Girl and What's His Name*

SET IN THE decade of grunge rock and ill-advised do-it-yourself body piercings, Aimee Herman's *Everything Grows* chronicles a sometimes heartbreaking, sometimes funny journey to acceptance, both of self and others. Eleanor Fromme is a witty, kind, and conflicted narrator who could teach many people in our nation a lot about empathy.
  JULIA WATTS, author, *Quiver*

EVERYTHING GROWS IS a work of healing. It describes coming out as a lifelong process of discovery. Friendship, disfunction, parenting good and bad, and learning to love are unspooled here against a background of exquisite caring. It is the rare read that leaves one a wiser person.
  STEVEN TAYLOR, author, *False Prophet: Fieldnotes from the Punk Underground;* editor, *Don't Hide the Madness: William S. Burroughs in Conversation with Allen Ginsberg*

everything grows

a novel

Aimee Herman

THREE ROOMS PRESS
New York, NY

Everything Grows
BY Aimee Herman

ISBN 978-1-941110-68-3 (trade paperback original)
ISBN 978-1-941110-69-0 (Epub)
Library of Congress Control Number: 2018962451
TRP-072

Publication Date: May 7, 2019

BISAC category code
YAF031000 YOUNG ADULT FICTION / LGBT
YAF037000 YOUNG ADULT FICTION / Loners & Outcasts
YAF058020 YOUNG ADULT FICTION / Social Themes / Bullying
YAF016000 YOUNG ADULT FICTION / Epistolary (Letters & Diaries)

First edition

COVER DESIGN AND ILLUSTRATION:
Victoria Black: www.thevictoriablack.com

BOOK DESIGN:
KG Design International: www.katgeorges.com

DISTRIBUTED BY:
PGW/Ingram: www.pgw.com

Three Rooms Press
New York, NY
www.threeroomspress.com
info@threeroomspress.com

"There are years that ask questions and years that answer."

—*Zora Neale Hurston*

For Romy

And for Andrew

everything
grows

before

Dear Elinore,

My mom used to read to me when I couldn't fall asleep. It was always The Giving Tree, I insisted. The pictures weren't anything special. I liked how sad they were. Kid books are always so happily ever after, you know? And life is just not like that. That boy just keeps taking and taking from the tree until there is nothing else. He carves into it, takes its branches, its apples, leaving just a stump. When I was a kid, I thought about how lucky this boy was to have a tree as his best friend, but what a moron I was to think that. The boy never gave anything to this tree. The boy never asked it what it wanted. Now I hate this book because it reminds me of how blind we are. Everyone just takes. No one really knows me and no one cares to. My parents they have no idea.

You probably read this book a million times, or at least know it. I've seen you in the hallways with your nose in some book—probably for pleasure and not because you have to, you're like that. We've got a weeping willow in our backyard. You know what this is? You probably do. I thought they actually cried like tears on their leaves sort of thing. They look like they're weeping, all hunched over like they found out some bad news and can't seem to recover.

I thought about this one day on the bus ride home from school. For months, I've been collecting ways to do it. There is a tree by the ravine near my house. It's really ~~beutiful~~ beautiful and maybe I've always kind of known that was the one.

1993

THE STORY OF MY FIRST HAIRCUT is legendary. Or at least it is in my family. It has circulated over Thanksgiving meals, in synagogue after prayer time is over and all that is left are slightly stale cookies to munch on during Oneg, and even when my grandfather was slowly dying in the hospital.

It was just after my third birthday. My thick, curly hair had gathered into more knots than a brush could untangle, so Dad grabbed the scissors from the coupon drawer and started cutting. Shirley (my mother) was too distraught to do it. After the first cut, I started to scream.

"You're hurting her," Greta, who was five at the time, yelled.

And then—according to this well-circulated story—I yelled: "You're killing it," meaning my hair. I guess I thought my hair, like everything else on my body, was alive. I didn't understand why my dad would try to cut a piece of me away. So, he stopped and I wouldn't let anyone near my hair again until I was almost six. By then, my head resembled a blond abandoned squirrel's nest.

I'M FIFTEEN NOW, SO OF COURSE I understand that hair is dead. My strands don't scream out when I'm at the hair salon. Though of course, Henny, who has been cutting my hair since I was eight, knows the story too.

Here is what my hair looked like before. It was beautiful, like shampoo commercial hair where the woman throws her head around and each strand glistens as though weaved with tiny suns. Strangers have even stopped me at the grocery store. Or they'd stop Shirley and tell her what gorgeous hair her daughter has. Grandma (Dad's mom) used to ask for my scraps after a haircut. Her hair was thin and straight. No one really understood where my curls came from. But apparently, I was blessed. This word was also used a lot to describe my hair. Anyway, it was long and thick and beautiful and then I cut it.

I don't believe I'm unusual. What I mean is, how else should a teenager react when they find out a classmate has committed suicide? Oh, maybe I should start from the beginning, though I'm not sure where that would be. Beginning of me? Beginning of when I started to realize things out about myself that made me feel different than others? When does this story begin?

We were in second grade together. He sat behind me. Also fourth grade, where I got my first 'D', which I don't think was fair at all, and seventh grade science class, and he is *was* in my English class this year. It's not like we were friends. Hardly. He was my bully. Threw frog guts at me in seventh grade during dissection. He called me "screen door" and "mosquito bites" in front of the whole class, and yet the teacher didn't even notice. Maybe he had a whole roster of people he bullied, but it sure felt like he had his hatred aimed straight toward me. But who cares about any of that now? He's dead.

I was down the block at Dara's house. Her mom (who knows everything about everyone) got a phone call (not sure from who) and went down to the basement where we were playing and asked if we knew him. I don't even remember saying goodbye. I just ran home, rushed upstairs to my bedroom, grabbed the scissors on my desk and started to cut my hair. When someone dies like that, things just stop making sense.

Of course, I understand why I was so upset. So, maybe *that* is where this story starts? But first let me explain what happened after the first cut. Again, I'm fifteen. I don't understand everything about the body, but I get that if I cut my finger, I will bleed and maybe cry, but blood and pain doesn't come out of a haircut. And yet, it was like I could feel every hair being pulled out of my scalp. I just stood in the middle of my bedroom, away from my mirror, because I didn't want to watch what was happening, and cut. The sound was like a slow rip. Not like paper, but well, like something else. My neck itched from the hairs falling against it and the floor caught my curls, creating a puddle of me. I just cut and cut, trying not to imagine him. Trying not to think about why a fifteen-year-old boy would want to kill himself. Trying not to think about Shirley and how I know about the time she tried to kill herself last May, but not about the other times, and there must have been more. Trying not to think about having to visit her on the weekends at that hospital. Angry about what she did, but still trying to be nice to her because she was in a mental hospital that smelled like rotten bandages. I used to call her Shirley in my head, though I'm not sure why. After she tried to leave us, I started saying it out loud.

I threw the scissors down on my bed and slowly walked to my mirror. My hardwood floor was now covered with my hair. Actually, it was really just a messy pile, but it felt like a lot. My hair had reached past my shoulders. The mirror now revealed my new 'do.

"Eleanor!" screamed Shirley.

Well, I couldn't hide in my room forever.

"What did you do to yourself?"

"I cut my hair," I said, plainly.

"I see that. Why?"

"I . . . I don't know. I needed to—"

"Francine just called me. She said you ran out of the house. She also told me about the boy in your grade."

I took a deep breath. Greta was the one who found Shirley, not me. But I had to help get her to throw up. She had swallowed too many of her pills. Greta was incredible. She called for an ambulance, tried to calm me down, took care of things. It's like she knew exactly what to do. I felt paralyzed. I didn't understand what was happening.

"Why would she take too many?" I asked, as though Shirley had forgotten the correct dosage of her anti-depressants.

"El," Greta said, "I think Mom tried to kill herself. Call Dad."

It's very strange when a parent does something wrong. You can't send them to their room and punish them. You can't take away their favorite toy; they don't have any. I never really got to react in the way I needed to, which was apparently by chopping all my hair off and leaving a messy patch of dirty blond nothingness.

Shirley pulled me into her and I could smell the haunt of cigarette smoke against her clothing. She quit while she was in the hospital, but I had a feeling she'd recently started back up. It was kind of like a secret we both knew about but didn't mention.

"Honey, I'm so sorry. Did you know him?"

"No," I said into her chest. "Yeah, I mean, not really."

"Can I make you something? Can I . . . what can I do?"

"Nothing. I just . . . I just want to be alone."

WHILE SHIRLEY WAS IN THE HOSPITAL, Flor—her best friend—watched us. Dad was traveling for work at the time. I missed him, but I got along really well with Flor, and she was happy to take care of us. Dad called every day to check on us. He even visited Shirley in the hospital when he got back into town. It's strange. They've been divorced for like six years now, but it's like they're nicer to each other now that they're not married.

Shirley's doctor at the hospital suggested we try a support group—for survivors of suicide. Dad, Greta and I went each week. Once summer arrived, Greta was hanging out with her friends more—before they all split and went to college—and stopped going to the group. Once Greta went away to college in August, Dad came with me a few more times. I thought about stopping, but actually, I really liked going. I didn't mind going alone. I guess it helped to be able to talk about it openly, to be around others who understood. Recently, Flor started to go with me.

"ELEANOR, DARA IS ON THE PHONE!"

I walked over to my desk to pick up the phone. We used to have only one phone in the whole house. It was in the kitchen with a cord long enough to reach the family room and even the front hallway. Then, we got cordless phones a few years ago. One in the kitchen, one in Shirley's bedroom and Gret and I have one in our bedrooms. I used to love how—depending on the channel—you could hear bits and pieces of neighbors' conversations. There was always some static, but I'd dig out all the wax in my ears just to hear whatever I could. My imagination would always fill in the rest.

"Hey," I said.

"You okay?" Dara asked. "You just ran and—"

"Sorry."

"Want me to come over?"

"Nah."

"Why do you think he—"

"I don't want to talk about it," I said.

"Yeah, okay. I mean, I guess it's extra scary because your mom . . . "

"I really don't want to talk about it."

THAT NIGHT, SHIRLEY TOOK ME TO the mall to get my hair evened out, whatever that means. I asked her if I could dye it. Up to that point, I was only able to use sun-in and my hair was already blond, so I didn't really see the point—though that didn't stop me from using it. Maybe Shirley felt bad or too tired to disagree, but whatever the reason, we went to the beauty supply store on the second floor, got some bleach and manic panic—I couldn't believe it!—and headed home.

"It fades," Shirley said, when we got home. "That's why I didn't battle you earlier. And . . . " she paused, " . . . I understand why this is extra hard, Eleanor. But you know I am better, right? I'm not looking to leave anytime soon. I love you. That has never wavered."

"Yeah, I know. I love you too. If it's okay, I'm gonna try this out."

"Please use an old towel," she said. "And put paper towels on the counter, in case anything drops."

Before the bleach. Before the cranberry-fizz-colored hair dye. Before I started to mourn my dull blond curls. I grabbed the heaping pile of my hair and put it into a plastic Food Town bag. I figured next time we visit Grandma's grave, I can bring her some. I know how much she loved it.

After the bleach. After the cranberry-fizz-colored hair dye. After I started to mourn my dull blond curls.

"Well, next time we lose each other in the mall, I'll easily find you," said Shirley.

"Ugh, is it awful?"

"Well, it certainly looks different from this morning, but it's not terrible."

I feigned a smile.

"Is your homework all done? You ready for school tomorrow?"

"Yeah. I don't know, I . . . Shirley, can I . . . can I ask you something?"

"Eleanor, you know how I feel about you calling me that. Go ahead."

"I feel like there must have been so many bad days. So, what turns a bad day into what you desperately hope is the last day? I mean, what makes someone decide: today I kill myself. Maybe yesterday sucked, but today is just too much."

"I certainly can't answer that for James, but for me . . . oh honey, I got to the point that I thought you and Greta would fare better without me."

"You thought dying would make our lives *better*?"

"I know. I know how ridiculous that sounds, but I wasn't thinking clearly."

"And now?"

"Now, with medication and—"

"But you were on medication. That's what you—"

"Better medication, more regulated. And going to therapy again has really helped. Brinna even mentioned me trying some group therapy. We've been making great headway and she feels like being around others could be really beneficial."

"It could get you to meet people," I said, trying to be optimistic.

"You have, right?"

"What? At the support group? Yeah, I mean, everyone is super nice, I guess. Didn't exactly go there to make friends, but . . . "

"But it gives you the opportunity to understand a little more. To know it's never about the survivors. To understand mental illness."

"Yeah."

Shirley threw her hand into my hair and tousled the tiny amount left. "I like this. Like Debbie Harry or something."

"Who?"

* * *

"THERE IS JUST NO WAY TO prepare for something like this." Ms. Raimondo stood in front of us, as she always does, but she looked different today, like her veins somehow wilted and all the blood inside vanished. I guess we all looked like that today.

James was dead.

"As your homeroom teacher mentioned, there are grief counselors who will be here all week into next, and you can go to them to process what's going—"

"Like instead of going to class?"

Ms. Raimondo just stared at Harris blankly. "Like because you *need* to."

"As I was driving to school today," she said, "I had all these words for you guys, but I guess I . . . lost them." She sort of smiled, as though part of her mouth didn't get the memo that it was supposed to lift. "It's difficult to know what to say when . . . " The rest of her words vanished.

I don't know how to feel. I just know I want to feel anything else but this.

"So, here's the thing," she paused. "We've been reading and taking apart poems in this class and addressing the complications of language, the feeling of being shut out or angry or emotional. There are times that it is just so hard to make sense of it all."

"Like Shakespeare?" Tiffany added.

"Sure," she smiled with her whole mouth. "Listen, I want to put aside today's lesson and introduce something else. Who here keeps a diary or journal of some sort?"

A few hands tentatively rose. I used to keep a diary many years ago and then lost interest. It was mainly just secret crushes or complaining about unfair rules. I guess not as riveting as I hoped it would be.

"Starting today, I'm going to ask you to keep a journal. I won't look at it, I promise. But I think it would be beneficial for all of you, especially with regards to losing one of our classmates this weekend. See it as a chance to reconnect with your thoughts and react in a safe space on paper. More specifically, I want you to write *to* someone. Anyone. Someone you've never met, someone you love. Whoever you'd like. By having a focus, it feels more like a conversation, except without the interruption, of course. I'm hoping it will be meditative, a chance to be with your inner thoughts. A destination toward healing," she paused, looking around the room. "So, uh, take out your notebook, if it's not already out, and start writing. Begin with 'dear' and then whomever you are writing to. This is more generative than anything else. What I mean by that is this doesn't need to be formal. In fact, it shouldn't be. Just let your thoughts and words fly. Roam. Be free."

"Are you collecting this?" Deanna asked.

"No, I'm not. Allow that to give you permission to write without edit, without judgment, without fear. And I want to encourage you to keep this going. When tragedy happens, writing can be one of the best medicines to make sense of things."

Behind me, I heard someone say, "Which one was he? I don't remember a James."

"Yeah, I don't know. I think he sat by the window? Maybe he had black hair?"

I stared at my blank page. Turquoise straight lines. I used to write letters to Dara when she went to summer camp. I loved feeling like I could say whatever I wanted without any interruption. I've written letters to Dad, even though he's just thirty minutes away. I wrote to Shirley when she was in the hospital. Sometimes I write to Greta. I didn't think I'd miss her when she went away to college, but I do. So much.

Ms. Raimondo is a newer teacher at our school, younger than the others. Sometimes I feel like I can see her thoughts grow inside her, but maybe that is just me staring way too hard because I think she's so pretty. When she walked into the classroom on the first day of school, I couldn't believe she was the teacher. She looked so cool, with double-pierced ears and purpley lips like she had eaten a whole bunch of pomegranate seeds before she arrived. On the first day of class, she had us write love letters to ourselves, which I thought was really strange. Then, we put them in an envelope she gave to us, which we had to address. She promised she'd mail them to us, eventually. When we forgot. After school that day, I went home and told Shirley all about her. She thought Ms. Raimondo sounded like a hippie, which I wasn't exactly sure was a good or bad thing. Shirley can be quick to judge at times.

I peered around the room and noticed a few people already writing. In front of me sat Aggie, slightly hunched with her dark glistening braid leaning on her right shoulder. Sometimes I forget Ms. Raimondo is even talking because the back of Aggie's head mesmerizes me. I've spent most of September trying to think of something to say to get her attention. She talks in class, but I haven't seen her talk to anyone else yet. She's new to this school, though I'm not sure where she's from. I've written pages of poems just about Aggie's braid. I wouldn't dare show them to anyone, of course.

It hurt to allow myself to think that James was gone. And then I couldn't quite understand why I was feeling this way. We weren't friends. The only words he flung in my direction were mean ones. But I guess it's that he succeeded. He did what Shirley has tried to do so many times. That's when I knew whom I needed to write to.

Monday, October 18, 1993

Dear James,

Ms. Raimondo looks like a grasshopper today, dressed in a long, tight dark green skirt and lime-green blouse. You used to be in this room, but of course we never spoke to each other. I kind of hated you. Or I was scared of you. I guess a little bit of both. You never raised your hand or spoke at all really. But I can hear your voice because it used to make fun of me. ~~It's so strange being at home without Greta. Quieter. I miss her more than~~ ~~I call my mom Shirley because~~ ~~I think Ms. Raimondo is really beautiful when she wears her hair back and I can see her ears.~~ ~~I still have a difficult time trusting Shirley since she~~ Why did you kill yourself?

✎

Tuesday, October 19

Dear James,

Something happened today in study hall. I can't stop thinking about it, and I figured I might as well tell you, since, well, you know.

By the time I get to study hall I'm so hungry, but lunch isn't for two more periods, so I often sneak in some kind of snack to eat while the teacher isn't looking. We aren't allowed to eat or talk, which is super annoying. Sometimes, though, I'll stick something in my pocket and sneak bites. Usually just loose cereal that I suck on to eliminate the loud crunching sound. Is that weird?

Today, I dipped my hand into my pocket and found only crumbs. I tried slyly emptying it out, dropping bits of flesh-colored preservatives to the floor.

"You know, if we were outside, birds would eat that. In here, you are basically just encouraging the cockroaches to come out of hiding." Aggie had tapped me on the back. She was sitting behind me, diagonally. That's right, two classes together, though not sure study hall counts as a class. And homeroom too, although that's just like a half hour or whatever.

I couldn't believe she saw me do that.

"Yeah, I . . . I was just . . . hey . . . " Wow. Real smooth, Eleanor.

Her voice was deep, not like the ocean, but more like Shirley's, whose vocal chords have been charred from decades of cigarette smoke.

"It's not like I'm judging, I'm just noticing," she said. I took all of her in. This was the first time I really could, since she was looking directly at me. She didn't exactly match, but from what I noticed through my many weeks of watching her, she never does. She had on a shirt with lots of stripes and an oversized vest (her father's?), a long skirt, and a tie that went well beyond her waist. "I'm Aggie, by the way," she paused and moved a little closer to me. "Agnieszka," she whispers, "but only my dad calls me that now. I feel like you're in all my classes and yet we've never talked to each other. Fromme comes before Glackhzner, so you sit in front of me in homeroom."

Agnieszka Glackhzner. A mish-mosh of letters. A song.

"Oh, uh . . . yeah," I dribbled out.

"My dad is a garbage man. '*Sanitation worker*'," she emphasized proudly, using her fingers to wrap around those last two words. "I've been brought up to locate garbage cans like exit signs. I've never had to make my bed, but I'll get punished if I'm caught littering."

I smiled. "Jeez . . . *sorry*. I mean, yeah, I didn't realize."

"It's all right," she smiled back, and I suddenly forgot how to breathe. "Eleanor, right?"

I nodded.

"Who are you writing your letters to? You know, from English class?" Aggie smiled. Her lips spread wide, and I quickly noted all her teeth, so white and slightly crooked.

"Oh, uh . . . "

"I mean, you don't have to tell me." Aggie brought in the corner of her mouth and bit down on her lower lip. Why couldn't I breathe?

The air had asbestos in it. Mold. Cancer. What was happening? Why couldn't I stop smiling?

"I'm writing to Richard Brautigan," she said.

"Is he an uncle or something? Or . . . "

"No, no. A poet. And storywriter too. A friend of mine I used to go to school with in Staten Island gave me a book of his. Oh man, I love his stuff. You've got to check him out. When Ms. Raimondo said to write to someone, he was the first person I thought of."

"Oh, uh, yeah." What?

"You're funny. Hey, I wanted to tell you in English class that I really love your new hair. It's awesome."

"Thanks." Finally, *a word.* "I'm writing to—"

"Sshhh," Mr. Greggs widened his eyes at us.

"Anyway," Aggie whispered, "you can borrow a Brautigan book, if you like. I've really got to stay focused this year. Second chance."

Second chance?

Wednesday, October 20

Dear James,

We had hamburgers with homemade french fries for supper. Not every letter needs to be about something.

Okay, *fine.* Maybe there is always something that can be talked about. Something of substance, I mean. What would you have said about my hair, James? Would you have pointed and laughed? What clever joke would you make of it? Would you call me cranberry bog or menstruation face?

The thing is, I guess I was distracted by you on Monday, and then Tuesday I couldn't stop thinking about my conversation with Aggie, but something else happened on Monday. After school.

Dara missed the bus in the morning, so I didn't see her until math—the only class we have together this year. When I walked in, she was already there, and she gasped. Really. Like out-loud-lungs-filling-with-everyone's-dead-skin-cells type of gasp.

"Eleanor! Oh my god! What happened?"

I threw my fingers on my head and felt around. "Oh, this? Yeah, I guess I made a mistake?"

"I almost didn't recognize you. You look like . . . " James, if you were in the room, I bet you would have laughed. Maybe you would have even egged her on. "You look like a *lesbian*." She whispered it like "lesbian" was a curse word.

"W-what does a lesbian look like?" I still can't believe I said that. I mean, Flor is a lesbian and she just looks like—I don't know—a person. Actually, she's the first lesbian I've ever met. Or know that I've met, I guess. She has short hair, but do all lesbians have the same haircut? I'll have to ask Flor.

Flor gives off a soothing aroma of peppermint and coffee. When she isn't drinking coffee—which happens all throughout the day, even at dinner—she is popping little peppermints into her mouth. Usually they are the kind you get from that giant bowl at the diner after you pay your bill. Flor always takes giant handfuls, stuffs them in her pockets and delivers them to a bowl in her house. Gret and I call them urine mints, and do not dare eat them, even when they are the kind with delicious bits of hard jelly in the center.

"They're always kind of damp," Greta once told me. "And you know why?"

I just shrugged.

"Because people go to the bathroom, hands damp from wiping not washing, and then they grab a handful of these. Pop 'em in their mouth. Gross," she said, sticking out her tongue. "Never eat them. No matter what, okay?"

When I first met Flor, I wasn't sure if I liked her. She is eccentric (I can't remember how I learned this word) in ways I have never experienced before. First, she's obsessed with the mail. Since she's no longer working—Shirley mentioned something about disability—she makes sure to be home every day the mail comes. Sunday is her day off. It is also a wasted day—*her* words: "A day without mail is a day unworthy of breakfast, showering, or conversation."

"I can't even housesit because I worry I would just open up mail that isn't mine, just to see what's inside. It's like a daily birthday present," she once said.

"But isn't it just bills and junk?" I asked her.

"Yeah, but someone still took the time to lick that envelope, tear off a stamp, and slip it through a blue mailbox. Time and appreciation, Eleanor."

Flor used to keep even her junk mail until Shirley went over to her house and saw the piles and piles of magazines and envelopes, half-torn open.

"You can't just keep everything," Shirley said between cigarette inhales. "You've got to let go."

Maybe this is why they're such good friends; they aren't afraid to tiptoe around each other. They just *tell it like it is.*

"I'm a lesbian, Eleanor," Flor said a few months after our first meeting, "So I've learned to get used to making room for myself in spaces that try to exclude me."

This was the moment I knew I really liked Flor. I liked knowing someone who understands how to exist even when others don't want her to because of stupid reasons like just wanting to kiss girls or whatever.

What happens when we say something out loud? Does it become more real? Is it any less real when we keep it to ourselves?

Anyway, where was I? Oh, yeah. Then math class started, and it was super awkward between Dara and I, and we didn't see each other again until our bus ride home. We always sit next to each other and we still did, but most of the ride was in complete silence.

"Hey, listen," I started, "it's . . . I don't know . . . I left your house and I just wanted to scream. Didn't you? I mean, we didn't really know him, but he was our classmate for so many years. And then I thought about Shirley and almost losing her in the same . . . anyway, so I just cut my hair. That's it. It'll grow back. Who cares?"

"No, yeah, I know, Eleanor. I'm sorry. I didn't mean to . . . say what I said. I think I have a gay uncle so . . . "

"So . . . what?"

"So, a gay person is probably related to me. So, it's not mean."

"I don't understand. And anyway, so what if I was a . . . a lesbian?"

James, I can tell you this because you're not my bully anymore, you're just a piece of paper. Before I became an atheist—my parents know, though they wish I'd reconsider—I had my Bat Mitzvah. That was kind of the end of my Jewishness. I was newly thirteen, begrudgingly (vocab word!) finished Hebrew school and completed the whole experience. I lead the minyan, read from the Torah, all of it. Anyway, at the party part, my friend Kelly kept asking me to dance. When Good Vibrations came on by Marky Mark, she grabbed me, and we just swung our limbs around like animals. It was incredible. I mean, everyone was dancing. When it was over, she yelled into my ear that she wanted to give me my present. I told her she didn't have to get me anything, but that I could just open it later. But she kept insisting. So, we left the room—my Bat Mitzvah was in this giant hall where, like, weddings probably happened. We went down the stairs and into this smaller room. I just looked at her because she didn't seem to be holding a gift, and then she kissed me.

You probably think it's lame or gross to imagine two girls kissing. I could tell you that I was shocked. I could tell you that I immediately pushed her away and wiped my lips, but the thing is, I wanted only one thing for my birthday and it wasn't until Kelly kissed me that I realized what it was. It's like my whole body opened up and I became something else. I remember walking in on Greta and her high school boyfriend Vegetarian Todd kissing and I couldn't get over how gross it looked. But I guess it's gross until it happens to you by someone who means something.

So when Dara called me a lesbian, it was like something got louder in me. After my Bat Mitzvah, every time Kelly and I saw each other, we kissed. A few times, Kelly took off her shirt and let me stare at her and once, she even let me touch her. She never really wanted to touch me. She called me her secret boyfriend. I didn't think much of it then. I just liked how she made me feel. Less than a year later, she moved away. Her dad got a job in Texas, and we wrote for a little while, but then she stopped, and I stopped and well, I guess it went away . . . you know . . . the feelings.

"I just think it's weird, El," Dara said. "I mean, you cut your hair and made it . . . purple. I guess it's not like you."

"Okay, well, maybe it isn't. But maybe I don't even know what I am or who I am or . . . "

"You weren't even friends with James."

"Dara, are you kidding me? It's so much more than that."

"Just tell me if you are. That girl Jacqueline who was in our science class last year? She shaved her head and then told everyone she was bisexual. I mean, you and I have had sleepovers. We've slept in the same bed! I changed in front of—"

"Okay! Okay. Yes. I am. A . . . lesbian, or whatever. Jeez. I don't know, I never said it out loud. Can we just . . . can we not—"

"Oh my gosh, you *are*? Wait, I was just . . . I mean, I didn't think. Eleanor, I . . . I'm not sure how I feel about this."

"We've been friends since we were seven. Why does this even matter?"

"I'm not sure. Can I think about it?"

"Can you think about how this doesn't even affect you?"

James, there's no need to continue the rest. I can't believe I told Dara something I barely ever thought about (actually, even as I write that, I know it's not really true—I've thought about it more than anything else) and now suddenly it was apparently the end to our friendship. I mean, I guess I kind of have feelings for Aggie, but I just saw it as like, a friend-crush, even though she's not exactly my friend and . . . oh, you wouldn't understand anyway.

~

Thursday, October 21

Dear James,

Tonight, I had my suicide support group. We meet every Thursday. Flor came along and while we were on our way there, I asked her about what it's like to be a lesbian. Super weird, I know, but I couldn't stop thinking about it.

"What's it like to be a fifteen-year-old?" she immediately asked back.

"Umm . . . "

"Eleanor, why are you asking me this?"

"I don't . . . I don't know. I guess I just wanted to know more about you."

"Okay," Flor was looking at the road (since she was driving), but I could see her face tense up as though she was thinking big thoughts. "Well, it's been a long time, I'm almost fifty. Wooh, don't say that out loud much. It's difficult and wonderful and challenging and . . . even at my age, I still have to come out to people. You never stop. I've had some good reactions, some horrifying ones. I've lost friends. I've gained friends. Funny, when I first met your mom, I thought she was gay. I thought everyone at the book club was gay. Maybe that's wishful thinking. And when I realized she wasn't—nor was anyone else—I wasn't mad or anything, I was just worried. I really liked your mom and didn't want to lose her as a friend. It had happened so many times before. Of course, she didn't care one bit. I'll never understand why something that has nothing to do with anyone else makes people so uncomfortable."

"What do you mean?" I asked.

"If I found someone, I couldn't even marry them. Shouldn't everyone have the right to just . . . love and get married if they want? I'll never get used to that. I'll never understand."

That night at group, there were a few new people. I've been going since June and I've seen lots of people come and go. Shirley occasionally checks in with me to make sure I still want to go, and I do. I feel less alone when I'm there. I also feel really grateful because a lot of people in the group actually lost their family members. I'm lucky I still have a mom.

"Eleanor, I made coconut chocolate cookies, the ones you love!" Delia insisted on bringing baked goods each week. She said that it allows her to funnel her sadness into something better. There was always coffee too, and some other snacks. I know, who cares, right? But I'm telling you this to set the scene, James. Because of what happened a little later on.

I spoke a lot more in the beginning, when everything was raw, but now, I prefer to just sit and take it all in. Delia spoke about her husband, who she found in the basement. I guess he was hiding a bunch of bad pictures too, that part I didn't really understand. But Delia said something about him leading some kind of double life. Delia always talked about her confusion of missing him and hating him at the same time.

A few other people spoke too, and then Peter, the social worker, asked if any of the new members wanted to speak.

I guess some people just need to be asked because right then a woman started speaking. She had a haircut just like my sixth-grade teacher. Do you remember Mrs. Gryzynsky? I know you weren't in that class, but I feel like everyone knew her. She was so strange. She was really short and always wore bright, bright red lipstick. Her hair was cut like a mushroom.

This woman had one of Delia's cookies in the palm of her hand. It's like she was petting it, like she didn't know it was edible.

"I lost my boy. My only one," she said. Her voice sounded scratched like someone with giant fingernails tore up her vocal chords.

"Would you like to share?" That's what Peter always said. A few times, he has mentioned that it was a question that allowed more openness to answer. Like we can talk about more than just who we lost or almost lost. We can also talk about our day or whatever.

"I don't . . . I'm still trying to understand. How can a parent ever survive this? I mean, . . . I just didn't know . . . " Her voice trailed off.

Patricia, who lost her brother last year, handed the woman a tissue. "There's lotion in it," I heard her whisper.

"If you feel able, would you share your name and maybe anything about him you might like?" Peter has a really soothing voice, which definitely helped me to open up in the beginning. He also has a monstrously-large moustache. James, remember our music teacher in middle school? Mr. Jerricks? His moustache was like three fingers wide. Peter's is even thicker.

"He was only fifteen," the woman said. "He liked to cook, bake all sorts of things with me. He listened to music a lot. I can't remember the names of the . . . I'm Helaine."

"Helaine, thank you for being here with us today," Peter said.

"James is his . . . was his . . . name," she added.

Your mom. Of course. In this moment, I wish you weren't just a piece of paper. I wish you could have seen her face. Puffy and red and wet and I don't know . . . like her brain melted or something. Not like she didn't make sense, no, not that. More like, she was at a loss for words. For understanding.

I didn't know you liked to cook. I don't really know anything about you, really. I wonder what your favorite recipe was. James, did you leave a note? Did you tell anyone beforehand? Who was your best friend? Did you ever get to be in love? Did you ever kiss anyone?

At the end of group, people started folding the chairs, putting away the cups and napkins, grabbing the last of the cookies, chatting a bit. I motioned to Flor that I was going to talk to Helaine. When she mentioned your name, I think Flor understood as well.

"Hi," I said to her.

She was looking at one of the few pieces of art on the walls. Some kind of landscape with a setting sun.

"H-hi," she said, still staring at the painting.

"I'm fifteen too," I said, hoping maybe she'd make the connection. She turned to face me. "Oh."

"Um, I knew him. James. I mean, we weren't exactly friends, but—"

Suddenly her skin grew pinker. "You did? You . . . did you have any idea? Did he tell you—"

"No, no, I . . . we didn't speak, but he was in my English class. He didn't really talk in there either."

"What's your name?"

"Eleanor," I said. "Eleanor Fromme, but I doubt James ever mentioned me."

She shook her head.

"I'm . . . I'm so sorry for your loss." Even as I said it, I hated every word. Why do we apologize when someone dies as though we caused it, as though we could have stopped it? Could I have?

"Thank you, dear. Tonight was . . . good. Maybe I'll get Burt to come."

"James's . . . "

"Father. He blames himself. He . . . he's a pastor. Always hoped James would be more . . . oh, I don't know . . . Christian." She smiled.

I definitely didn't know what to say to that.

"May I . . . may I ask what causes you to come here as well?"

I took a deep breath. "My mom."

"Oh, Eleanor, I'm so sorry—"

"Actually, she's still alive. I mean, she tried to kill herself, but she's okay now. I'm not so sure what okay really means. I'll always be waiting, you know? Scared that she might try again, even though she promises me she won't. I see her every day, but what happens when I'm in college and it's just her and—"

"So much for a young person to think about," she said.

"Yeah, well, I'm sure I'll put her through a lot too," I laughed.

"Maybe I'll see you next Thursday, Eleanor."

James, I can't pretend that it wasn't strange to speak to your mom after there were days I'd go home after being bullied by you and thinking a monster must have raised you to turn you into one. But she's warm and even in her sadness, she seems so kind.

On the ride home, I told Flor about Helaine and feeling guilty that I still have my family member, while so many people in group lost theirs. Sometimes I feel like an imposter.

"Eleanor, you are everywhere you are supposed to be," Flor said.

P.S. Your mom smells like banana bread.

―――

Friday, October 22

Dear James,

It is so strange to ignore someone I used to tell all my secrets to. And I wonder if Dara feels the same way. On the bus to school, I had to sit next to Ross, who smells like old grape jelly sandwiches. Dara and I always sat together. I thought maybe she'd apologize. But it's like I was invisible to her. And then of course, I had this terrible fear. I mean, she's the only person that knows that I'm . . . just write it, Eleanor . . . A LESBIAN! What if she tells people? What if the whole school replaces you as my bully. ~~What if~~ James, you got to die with all of your secrets. I guess we all have them.

I don't even know who your friends were. Sometimes I wish I could talk to one of them and ask what you were like. I don't really think you were the monster I thought you were. After meeting your mom, I realized there must have been some of that kindness in you too, right?

There is a poster in our health class with a boy in mid-punch leaning toward a scared-looking boy. I think they're in a cafeteria, maybe? In giant bold lettering, it says: Bullies Get Bullied So Don't Be A Bully! I'm sure someone was mean to you and you just did what you saw. Mr. Giore (my history teacher) said that history happens over and over, so there is no past, just present-tense re-runs.

Greta used to bully me all the time. She'd boss me around and if I put up a stink, she'd yell at me. Sometimes she'd steal my favorite toy and hide it. She was worse than when Dad and Shirley would punish me. I'm sure I've bullied too. Maybe I've even bullied Dara. Bossed her around. Made her feel bad. I don't know. What things can we forgive? And are there things we just can't let go of? James, writing to you really digs at my apple core. I know I'm still so mad at Shirley for doing what she did. Maybe I won't ever forgive her. But being in that support group helps. Maybe that's why I stay, so I can try to let go of what she did. So I can trust her again.

—⁓—

Sunday, October 24

Ms. Raimondo said that to tell a story, one must start at the beginning. But who remembers that? I couldn't speak when I began. I can't remember what my first word was, probably Mom or Dad but certainly not enough vocabulary to tell my story. Or a story.

But Ms. Raimondo said something else, which I guess is why I'm writing this. She said that stories find their meaning once they are written down. You were there that day, weren't you? When she said that? It meant something because I actually wrote it in my

notebook and I'm not really the best note-taker—I usually start
and then lose interest—but I wanted to understand it better.

Anyway, I never told anyone about that night. Last March.
Maybe if I write it down, I can let go of it. Forgive you, maybe. It
was so cold outside, but I had to get out of my house. Shirley had
her book club people over. Every month they discussed romance
novels as though they are . . . I don't know . . . works of art or
something. But that's how Shirley met Flor, so I guess good things
come out of weird things, right?

Everyone was smoking cigarettes, and it was like the tar was
tiptoeing up the stairs, into my bedroom. I piled on a sweater over
my long-sleeved shirt and another sweater over that with long
thermal underwear beneath my sweatpants and I felt like a polar
bear swallowed by another polar bear. Plus, two scarves, my winter
coat and my Walkman with a mix tape made by Dara. I remember
everything.

"Bored! Gonna take a walk around the block! Be back s—"

"Wait," interrupted Shirley. "Are you kidding me? It's freezing
out there."

"I know. I'm bundled. But it reeks of smoke in here and my
lungs are screaming. I promise I won't be gone too long."

Shirley looked at the others. "Okay, but just around the block
and then back," she said.

I walked out, pushing the headphones over my ears and
preparing for some perfectly picked out music to accompany me
on my walk.

James, I just realized this was before. Shirley was . . . *Mom*.
Helaine is probably going to think this way too. Before you hung
yourself and after.

Here is something to know about my neighborhood. I live on a
cul-de-sac. The great part of this is that when I was younger and
the thought of playing outside was enough to make me happy, I
didn't have to worry about oncoming traffic when playing catch in

the middle of the street. Anyone who drives on our block already
lives here. But I decided to make a right turn and travel out of the
cul-de-sac, heading toward the 'shady development'. I titled it this
when I first noticed the tall trees turning into each other like
clasped fingers. The branches became like an umbrella shading
me from the summertime sky when I was zipping away on my bike.
In the winter, without all the leaves, they just looked like trees with
bad posture, leaning. But it's my favorite place to bike through in
the warmer months. Each house is so different from the other and
since the houses are much older and have been there for many
decades, the trees are tall and wild.

Anyway, I was listening to the Pixies in my eardrums and feeling
like a dragon as my frozen breath escaped me, creating a white
smoke from between my chapped lips. I was singing loudly—I
remember this—because I was the only one who existed or at least
it felt that way. I don't really know too much about the Pixies,
except for the way they make me feel, which is alive and excited. I
wonder what music you listen to. Your mom couldn't remember.

And then I felt something.

"Hey!"

I felt you before I saw you because the music was loud, and I was
lost in my thoughts.

"What?"

"Hey, what *are* you, freak?"

And I remember everything as though it was a movie I was
watching, but I was in it. I didn't know it was you at first, because it
was so dark. You were in one of those winter sock hats and your
jacket was dark. Actually, everything was dark except for the
streetlights that had been illuminating my walk.

I took off my headphones because I was scared and wanted to
be alert.

"You go to my school, dyke."

I kept walking. And if I was a dragon before, I suddenly became

Jackie Joyner-Kersee. Although, I wasn't exactly running, more like power-walking, which is what I do in gym class.

"Am I scaring you, lezzie? I know what you are."

You were smoking a cigarette.

"Or maybe you're a fag," you said. "Which one? Huh? You a dyke or a faggot?"

I could still hear the music blaring through the speakers of my headphones. Of course, I didn't answer you. I didn't know what to say. James, you really frightened me. And then, suddenly I was on the ground because you pushed me, pulled at my sleeve, and I fell.

I could hear the crackle of the paper burning up with each suck of your cigarette between your lips, and do you remember what you did next? You blew that smoke right into my face.

Here's the thing: I'm not going to pretend to be some fearless superhuman. My body was trembling beneath every single layer, and I think my complete silence was due to the fact that every word that wanted to come out was frozen inside me. I've never been in a fight before, so I can't even say if I can pack a mean punch or not. There was that time Heather S. thought I was staring at her boyfriend in Spanish class last year and she told me she was going to beat me up after school. I was terrified of the day ending. I wound up hiding in the library until I knew all the buses had left and then called Shirley from the payphone to pick me up. Yes, I was staring, but only because I thought his jean vest was so cool and I was trying to read the pins he had on the back. Anyway, maybe I've got a badass boxer living inside me, but I wasn't exactly in the frame of mind to figure it out that night.

You said some other stuff that for some reason I blocked out and then. You. Spit. On. Me.

You were so close to me that I could feel your hot breath on my neck. I remember you kind of smelled like Vick's VapoRub.

"My dad, he . . . he wants me to be everything he is. Go to church, pray every single day. It's bullshit. He wants me to be real . . . you better not tell anyone about this, dyke."

And then you spat on me once more and I could taste the tobacco in your saliva on my skin. So gross.

I always wondered if you were afraid I'd tell. Or if you even cared. And I'm not sure why I didn't. I guess I didn't know how to tell it. I guess I was afraid that if I said the words out loud that you called me, they would become more real. What I really wanted to ask you was: how did you know?

I have lived in this neighborhood for most of my life. We moved here when I was six and everyone on my block pretty much knows each other's business. The Fiore's live next door and when Gabby, who is one grade above me, found her father french-kissing her mother's best friend, everyone found out. It's kind of like a game of telephone, where the real story rarely remains in its original form. But in this particular case, her father really did have an affair, and now I think they are having an open relationship or something.

When Shirley set off the fire alarm because of her cigarettes, the fire trucks came. Oh man, they all couldn't wait to feast on *that* gossip. It wasn't the first time she fell asleep with one lit. I don't even want to talk about that.

David Werzloski moved into the house at the corner two years ago. In second grade, he showed me his penis. Just pulled his pants down right in the middle of Mrs. Rossi's math lesson and I couldn't believe how wrinkly it was, kind of like a crumpled-up fruit roll-up.

And Rachel, Tina and Tiffany live three houses away with their parents and new dog named Rover. The Pashmis across the street. The Jacobs. The Gowers. The McDonnells. The Goldbergs. Dara and her family live about six houses down. There are more boys than girls on our street. The Goldbergs have triplet boys who are Gret's age. One enlisted in the army, the other two went to some college in Oregon, I think.

My point. My point is that I feel like we all know each other in some way. I've trick-or-treated at everyone's house. Beyond just this cul-de-sac, all the streets connect. I sold Girl Scout cookies when I was briefly a Brownie, just until I got to go to Sesame Place. Then, I decided I didn't like being called a dessert that I couldn't even eat because during that time Shirley prohibited sweets from our house. I've been to sleepovers and played Monopoly in these houses and swam in their pools and went to Halloween parties and even accompanied Shirley to a Tupperware party one evening at one of these homes.

When you pushed me, I stopped feeling safe. I was so afraid to go to school that Monday, but you acted like nothing even happened. Didn't address me or taunt me or anything like that. Actually, I feel like that was the last time you ever bullied me.

〜

Monday, October 25

Dear James,

It feels kind of weird to be writing to you like we are old friends or something and I'm just catching you up on what you've missed. It's been a week. Just one week since you've . . . the ribbons people tied to their car antennas and backpacks are mostly gone. The wind took them away. Your picture will probably be in the yearbook under some kind of heading like: 'In Memory Of' or something like that. And then what? We move on? Nothing changes, and everything just keeps growing around us. I keep thinking about your mom. I hope she comes back to group. I hope your dad comes too.

Anyway, today Aggie and I sat together during lunch. It was incredible. I didn't even realize we were in the same lunch period, and then I saw her. She actually motioned for me to sit next to her!

"Do you think your thoughts are strange?" I asked her.

"Yeah. Sometimes."

"I feel like I'm thinking things I was trying not to think about and it's . . . I don't know . . . "

"Why don't you want to think about them?" she asked.

"It's like breathing. We can hold our breath and stop for a second or two, but eventually we have to go back and let the air in. Maybe I can try to not think for a second, but then my thoughts just come right back."

Aggie smiled. Today, she had on some kind of shiny lip-gloss. I couldn't stop staring.

"Maybe they keep coming back because they are still forming."

"Maybe," I said. "Anyway, let's talk about something else, okay? Tell me about . . . tell me something that you haven't told me yet."

Aggie had just grabbed a large bite full of her tuna and capers sandwich, so she dragged her finger through the air as a symbol of *hold on*.

"Well, we haven't been friends for very long, so there's a lot on that list! I don't know . . . umm . . . I pierced my own belly button last year, which was a painful mistake."

"Bloody?"

"Infected."

"Oh, well, my parents pierced my ears when I was a baby, never even asking me if I was cool with it. Once I was old enough, I unplugged my earlobes just as soon as I could. The hole is closed up now." I grabbed my earlobe and twisted it toward her. "See?"

"Looks to be," Aggie smiled. "Oh, I collect envelopes."

"Like, new ones?"

"No," she laughed. "The ones from junk mail or bills. It's the insides that I like the best."

"The letter?"

"No, the *lining* of the envelope. It's always cool patterns and I used to dream of cutting them into tiny squares and gluing them together like a paper quilt. Can't really say what I would have done with it. I imagine tiny, hidden stories inside the patterns. Like morse code. I've always wondered if other people notice how beautiful the inside of an envelope is. My dad knows about my collection, so he always saves them for me. Right now, I keep them in a giant envelope. Oh, my gosh, I just realized how funny that is."

"Like those wooden Russian dolls that fit inside each other. A doll inside a doll. An envelope inside an—"

"What's something that you collect?"

"I collect a bunch of stuff, but I used to collect . . ."

"What?" Aggie leaned in.

"Oh gosh, please don't think I'm strange, but I used to collect my fingernails. Like baby half-moons. I kept them in a cigar box my dad gave me. Weird, I know."

Aggie grabbed my hand and brought my fingers to her mouth. "How about I add to your collection?"

She pretended to bite my nails, and I laughed hard enough to feel my apple juice slosh around in my stomach.

"I'm glad you moved here," I said. I could feel my entire face and body blushing. I only hoped Aggie hadn't noticed.

"Yeah, me too. Hey," she brought her hands to my cranberry fuzz and sloshed her fingers around. "You getting used to being hairless?"

I smiled. "I keep forgetting that. I don't really have a habit of checking myself out. Yeah, it's weird, but I feel more *me* like this."

"What do you mean?"

James, I didn't really know how to answer her. The thing is, there's something else that's been kind of growing inside me for a while now, but you know like when you don't have a word for something, you kind of just twist your way out of that sentence? Am

I making sense? Probably not. What I mean is, I *feel* something in
me, ~~something that feels incomplete~~. Something that feels
unspoken. When Dara called me a lesbian, I thought that might be
it, except that feeling remained. That feeling that something else is
still there waiting to be found.

"You know like when we're really young and our parents dress us
and maybe it's something we like, but then you look back on
pictures taken and you're like, 'I would never have picked that!'"

"Definitely," Aggie laughed.

"Maybe I'm just still figuring out to dress myself. How to look.
Even though this haircut was definitely not thought out, I am
starting to recognize myself a little more."

"Hey, do you want to have a sleepover this weekend? If you're
not busy, I mean?"

Oh my gosh oh my gosh act cool, Eleanor.

"Sure, okay." Inside, every single organ in my body grew teeth
and lips just so a smile could form. My lungs, my intestines, my
liver were all beaming!

James, have you ever met someone who made you feel like you
wanted to understand everything about yourself?

～

Wednesday, October 27

Dear James,

Today in class, Ms. Raimondo said that there is a book out
there for everyone. She said it because when we were discussing
a poem by James Baldwin, Greg blurted out—he never raises his
hand—that it was just too hard to understand, and poems are
only meant for too smart people. *Too smart people*, James? Ugh,
anyway, I've never heard of James Baldwin before, but Ms.
Raimondo said that we'll be reading some more of him later in
the year and I kind of got excited about that. The poem was

called "The Giver". It felt like a riddle and maybe I still don't quite get it, but Ms. Raimondo said it's less about the gifts we give, but rather the action of it. And that the feelings we have when giving the gift aren't always fully received. Giving gifts don't always solve the problem, she said. James, I'm not sure why but I felt such relief in this.

This past weekend, I thought about what would have happened if you weren't my bully and we somehow made our way to friends. We'd share jokes and maybe even read the same books and talk about them and who knows, maybe even study together. And if we had been friends, maybe you wouldn't have . . . but then when we read this poem, I realized that we can gift-wrap all sorts of things and it doesn't mean it will bring happiness or even cure madness (Ms. Raimondo mentioned that part). We can give, but it may never be enough. We will always run out of food, out of houses, out of . . . hope.

Yeah, I guess this poem is pretty sad too.

～

Thursday, October 28

Dear James,

I have two small closets in my bedroom. When my parents were still together, and life seemed defined by rules, one was designated for my warmer-month clothes and the other for winter. Nowadays, I fit all my clothes into one closet and use the other as my hiding space. I kind of see it as my tunnel toward being whoever I want to be.

In it, I've hung a Whitney Houston poster where her hair looks so beautiful and curly, placed my favorite pillow and my small, battery-operated radio/tape player. My closet is just big enough to sit inside, with my knees semi-comfortably pressed into my chest. I guess it's not much of a hiding space since my whole family knows I go in there sometimes when I don't want to be bothered.

I often close the door when I'm in there and the only light coming in comes from the gap between the door and the floorboards. I imagine my body as though it hides its own trap door. Sometimes I take off all my clothes, so the darkness becomes like a fifth wall, and then just feel around. I pretend everything is as it should be. I knead my small breasts in a way that pushes them down like that time Dad and I made challah together and I could feel the tough dough get more elastic and even with each push of my palm. I imagine planting seeds in my vagina, waiting for something different to grow. James, good thing you're paper now, because you'd probably stop reading this, but this is how I feel. I'd watch the roots slowly pour out, twist and turn. My vagina would be replaced by a fern or banana tree. Or, maybe just a giant hand would emerge and scoop out all the woman in me.

It's like I'm a meal on a menu with the wrong name. My ingredients make it seem like I'm one dish when really, I swear I'm another.

╼

Saturday, October 30

Dear James,

Today, Aggie comes over for the first time and I just can't wait. But James, I want to tell you about group this week. Flor didn't come because she had a date—which she seemed super excited about—so Shirley dropped me off. You probably want to know if your mom was there.

"I want to shape tonight a little bit, if that's alright with everyone," Peter said. Usually he takes a back seat to the discussion. He kind of just nods his head, but not in a way like he isn't listening, more like knowing that it's about us and not him.

"I'd like to encourage everyone to speak. Of course, if this feels uncomfortable or impossible, then of course you may pass. But I am going to place a question in the air for everyone and hopefully embolden some thoughts." Peter twisted the end of his moustache. He did this a lot when he was listening. It's like it turned his thoughts on or something.

"There is very often guilt involved with survivors. We've talked about this in here. A sense of 'I should have said this'. What do you want to say in this moment? For some of us, we've had only weeks apart from the tragedy. Others, months, even years. But as we know, the questions and thoughts never stop. So, tonight, I want us to fully address our loved ones. Talk to them. Say what we didn't. Speaking it out is a path—a long, windy one—toward healing."

Maeve, who lost her sister, started to speak. "There were times I just wanted you to finally go. Our whole lives you kept trying and it became so painful. I stopped . . . I stopped trusting you. I could never get comfortable. And then, when you . . . when you finally . . . I was relieved." She pressed her hand against her mouth.

James, I'm not sure why I'm telling you all this. I guess every letter to you is full of this doubt, this sense of why do I need to give these words to you? But Thursday's group gave me this sense of understanding a little bit more about speaking out loud. Even when the words feel like they are too late.

"Maybe we were too hard on him," your mom spoke.

"If it's alright, I want to encourage you to speak directly to him," Peter said.

"Yes, of course. Sorry. My husband . . . I tried to get him to come tonight . . . he . . . he's not . . . he blames himself. He expected James to be a certain way. But we do that as parents, we want for our children what we didn't have. We never want them to suffer. And yet . . . he was suffering the whole time."

James, as your mom spoke, she held onto a handkerchief so tight, I watched her knuckles scream.

"I should have just let you be *you*," she said. She pressed the handkerchief to her eyes and nose.

Like I said, I don't usually talk, but I felt a pull.

"My mom just attempted, but it hurts just the same," I said, "because it's like even though she is still here, I'm still scared that she'll . . . sorry, *you* . . . will try again. And also, it's hard knowing how you tried so hard to leave us." I looked at Peter and said, "Her being here is kind of like a consolation prize."

"What do you mean by that, Eleanor?" Peter asked.

"I guess it's like . . . well, I used to watch The Price is Right with my grandma. You know that show? People have to guess the price of things and then the winner gets to play something else. Sometimes they get to choose between door number 1, 2, or 3. You just know they're all hoping for a car. Or like a dream vacation to Hawaii or something. Usually people are excited no matter what it is, even if it's just a washing machine. But sometimes it's like a suitcase made of broccoli and you can tell the person is excited to be on television, but pretty disappointed. My mom meant to die and when she didn't, I'm sure there was a part of her that felt bummed, you know? She tells me she's sorry and that she wants to be here, but it's still hard to accept."

James, I could just feel everyone stare at me. I got super self-conscious. And then your mom said something.

"You know Eleanor, sometimes we make a decision and moments right after, we wish, *wish* we could change our minds."

After group, during cookie-hoarding time, as I like to call it, I spoke with your mom for a bit.

"How are you . . . how *are* you?" I asked her.

"Each day still feels empty, missing."

I didn't really know what to say to that.

"Eleanor, would you like to come over for supper sometime?"

"Yeah, I'd like that."

"And your mother too. We'd love to have you both."

When I got home, I talked to Shirley about Helaine and her invitation. I gave her Helaine's phone number, and Shirley said she'd set something up.

~

Sunday, October 31 (HALLOWEEN!!!)

Dear James,

Aggie and I were up until 5 a.m., finally falling asleep against each other, her braid on my shoulder, her scent leaving footprints on my skin. Can you believe it? She read me stories from a Richard Brautigan book called *Revenge of the Lawn.* I told her that title made me think of what would happen if someone forgot to mow their grass and it became so wild it took over the world. She laughed, and when she smiles it makes my whole body feel like it's glowing. I tried hard to listen while she read and not lose my concentration from the shape of her lips and wideness of her dimly lit hazel eyes.

In the morning, we ate pancakes smeared with organic peanut butter—the kind where the oil becomes the main ingredient, holding the good stuff hostage—and tons of maple syrup. My Aunt Renita gave it to us last Chanukah. That was before she divorced my Uncle Greg. I always liked her better, and now I never get to see her because my Uncle Greg is Shirley's brother. Divorce sucks.

James, I feel like I really got to know Aggie last night. We shared so much with each other.

"I mean, I really liked Staten Island, but I think my dad needed a change. He's a little better now since . . . " Aggie said.

"Since what?" I asked.

"My . . . my mom died two years ago."

"Oh, Aggie, I am so sorry."

"Yeah, it's still so weird to say out loud. She . . . " Aggie looked down at the floor. I watched as she poked her fingers into the tiny holes created from her hair weaved into itself. "This may sound strange, but I'm grateful to have been left back. When she died, I just couldn't handle things, I was so angry. It's like our house just crumbled, you know? How was I supposed to still go to math class and do that stupid physical fitness test in gym? Ughh . . . why do we even do that *every* year? Anyway, my grades just tanked and I was left back."

"What . . . happened to her? To your mom? I mean, if you are okay talking about it. I don't want to—"

"Breast cancer. She had it for awhile. We really thought it would just go away. And it did. I mean, it vanished for a few months, but it was always there, like wind, you know? Wind is just really angry air. And cancer is just really angry cells, I guess. She used to brush my hair every night. Every single night. She'd sit behind me and I could feel every hair on my head being touched by her. Pulled at, but never hurting, you know? And she'd just listen as I told her about my day. Who I crushed on. Who I was mad at. What I was learning in school or having trouble with. Obviously, I could brush my own hair, but it soothed her to do it, even before she was sick. For that reason alone, I don't think I could ever cut my hair. It has memorized her brushstrokes."

"Oh, Aggie," I dripped out.

She grabbed her braid, resting on her shoulder, and swung it toward her back.

"So, I just stopped going to school. My dad was grieving pretty hard then too, so for weeks we just sat on the couch together watching old episodes of *Murder She Wrote* and *Cagney and Lacey*, my mom's favorite television shows. She recorded almost all the episodes. But then the school finally called my dad. I guess that's some kind of felony. They said I was in danger of failing my classes and that I went over the limit of absences. My dad . . . he's pretty tough. I mean, my mom's death definitely softened him. But when they called him, he didn't even argue. He just cried. My dad cried on the phone to the principal."

For a while, we sat in silence. I just wanted to glue myself to her, so she could feel bigger or stronger.

"Sorry," Aggie looked up at me with damp lashes. "I didn't mean to get all dark. It brought my dad and I closer and I'm glad we're here. We needed to leave Staten Island behind. And I got to meet you."

This made me smile so big, I thought my cheeks would crumble.

"So, you still haven't told me who *you're* writing to."

"I've been writing to James."

"James? The kid who—"

"Yeah."

"Were you friends? I didn't realize . . . "

"No, I mean, not at all. Actually, he bullied me. I guess writing to him helps me understand a little bit more. Actually, it's helping me to understand *myself* more. Shirley . . . my mom . . . she tried to kill herself earlier this year."

"Eleanor." I watched Aggie's eyes grow larger.

"Yeah. Speaking of it getting dark." I tried to smile, which was easy to do around Aggie. "Anyway, I'm still working on forgiving her and understanding all that. I go to a suicide survivor support group once a week. Actually, I met James's mom there."

"Really?"

"Yeah." I took a deep breath and could feel my lungs expanding. "She's really nice. And the group helps me to be around others who understand. It's all just so hard."

"Definitely."

"Ugh, it's bad enough being a teenager with a body that's changing whether I want it to or not."

"What don't you want?" Aggie asked.

No one ever asked me this, James. After this horrible year of almost losing Shirley and Gret going to college and barely seeing Dad, no one has asked me what I want or what I don't.

"I don't want what I know I'm supposed to be getting."

"What do you mean?" Aggie asked.

"Breasts. And . . . don't make fun, but I haven't gotten my period yet."

"Oh! You're lucky. I got mine in fifth grade, can you believe it? I feel like an old pro now. I actually really like tracking my cycle. My mom gave me a calendar when I first got it. I got in the habit of writing it down. It's kind of beautiful to get to learn my body like that. She was all about how the moon follows us, changes its shape as we do. As women, you know?"

"I guess I don't feel that way at all. I feel like I don't know my body."

"Well, you've got your whole life to learn it, right?"

Aggie grabbed my shoulders and shook me a little and then we collapsed. There was so much more I wanted to tell her, James. But I was scared she'd stop being my friend like Dara. We just became friends, some things I need to stuff further down until they get too big to fit into my pockets.

It is almost noon now and Aggie's fork still rests against the plate she ate on. I'm not ready to wash it. Nothing is the same, yet *I* am. Or perhaps I am not. Perhaps I will never be the same and the same no longer exists.

Last night, Aggie said that we are onions. Always unpeeling, making people and ourselves cry as we unwrap. I have so many more layers, James. I feel like I'm just starting to unravel and see what has been hiding in me. What was hiding in you? Were there things you were afraid to unwrap?

Monday, November 1

Halloween used to be my favorite holiday and I didn't even dress up. I guess eighth grade was my last costume celebration; I was a news reporter. Did you like Halloween, James? Aggie was going to stay over and help hand out candy, but then she remembered she had a math test today and had to study, so I wound up giving out candy with Shirley. I thought it was going to be lame, but actually it gave us a chance to talk between doorbell rings.

"Why'd you get such crappy candy this year?" I couldn't help but ask.

"What do you mean? What's wrong with Tootsie Roll Pops and Smarties?"

"Usually you get chocolate," I said.

"Yeah, and then I wind up eating what's left. Best to get rid of the temptation. But don't worry," she smiled. "Flor is coming over later and she's giving out the good stuff. I'll ask her to save you some."

"Thanks."

"How . . . how has school been since . . . "

"The grief counselors have gone, so I guess we're supposed to be over it by now."

"Well, it doesn't exactly work that way, you know that. Did James have many friends? Have they thought about memorializing him in any way?"

"He was a bully, Shirley."

"Eleanor, you know I hate—"

"Well, he was. And I'm sure he must have had some friends, but . . . I don't know. The thing is, I'm still trying to figure out why it all upset me so much. It's like I feel this need to understand why he would . . . why he needed to . . . "

Suddenly, Shirley was holding me, and something must have opened up inside me because I was weeping. Really, James, like chest heaving and snot everywhere.

"We may never know, sweetheart. And I wouldn't dare tell you how to feel, but—"

"But?"

"But the reason was his. It doesn't matter so much now. What matters is what remains."

"What do you mean?" I asked.

"Eleanor, when I was feeling depressed, if I had tried to tell you, if I had successfully articulated what was going through my mind, it wouldn't have necessarily solved anything. In fact, it wouldn't have made you feel better. It may not have even helped you to understand. Sometimes life and who and how we are just doesn't make sense. It just is. We work with what we've got."

"But he couldn't. He couldn't work with it."

"No, but again, it's about the remainder. Being as alive as you can possibly be. To understand who you are and . . . well, keep going, I guess."

Shirley wiped my nose as though her fingers were a tissue. Gross, I know, but that's what moms do, I guess, and all I could do was smile.

"I'm not ready to call you Mom," I said, nervously.

She just stared at me and I worried she was going to break down. Then, she said in an almost-whisper, "I understand. You let me know when you are, okay?"

"Yeah, okay."

Then, the doorbell rang, and we had a slew of ghosts and Power Rangers and some costumes we weren't exactly sure of and the night rolled on.

〜

Tuesday, November 2

Dear James,

Dara actually talked to me today. She dropped a note on my desk in math class.

> *Eleanor, can we talk? I feel like it's been 4ever. Maybe we can sit together on the bus after school? Dara*

Before I headed out the door after class, I turned to look at her and nodded. I may have smiled a little too. I guess I figured she hated me and had no interest in making up. It didn't seem like she told my secret to anyone.

On the bus ride home, it felt so strange to be sitting next to her again even though it really hadn't been that long. And yet, I felt like so much had changed. Although my hair was growing in, I really liked it short. I've begun to play around with it a little, using gel and mousse, some days slicking it back or letting it be like a wild thunderstorm jutting from my scalp. Shirley keeps asking if I'm going to let it grow out, but after cutting it, I can't imagine it the way that it was. This is me now.

"Hey, I bought a bag of your favorite chips—barbecue. Want some?" Dara opened the bag and brought it closer to me.

"Sure." I leaned in and dipped my hand into the bag.

"So, what's up?" Dara crunched on a chip and half of it plunged into her lap. Barbeque powder rained like New Year's Eve confetti on her thigh. She swatted it away, waiting for my response.

"I failed my Spanish test," I blurted.

"Oh yeah? I'm doing pretty good in Spanish. I can help you with conjugation or whatever."

"Yeah, maybe. What's up with you?"

"My parents are probably getting a divorce."

"Oh, I'm sorry, Dara."

"My dad was sleeping in the basement for weeks and I finally just asked him what was happening. They're calling it a separation, but . . . "

"Well, maybe they'll change their minds. You never know." I said this, knowing they probably won't.

"Maybe. Remember the beach this summer? Feels like so long ago. I had a feeling then. They were being so nice, and I don't know, something felt off. Remember?" Dara's voice drifted and I could tell she was quite sad about it.

"Yeah. Gosh, that really did feel like so long ago."

I spent two weeks in July—before Gret went away—on Long

Beach Island at Dara's family's beach house. We lived on hot dogs and fried everything and one night, we walked outside in our pajamas and howled at the moon (kind of) and fell asleep in the sand underneath more stars than we could ever count in our lifetime.

"I thought maybe you'd apologize first," she said.

"I'm not sure what I'd be apologizing about. You're the one—"

"You just ran out of my house that day! Didn't call or anything. And then you came to school and all your hair was gone. I'm supposed to be your best friend."

"You are. You were."

"And you're . . . you know . . . and you didn't even tell me that."

"Gay? Did you happen to think that maybe I wasn't ready to even say anything? I haven't even told anyone yet. Have you?"

"No, Eleanor. I wouldn't blab. It's yours to tell, but. Are you really? I mean, how do you even know?"

"How do *you* know?"

"How do I know what?"

"How do you know you're not gay?" I asked.

Dara just looked at me as though I had asked her the most ridiculous question.

"Eleanor, please," was all she could say.

James, everything changes all the time and it's so easy to forget or not pay attention to it. With my hair short, I can see the passing days as it slowly starts to even itself out. I feel like whatever has been growing inside me has gotten louder in these two weeks. And maybe some things are finally ready to come out.

Oh, and I guess Dara and I are still fighting. We spent the rest of the bus ride in silence.

〜

Tuesday, November 2 (later)

Dear James,

I threw out that mix tape I was listening to the night you pushed me. Actually, I thought I had already. I didn't want to be reminded of that night. But when I was looking for something under my bed, I found it. I pulled out the thread, watched it unravel and get immediately tangled. Then I threw the tape in the garbage can in my bedroom. I think it's time for a new one. New music. Maybe I'll make you one. One I would have given to you if we were friends.

~

Wednesday, November 3

Sometimes school feels like a rerun of a cancelled television show. We see the same people in the same mint green hallways wearing the same outfits having the same conversations. It's not that nothing happens, it's just that we so quickly forget what came before all this.

~

Thursday, November 4

Aggie asked if I wanted to come over to her house this weekend and I wanted to scream out YESYESYES, except I'm spending this weekend at Dad's. He's been out of town a lot lately and we haven't spent a full weekend together in almost a month. Dad used to be my favorite parent and I guess he still is, but I don't see him very often. I bet you liked your mom best. She seems really nice. Oh! Shirley and I are going over to your house for dinner on Friday night. Really weird. Can you even imagine if you were still . . . well, I guess if you were still alive I wouldn't be going there. I never would have met your mom. And I certainly wouldn't be writing you these letters.

I thought Shirley was doing better, but the other day she didn't even get dressed and I've learned that's a sign. Maybe she just felt like being lazy. I mean, if it were up to me, I'd stay in my pajamas all day. I'd even go to school in them, who cares?

〜

Friday, November 5

Dear James,

Last night Flor and I went to group. On the way there, I asked her how her date from last week went. In the time I've known her, she's never gone on a date before, or at least she never mentioned it.

"We went to an Italian restaurant near her house. They serve family style."

"What's her name? What's she look like? Will there be a second date?"

"You're rather interested, aren't you?" she said, smiling. "Her name's Theresa. I met her at the library and we just started chatting. She's taller than me, more slender. Dark hair. Glasses."

"You think you'll see her again?"

"We saw each other a few days ago. We'll see how it goes." Flor smiled in a way I hadn't seen before. She looked truly happy.

"I'm worried about Shirley," I blurted.

"Eleanor, there's no need. She's—"

"She didn't get dressed at all the other day. When I got home from school, she was watching her soap operas. She looked like she hadn't moved from the couch all day. I don't know. I feel like I need to pay extra attention to these things now."

"I understand being worried but give her a chance to have bad days. She's human."

"I guess." I wandered my eyes toward the moving landscape out the window. McDonald's, bank, jewelry store, another McDonald's, Wendy's, strip mall, strip mall, strip mall, tree.

"So . . . anyone catching *your* eyes these days?" Flor never asked about my dating life, mainly because I've never been anywhere close to having one.

"Maybe a little, but—"

"Oh? What are they like?"

James, I wasn't thinking this then, but I do think it's interesting that Flor never used a he or she.

"I don't know. I don't really want to talk about it. Not yet, at least."

You probably don't care about this and would much prefer to hear about your mom. It seems she finds group to be really helpful. She even told the group that she started seeing a therapist, which I guess is a big deal because she said she'd never seen one before. She's still hoping your dad will come join the group sometime, but so far, it's just been her.

She asked if I like fried chicken. I bet your mom is a really good cook.

⌇

Saturday, November 6

Dear James,

Your house smells like cooked carrots and pine trees.

Shirley and I got there a little early. Your mom was still in the kitchen, frying chicken. I offered to help, and she let me whip the potatoes with the electric beater. She even gave me an apron to put on, which she said was yours. Her and Shirley talked a bit while I whipped, but of course I was listening the whole time.

"Burt is at church. He is meeting with a couple tonight who are getting married in a few weeks and they've been having counseling sessions. He sends his regrets."

"How is he . . . coping?" Shirley asked.

"We're both just without words. I haven't even been able to go in James's bedroom. I don't want to open the door. I don't want his smell to escape." She blushed. "I went in right after and then . . . he's just . . . he's everywhere."

James, there is so much I wanted to say. I wanted to tell her how I used to be afraid to go anywhere near Shirley's bedroom while she was in the hospital—we found her in her bed. That every time I even looked in the doorway, it was like replaying that day all over again. But I didn't. I just mixed the potatoes and let them talk.

"Helaine, if you ever want to talk, I am here. So is Eleanor, of course." She looked at me and I tried to force a smile.

"Actually, I wanted to see if Eleanor might want some of James's tapes. Eleanor, I remember during group that you mentioned you liked the Nirvana band. James was quite enamored, to put it mildly."

"Oh, uh, yeah. Sure."

"His bedroom is just up the stairs to the right."

"I thought . . . I thought you didn't want to open his door. I mean, it's fine. I don't need to—"

"Just close it when you're in there and then when you leave. It's okay, dear."

James, I'm not sure what I was expecting when I went into your room. Obviously, bedrooms tell a lot about a person. I mean, if you were to go into my room, you'd learn that I love the color purple. Dad painted my walls when I was seven. Honestly, my love affair with purple kind of ended a few years ago and I much prefer blue and green, but I've been too lazy to even think of repainting or asking Shirley if I can. I have a poster of The Scream, you know that painting by ~~Edward~~ Edvard Munch? I've got a photo of whales because I used to want to be a marine biologist but changed my mind. Just haven't taken the poster down. A poster from the movie Fried Green Tomatoes. I liked it, but between you and me, I have a

Saturday, November 6

Dear James,

I thought maybe I missed an important detail about when I was born, so I figured my dad could fill in the details that Shirley had missed. I know this sounds CRAZY, but the way I've been feeling lately, maybe the doctor took something away and everyone just forgot to tell me.

"What do you remember about my birth?" I asked him.

We were both too full from taco night to engage in talk of dessert.

"I remember that after her water broke, she just went about her day."

He stopped, smiled, and I noticed his eyes getting watery. "She mopped the floor, laid down on the couch and turned on *M*A*S*H*. Your mom must have seen that movie twenty times. Ask her and she'll tell you she notices something different each time. She didn't call me until the credits rolled."

"Were you mad?"

"Mad? Why?"

"That she didn't call you right away?"

"No, I'd come to expect the oddities of your mother."

"So . . . then she called you. And you . . . what? Came to pick her up? Brought her to the hospital?"

"Actually, she asked me to stop at the deli first and get her a corned beef sandwich with extra mustard. And a Dr. Brown's cream soda. Once we got to the hospital everything just happened so quickly."

"And then I just popped out?"

"Something like that, kiddo."

"And how'd you feel when you saw I was a girl? Or—"

"You know, in those days, people didn't know beforehand what sex the baby was. Or *we* didn't, at least. We found out that moment you arrived. I think we both wanted another girl so much that we believed we'd wished you into one."

"So, you had names picked out in case I was a boy too?"

"Yes. Evan."

Evan. I liked the sound of that name. I knew no Evans, so it had a sense of mystery. It was kind of plain but also close to the word *even*. You know: flat, smooth, uniform, steady. These are the things I wanted. These are the things I longed for. Instead, my parents wished me into a *girl* and now I'm curved and loose. I want to feel like an Evan, but instead I'm an Eleanor.

"The thing is, I . . . well, I guess I wonder if I looked okay."

"What do you mean?"

"Like, was I extra bloody or did I have any organs born on the outside or . . . Well, I know Mom *smoked* during the whole pregnancy. Doesn't that cause some kind of side effect? Was I . . . *missing* anything?"

"In those days, Eleanor, we had no idea about things like that. The doctors even smoked in the room with you! But you came out fine. Don't you think? All we kept saying through the whole pregnancy was we wanted a healthy baby. Everything else really didn't matter."

"But . . . but you just said you *wished* I would be a girl."

"Yes. And we were blessed with two."

"Yeah, yeah, I guess."

James, you know how you feel after you're sick with a cold? Like you've spent days unable to breathe, all clogged up, sneezing and blowing your nose and it starts to hurt because the skin is all red and chapped and you think to yourself: I'm never going to breathe again! My nose is always going to be red and sore and this is my life! But then ~~miraculosly~~ miraculously you get better and your nose clears up and you can suddenly smell everything. But it's like your nose is improved, better than it was, and you can smell things you weren't able to before, or at least it feels that way. Is this making any sense?

What I am trying to say is that I feel super aware of my body these days. It's only a matter of time until I start ~~menstrating~~ ~~menctrating~~ menstruating and my body will feel less like mine. I've already started to grow some hair under my arms and on my legs and Shirley keeps saying that I need to start wearing deodorant because I guess puberty has a smell or something? But James, what if I don't want to get my period? What if I'd prefer to skip it. Bigger boobs? No thanks. Don't I get a say in all this?

Anyway, I'm wiped. Goodnight.

Sunday, November 7

When I got home from Dad's, I screamed a hello to Shirley and then ran up to my room. I told her that I forgot about a homework assignment, but the truth is I couldn't wait to open your journal. I thought about just devouring the whole thing at once. But it's like that time Shirley bought a chocolate cheesecake to celebrate . . . wait, what were we celebrating? Oh, when Gret got into college! Dad even came over and we each had a slice. Gret's was tiny because she was already worried about freshman sixteen or something about gaining weight when you go to college. That night, I woke in the middle of the night and ate the rest of the cake. Can you believe it? I definitely paid for it the next morning because my stomach felt like I swallowed a brick building, but it was so good.

What's your point, Eleanor, is what you'd be asking me right now. My POINT is that once I ate the rest of the cake, it was gone. Nothing left to go back to. I guess I just want your voice to remain, to learn the mystery of you slowly. So, if you can believe it, James, I limited myself to the first three pages.

Dear Elinore,

Sometimes I feel like being somewhere else is the only way I could be me. Floating around in space with the stars and planets and dust and rocks and whatever else is up there. I'll never be able to really be me here. My dad is really religious. My mom is too, but also cool with me being different sometimes. I think she probably knows. When my dad is not around, my mom lets me cook with her. We make all sorts of things. She taught me how to make ~~Gocci~~ gnocci. We bake. She gives me recipes and then I measure things out. It's like science, but I like it. My dad is very traditional and would call me all sorts of things if he knew how much I loved to cook. He already calls me the names anyway. I hate him. Something changed when I reached ~~to~~ 8. Earlier than that even. It's like I could do whatever I wanted until 6, and then things started to matter more. I cooked with my mom and baked with her. She even got me a Betty Crocker cookie cookbook for Christmas one year and man, I loved that. All the pages were stained, full of food from all the recipes I tried. Then it wasn't cool anymore. Dad said I was becoming a sissy. A fairie. Yeah, he actually said this. I have no friends or people who actually tell me I am OK. I am just reminded of what I am doing wrong. That I am not and never will be enough.

DEAR ELINORE,

I USED TO LISTEN TO MICHAEL JACKSON'S SONG "BEN" OVER AND
OVER. I HAD IT ON A RECORD, SO I JUST HAD TO LIFT UP THE
NEEDLE TO PLAY IT AGAIN. YOU KNOW IT WAS ABOUT HIS PET
RAT, RIGHT? RATS ARE SO UGLY AND PEOPLE RUN FROM THEM. I
WENT TO NEW YORK CITY ONCE WITH MY AUNT AND UNCLE
AND SAW THIS REALLY GROSS ONE ON THE SUBWAY TRACKS.
HALF A TAIL WITH A BIG BLOODY ~~SCKAB~~ SCAB ON ITS SIDE.
AFTER THAT, I THOUGHT HOW MUCH I HAVE IN COMMON WITH
RATS. I MEAN, PEOPLE DON'T EVEN UNDERSTAND HOW SMART
THEY ARE. THEY'RE JUST TRYING TO DO THEIR OWN THING, YOU
KNOW? WE THROW OUT OUR ~~PREDUDICE~~ PREJUDICES AND MAKE IT
SEEM LIKE THEY'RE ALL BAD. BUT THEY AREN'T.

NOBODY GETS ME. NOBODY.

Dear Elinore,

I wish I could write like Kurt. Sing like Kurt. That's why I started smoking cigarettes. I wanted my voice to sound scratched up like his. I don't know. I guess I thought maybe if I sucked on a lot of cigarettes, my voice would get all gravelly and cool-sounding. Basically I steal them from my dad, who smokes them in secret even though we all know about it because it's not like they don't smell or anything. So far, I haven't noticed a difference in my voice, but it hasn't been that long. I want to look like Kurt too. It's like he's so cool, he doesn't care what anyone thinks. He'll wear a dress and no one calls him a fag because he's Kurt Cobain. I feel sick all the time. My dad makes me feel like I'm sick. I wouldn't choose this. I didn't ask to be like this. I just keep listening to Kurt, letting his words drown out everything else. Everyone else. Brian was my best friend 1st grade to sixth. Then, something happened. It's like he figured it out. Shit, I'm lying even to this page. He let me touch him. Once. After camp, when he came over my house. My parents weren't home, and we were in my room listening to music and it kind of just happened. He didn't stop me. He was touching me too. The next day, I was a ghost to him. After calling his name ten times and being ignored, I got the hint. I stopped trying to have friends after that. Maybe I loved him. Maybe I realized it would always be like that.

Monday, November 8

Dear James,

I fell asleep clutching your notebook. We sit in classrooms for years and years. Same faces. But we have no idea what we are all swallowing deep, deep inside us. Why were you writing to me, James? *Me?* And why did you choose me to bully? Do we hate the people we recognize ourselves in? I mean, parts of ourselves that we can't exactly be? I can't believe you were . . . *were you* . . . gay. Too.

Today in English class, we discussed a short story we read for homework by a guy named Sherman Alexie called "What You Pawn I Will Redeem." I liked it because it took place in one day and he separated it by hour. This homeless guy needed to get money to buy back his grandmother's regalia from a pawnshop. And every hour he gets money, but then winds up spending it. Anyway, during the discussion, Ms. Raimondo said it is never really about what you are striving to get or achieve, it's the journey. Then, Matthew said something annoying.

"But who cares about the journey if you never get what you want? No one cares about everything you failed at, right?"

"I don't know," said Aggie. "I think failure is kind of important too. Like we should be encouraged to fail more."

"Are you kidding me?" said Janae. "If I fail, my parents would kill me. There's way too much pressure to get good grades."

"Yeah, but like, we often remember the failures. I know it sucks, but don't you think that's when we learn so much more?" Aggie said.

"Aggie, that's an insightful point," Ms. Raimondo said. "Even when we fail, we are still achieving something—"

"Tell that to my dad," Janae interrupted.

"What we achieve is the desire to thrive. We cannot always be number one. We cannot always get A pluses on everything. As much as we may want to," Ms. Raimondo smiled. "But the thing is, our protagonist experienced so much life in those hours of trying to make the money he needed. *That* is really what this story is about. The real adventure is in the struggle. To risk. What is lost."

James, I can't even begin to express how today's lesson affected me. Sometimes it feels like Ms. Raimondo is digging out all the secret questions in me. During lunch, Aggie and I talked more about the story. She loved it too.

Wednesday, November 10

Dear James,

I was ten when Shirley and Dad told Gret and I that they were divorcing, and it was over a game of cards. Shirley was leaning against the counter, smoking, while Dad, Gret and I played Rummy 500. I remember that I kept playing even after Dad told us. I was so focused on my cards and matching suits, that I barely heard him utter *'separation'* and then *'divorce'*. What broke my concentration was Greta. She was crying so loudly, my ribs jumped. *Really.* I mean, she can get loud when she sets her tears loose.

I really wasn't that upset, nor was I surprised. It was only when my dad officially moved out that I realized things were never going to be the same. I've been conditioned to expect the worst when playing cards because that is when the bad news is often brought out. I remember learning about this in science class. *Conditioning.* When my grandma was dying, Dad told me over a heated game of Gin Rummy. And when cousin Bertie was diagnosed with leukemia, Dad and I were playing Uno. I realize now, whenever I play cards with friends, I have a terrible feeling in my stomach like someone is about to die or something.

I mention this because I went to Aggie's house after school today and when she suggested a card game, I noticed myself start to sweat. *A lot.*

But nothing happened. In fact, we played Spit and the whole time we shared stories from childhood.

"My mom was a big feminist. I mean, she used to give me all sorts of books to read to learn about all the waves," Aggie said.

"Waves?" I asked.

"Well, the one we know most about is second wave. But first was like all about women's suffrage."

"Oh, yeah, right." James, I had no idea there were different types of feminism, but I was too embarrassed to ask questions.

"My mom was a bra burner, big time hippie in her prime. She mellowed once she married, but she always taught me the importance of being a feminist. You're one, right?"

"Oh, uh, I guess. I mean, I've never called myself that, but . . . "

"Women are not equal, Eleanor, and until they are, we need to keep fighting."

"Definitely."

"My mom actually bought me my first vibrator."

"What?"

"She felt it was important I celebrate myself and never feel shame. Oh, Eleanor, I wish you could have met her. Have you . . . have you ever . . . "

James, I was just about dying at this point. Talking about *masturbation* with AGGIE?!!!

"Uh, yeah. I mean, not with a . . . a . . . "

James, I was so sweaty at this point, I could have swam home in the ocean of my perspiration.

"Don't worry. I'm not going to ask for details. I can already see how uncomfortable you are." Aggie smiled and pinched my arm a little, teasing me.

James, you probably won't believe me, but I actually told Aggie all about it. Well, maybe not everything.

Shirley had all her book club people over and they were discussing—I will never forget—*Carleen's Lost Lover.* They loved reading excerpts out loud that usually just made me blush when I eavesdropped, but that never stopped me from pressing my ears to the floor of my bedroom and listening to their slightly muffled words.

There was a scene they read that was kinda . . . sexy . . . I'm shy even writing that down, but I lay down in my bed and started to imagine what they were reading and then, I guess my imagination took over.

That's where I stopped. I couldn't tell Aggie the rest because then she would have known what I was thinking. But the thing is, James, that was just the beginning.

My hands moved down and I began pressing on myself. On my . . . *self.* Between my legs. Just pressing and poking. I imagined my fingers as fan blades, spinning into me. I couldn't believe how good it felt. The intense pressure.

Images grew inside my head. Aggie's braid against her bony shoulder. The weight of it and how soft it is and that first time she let me touch it and unravel it and a few hairs fell out and I remember finding them on my comforter the next day and putting them in my mouth and tasting her shampoo and her breath kind of sweet like pancake syrup and her collarbone which my fingers dug into and her lips pink pink pink her bottom lip bigger and thicker like an inch worm and the way her tongue comes out to lick them and the spit, her spit creating bubbles and her teeth wrangling them in and her fingers so skinny in my hair which is still quite patchy and her legs around me and we are breathing so heavy and hard, our lungs almost break free and her lips are over mine and my cheeks swell around hers and we are on fire and we are burning and then my lungs went from inflated hot air balloon to deflated Santa ornament on front lawns during Christmastime.

How could I possibly tell *that* to Aggie?

James, of course this wasn't the first time. The first time was when I was eight. No, nine. Yeah. And it was kind of accidental. I woke up all sweaty from a terrible nightmare, which I certainly can't remember now, but I remember at that time it haunted me away from sleep. My blanket was all bunched up at the foot of my bed; my sheets were coming off at one of the corners, and my pillow was no longer by my head. It was being held captive between my legs and with each twitch and shake, I was feeling something. I just kind of rocked on my pillow and the friction was unlike anything I had ever felt.

Once, my friend Hannah told me she got excited when she went horseback riding for the first time. Since then, I have a fear of horses. I would be mortified if I orgasmed from being on an animal!

Kate likes to masturbate with her mother's shoulder massager. I was over her house last year for her birthday party and we all took turns pressing this vibrating plastic contraption between our legs (underpants left on, of course) and there was a lot of hesitant shrieking. Dara told me that she never masturbates—tried it once and just didn't get anything from it. I think she's afraid to turn herself on, or maybe she just doesn't want to share her own stories.

~

Thursday, November 11

Dear James,

Tonight in group, I talked a lot more. Maybe because I've been a little worried that Shirley is going to try and hurt herself again.

"About a month before Shirley . . . I was in my bedroom and smelled something really strange. Flor wasn't over; it was just Shirley and me. I went into her bedroom and noticed a lit cigarette between her fingers. She had fallen asleep and the ash burnt her hand. I can still smell that sizzling flesh like over-cooked hamburger. So awful. Surprisingly, the burning didn't wake her up. I was finally able to nudge her awake. She claimed that she just hadn't slept the night before and must have been in a deep sleep. I believed her in that moment."

"Eleanor, have you shared this memory with your mother?" Peter asked.

"Not really. When I visited her in the hospital, my sister and I went to a . . . like a meeting . . . with her and her doctor. He asked us to share our fears with her. First, he had us write down a list and then he had us read what we felt comfortable sharing out loud. I remember telling her how scared I was that she'd fall asleep again while smoking. I begged her to quit. My sister did too. She stopped, sort of. I think she still sneaks in a few every so often because I can smell it on her, even though she insists it's just 'ghost smoke'. That's what she calls it. She sleeps with her bedroom door open now."

"Was that her decision, or . . . " Peter asked.

"I asked her. I haven't been able to go in there. I think she understands why."

"Eleanor, would you like to share anything else you remember from that time?" Peter looked at me with his earthworm mustache.

"When I was seven years old, my mother quit smoking for the fifth or sixth or thirtieth time in her life. Hard to keep track. Anyway, it was wonderful. Suddenly my own sense of smell became intensified. Secondhand smoke is a killer, you know. All the ashtrays were thrown away, and there were a lot of them. The air was clean without a thick interruption of smoke and coughing. I really thought it was a smooth break-up, but I soon learned that Shirley was having an affair on the side.

"I was supposed to be at Dara's house—my friend, my *ex*-friend. I ran home to get a few of my dolls because we were playing our favorite game, Broadway Show, where we sat all of our dolls next to each other as our audience, and then we sang songs like famous Broadway stars. Shirley was alone—I'm not sure where Greta or my dad were—and I could smell her affair the moment I opened the front door. I quietly snuck upstairs to my room, and then stopped, inhaling the smoke. I think I only noticed it because I had become so used to the cleaner air. It's like the walls lost weight, no longer suffocated by pounds of cigarette smoke.

"Slowly, I walked into Shirley's bedroom, which has its own bathroom. The door was open and she was sitting on the toilet, smoking a cigarette and blotting her arm, which was bleeding. She didn't see me. I never told anyone that I had seen her like that. I didn't understand then what had happened. Later, I realized she had been cutting herself. Blood and smoke flushed down the toilet. Then, three weeks later, Shirley tried to kill herself. The first time or the fourth time or the twelfth time. I didn't want to know then, and now it is too late to ask. Dad had Gret and I stay with Grandma, while Shirley was in the hospital. I actually didn't know what was going on. They kept saying Shirley was sick, so I figured she was away because she was contagious. I wasn't scared. I didn't even ask questions."

"Did your parents explain to you what was happening?" Maeve asked.

"Not that I remember. I started to piece it all together years later. I guess that's why I'm so nervous now. She keeps trying to tell me that she is fine. But how can that be? She tried so many times and she's still here. It's only a matter of time—"

"But Eleanor, did you hear what you just said? She is still here." This was your mom talking. James, I feel like your mother is a warm hug wrapped up inside a human being. It's like everything she says is so comforting.

"Yeah, but it doesn't make my fear go away," I replied.

—

Sunday, November 14

Dear James,

I was all set to go to Dad's this weekend, but he had to fly to . . . somewhere . . . for some kind of trade show for work. Of course he was apologetic, but I was disappointed. He promised he'd make it up. Shirley had some sort of plans with a new friend she made from her therapy group, so Flor asked if I might want to go into the city and have an adventure.

"We can eat out somewhere fun and go to a museum. You think you might like that?"

"Nah, I'll just stay home and watch television or read a book or something."

"Nope."

"Nope?" I said.

"Eleanor, this has been a doozy of a month. Let's go to New York and breathe in my favorite childhood smells. It's been awhile since you and I hung out together and—"

"That's because you've got a girlfriend now," I teased.

"Okay, okay. Fair enough, although Theresa and I haven't exactly used that terminology quite yet. Let's have some fun in the city."

Have I mentioned how much I love Flor? It's impossible not to notice how wonderful she has been this year with Shirley getting sick and Gret leaving for college. Really, I felt this way about her even before all that. She's pretty amazing. In Spanish, her name means flower. She once told me that her mother never had any names picked out and wanted to wait to give birth before she made the big decision. When Flor's mom first locked eyes with her, she noticed all her folds and pinkness. "*Tú eres mi flor salvaje*," her mother cooed. Flor's father is/was Colombian. Is and was. He is still alive, so I assume he is still Colombian, but Flor always talks about him in the past tense. He grew up in Florencia, so in that moment I guess everything just seemed so perfect. Florencia Erlene Leandro Acacia.

James, I wonder where you went when you visited New York City. Did you go to a museum? What did you eat? Did you like how loud and tall everything is?

I chose the Metropolitan Museum of Art and suggested we head to this big bookstore on Union Square afterward, which Aggie told me about, called The Strand. She said it was as big as our school, just full of every book you could ever think of. New ones and old ones and signed copies by famous writers.

Flor parked her car by the bus station off route 9 and purchased two round trip tickets. On the ride there, I looked out the window, thinking of you, James. Lately, I wonder about what would have happened if we were friends and you told me what you told your notebook. I'd react without judgment. You'd be shocked and then I'd say something like, I am too. We'd laugh because we'd both acknowledge how scared we both were about coming out.

Actually, I've been thinking about that a lot too, James. I think I might be ready, whatever that means. I feel like I want to do what you weren't able to. Then, maybe anyone else who might be feeling the same way would feel comfortable to come out as well. I can show people that it's really not a big deal.

We had things in common, James. We could have been friends, I could have helped you. You'd still be here. But you felt like the only one. No one is the only one.

At the museum, there was a neat exhibit with a really cool painter named Kandinsky. I kept staring—which Flor encouraged—in order to find the meaning. I don't really know much about art besides that I like when it makes me feel something, and I definitely *felt* things. It's like he creates these animals . . . no, musical instruments out of lines and shapes. I thought about that time I was nine years old and I found a finger on the Jersey shore. At first, I thought it was a slice of driftwood, a crab corpse or an unnamed beast from the ocean's floor. If Greta were with me, she would have screamed its remaining skin off. But

I was alone, and a reaction was unnecessary, allowing me a chance to really look at it. I remember picking it up and carrying it in my palm as though it were a tiny fetus. Gross, right? At that time, when I was nine, I probably would have just described it as an uncooked french fry. It didn't feel like much. I remember that. It was water-logged and soggy, but also stiff and discolored. The fingernail was gone; the water stole it away. I found a shell, big enough to act as its sofa and placed the finger inside. The sand huddled around the shell and I hovered above it all.

I wondered what it would feel like to lose a part of me. What if I lost a finger? Or a whole hand? Or the ability to see? If I had stayed in that spot long enough, would more body parts begin to wash ashore? At that age, I had an unspoken fear of disability. If someone passed by in a wheelchair or with a disrupted face, I would fight the urge to stare and look away simultaneously. I worried it was contagious. Now, I think scars are beautiful and disabilities are almost like a super-power. There really is no *normal*.

I can't recall how long I sat with that finger. It could have been hours, but probably just minutes. I compared it to mine: its pale sausage thickness to my pale bony tightness. I wondered if it came from a man or woman and did it matter? My fingers curled in and out of my palm, blinking—an attempt to prove they worked and were okay. There was a moment during this when I began to cry. I wouldn't even have noticed had I not caught the exact moment of when my salty tear fell right onto this finger. It's like we were united. A part of me had entered it.

Looking at the painting, I felt this sense of being part of it somehow. I guess this happens anytime you experience something—even if it's something not exactly meant for you. Like when I listen to music and feel like the lyrics were meant for me. Or with that finger, like I was supposed to find it. Someone else's loss can lead us toward our own discoveries. Like the story we read in English class! Oh my gosh, you'd think I was such a dork, James.

Anyway, I felt like I could see a laundry machine of tumbled people and emotions in the painting. I wrote down a bunch of stuff in my notebook, but when it came time to actually talk out loud about how I was feeling, all I could do was smile. Funny, but I felt like maybe Flor knew exactly what I felt because she was smiling too.

After the museum, Flor and I were exhausted. Looking at art is far more tiring than riding my bike. It's kind of strange that way. Flor joked that the air is drugged so that paintings, which might normally seem ordinary, will appear fascinating. The Met is also really big. I don't even think we saw a fraction of it.

"I'm not sure I'm up for the bookshop," I said, sleepily. "Or maybe we can go someplace to eat first?"

"You read my mind!"

Flor grew up in Queens, lived a few years in the Bronx, then Brooklyn, and then moved to New Jersey. In New York, she never has to ask for directions. Even when I felt like we were lost, she always found a way to where we needed to be.

"I know a great spot downtown. Well, actually it's been awhile since I've been there. The truth is, the last time I was there I was on a date." Flor blushed a little. "Yeah, I can't imagine this place closing. Best pizza I ever had."

At the pizza place, all the tables were covered in red-and-white plastic tablecloths with a few cigarette stains creating occasional polka dots. It was nowhere near fancy, which I liked. All I could think about was Flor there with some woman, nervously sitting across from one another, asking questions back and forth to test compatibility. I imagine a date to be kind of like an interview without the possibility of a paycheck at the end. You dress up. You're on your best behavior. You hope for the best. I've never been on a date yet, not one that really mattered to me. Maybe my first date can be here.

The waiter arrived at our table wearing the same colors that decorated the whole place: red, white, and green. He was really tall, so Flor and I both tilted our heads way back. "We'll have a large pizza with olives . . . " Flor looked at me and I nodded. "And peppers and onions. Also a root beer for her and a diet coke for me."

"It smells good in here," I said.

"Wait until you try the pizza."

"Thanks for all this, Flor."

"I keep thinking about what you said to me in the car the other day. I worry I was dismissive, but the thing is, your mom is actually doing a heck of a lot better."

"I guess."

"She's going to individual therapy, she's got her group therapy. She's meeting people, she seems to be adjusting quite well to her meds . . . "

"I wish I could turn it off, you know?"

"Turn what off, honey?" Flor asked.

"Just this worry. This fear. That I'm going to come home and find her. Like Gret did."

"Eleanor, it would be unfair for me to tell you not to feel that way. You might have that fear for a long time. But I would advise you to talk with your mom more. You don't need to pretend these worries away."

"But I don't want to worry her."

"Sweetie, she's gotten a lot stronger. Give her the chance to show you that. You're lucky," Flor paused. I watched her take a deep breath, one so big her entire body got involved. "I wasn't very close to my parents. I loved them, of course. And I know my mother loves me very much, but times were different then. I know your dad loves you very much too."

"You never really talk about your dad. How did he—"

"It's difficult to talk about someone who had such limited access to the happy parts of my life." I watched as Flor fumbled with the tablecloth, smoothing it out.

"Eleanor, things are going to get better. I'm watching you grow into this beautiful and smart human being. All brave and such an individual. I couldn't be that way with my father. And barely with my mother."

"Did they know?"

"I came out to my mother when I was in my mid-twenties. She was still living in Queens then. She made some kind of . . . mixed pot of the old and the new." Flor smiled big, biting her bottom lip. "That's what most of her dishes were called because she'd mix leftovers with *new*-overs. *Her* language. I don't even think my mother ever owned any cookbooks. She just kind of threw things into this giant green pot she's owned for decades—probably belonged to *her* mother—and it always came out brimming with intense flavors. Anyway, she ladled out a bowlful for each of us and then I just kind of blurted it out before I think either of us had the chance to take a bite. I didn't have to say anything. You know, I could have just . . . gone about my life and still she wouldn't know, but my mother and I . . . we weathered many storms."

Just then, the waiter approached with our pizza and it smelled better than I could have ever imagined.

Flor served us each a slice. Then, we curled our pizza a little so that the hot cheese wouldn't fall off, and took a bite.

"Mmmmm," was all I could say.

"Told you so."

"Keep going. With your story, I mean."

"My father . . . I don't ever . . . I don't talk about him because he wasn't a good man. And maybe I shouldn't tell you this, but I will because you're my family, Eleanor. I love you and I don't ever want to pretend with you. My mother did that . . . just pretended my identity away and I almost never forgave her. I still d—" Flor looked down at her pizza and I watched her chest rise and fall.

"For many years, my father abused me. When I finally came forth to tell my mother, she just could not believe any of it. 'Not your father,' she would say. 'He's a good man. A good man.' She'd just say that over and over. And I almost believed her. He finally left before she could kick him out. I haven't seen nor talked to him since. I think he's got another family now. Probably several. I've never really had a good man in my life. No friends or mentors. And I see how you are with *your* father and how he is with you. You're lucky, Eleanor. Really lucky."

All I could do was nod. I got up from the table and walked toward Flor. Her eyes were extra wet. I wrapped my arms around her and we hugged for a really long time.

"I love you," I whispered. "I'm lucky to have my parents, but I'm also really lucky to have *you*."

I let go and felt Flor still holding on. When she broke away, I walked back to my seat and took another piece of pizza, even though I hadn't even finished my first.

"So, after I told my mother I was gay, she just kept eating. Didn't look at me. Focused on the food on her spoon and just shoveled it into her mouth in the daintiest way. I waited. I waited and waited for her to say something, but she never did." Flor laughed a little. "And she still never has. She's met girlfriends and always calls them my *friends*. It's generational. It's cultural. It's a lot of things. She's never pushed me out of her life and she certainly could have. In fact, part of me was ready for that. My mom has invited my girlfriends over to family things, but deep down, I know it upsets her. She doesn't understand, probably never will. It's changed the way I make friendships or even keep them. Funny, I joined that book club in hopes of making some friends and when I met your mother, I knew she'd be in my life forever. There is just something really special about her. She accepts me. She never got strange when I told her I was a lesbian. You'd be surprised how many grown-up straight women subtly stop talking to me. Think I'm gonna hit on them or something."

"Flor, I . . . "

Flor put her pizza down and wiped her hands on her napkin. She stared into my face as though something in me or *on* me had changed. Did I have pizza sauce all over me? Something about this moment, this restaurant, this day was leading me right to the words that have been balancing on the tip of my tongue for months. No, much longer than that.

James, I was ready. This was the moment.

"The thing is . . . well . . . " I took a deep breath, tasting the olives stomped between my teeth. It was the strangest feeling, James, like my emotions were pushing me up against a wall, threatening, "say it, or else," and then the words just kind of fell out.

"I am too," I uttered.

How to describe the slow motion of a moment? In movies, I love this. The record scratch moment, the Tony/Maria moment in West Side Story. I used to listen to that record over and over from Shirley's massive collection. And when I finally saw the movie, I just loved that scene when they first noticed each other at the dance. Nothing and no one else mattered. And suddenly in this pizza restaurant, it was happening to *me*. Was I Tony? Maria? Neither, I guess. I mean, it wasn't quite like *that*. But I swear I heard a record scratch, or maybe that was just my stomach churning and gurgling from eating too fast. I could feel the aftershock of those three words in my body. My knees felt strange: twitching and shaky. My shoulders felt like they were collapsing, and I wasn't even depending on them. Was I even breathing? I felt like maybe I had stopped.

I watched Flor's face go from serious to surprised to not-so-surprised and did she know and what did I really just say and—

"Eleanor, are you saying you're . . . "

"Ummm, I'm saying . . . what *am I* saying? I'm sorry. You were talking about your life and your dad and—"

"Eleanor, don't you apologize, especially about something like this. I'm just trying to understand. I want to make sure I—"

"I didn't plan this, Flor. Not . . . not the *gay* thing. I mean, obviously I didn't plan *that*. But I mean, I didn't plan on telling you today. Or *any* day, really. I . . . and that's not why I cut my hair either. You know, everyone at school probably already thinks I'm . . . you know, Dara called me a lesbian even before *I* was ready to. It's hair. It's hair, Flor. I just don't get how length is attached to who or what I like. I mean, not all lesbians have short hair, right? Right, Flor?"

For a while, or maybe just seconds, Flor and I stared at each other. Our pizza, untouched. Our limbs still, even though I wanted to fidget. I wanted to bite all my nails off. I wanted to pull all my hair out or pick that pimple off my face that was starting to become more noticeable. I wanted to do something to break the silence. And yet, I also wanted to keep it going. I wanted the silence to last forever. I wanted it to coat me like the fancy blueberry maple syrup Shirley once bought that seemed so thick, it took forever to drip down the sides of my pancakes.

"I love you."

It was Flor who broke the silence. I smiled because I couldn't really say what I needed her to say, but that was enough to make me feel like maybe everything was okay, and nothing had really changed between us, especially when she said, "I had a feeling."

We polished off that pie as though we were ending a bout of starvation or breaking Yom Kippur or something like that.

After lunch, we decided to take the train to Union Square and head to The Strand. We were both reenergized from lunch and revelations, and I wanted to at least get a bookmark or something for Aggie from this trip. I also really wanted to see the miles of books she kept talking about.

On Broadway, I noticed the giant flag announcing The Strand, and carts of books right outside for just a dollar or two. No order really, just spines to sift through.

"Shall we go inside?" Flor looked at me with a giant grin. She knows how much I love books and reading. This was the best day I ever remember having.

When we walked in, a nice-looking lady with lots of earrings in her ears greeted us. When she said hello, they shimmied like tiny silver dancers.

I could not believe how many books were in one place, on tables and on shelves, from floor to ceiling.

"I have a book in mind for you," Flor said. "Let's see if we can find it together."

We walked straight back, past the new hardcover fiction and non-fiction books, staff recommendations and other themed tables. There was so much to take in and I started to get overwhelmed with how many books there were that I've yet to read.

"I used to know this beautiful poet," Flor said. "She was my teacher when I went to John Jay for a semester, before I transferred to a different school. It's like I was meant to go there just to meet her. We kept in touch for many years, just here and there. I'd write her letters and she'd occasionally write back. She kept busy. But she died last year, and I still think about the imprint she made as a writer, specifically as a *lesbian* writer, Eleanor. Her name was Audre Lorde."

"You knew a published writer?" I looked up and thought about all the people alphabetized on the shelves. Their lives. Their imaginations.

"Oh, Eleanor, I knew many."

We searched the Ls and I noticed that there were many books by Audre Lorde.

"This is the one," Flor said, handing me a bright orange book that said, *Zami* in giant thick capital letters and then a bit smaller, *A New Spelling of my Name.*

"Cool," was all I could say.

"There is a history of women and men, of activists who died just to be out as gay and lesbian. Hard to imagine maybe, but—"

"I want to know all of them," I said, excitedly.

Flor smiled. "Audre was a black, lesbian feminist. Fought for civil rights. Fantastic scholar. When you were in the room with her, you felt like you were part of a movement. I want you to read this book. At your leisure, of course. I know you have things to read for school, but . . . I guess I just feel excited to share the works of gay and lesbian writers with you, since you probably won't get a tutorial in school. Got to wait for college for that." Flor winked.

I opened the book and flipped through. All these words I didn't know yet but wanted to.

We browsed a little and then made our way to the register. I got a postcard for Aggie of Frida Kahlo, an artist she said she really liked and we made our way with bright yellow Strand bags toward Port Authority bus station to head back to New Jersey.

On the bus back, Flor began asking questions about Aggie.

"You *like* her, yes?"

"Yes," I said. "I like her. But she's not . . . I mean, I don't think . . . we're just friends."

"Got it," she smiled. "Well, I like watching you with her. You seem . . . what words am I looking for . . . celebrated when you're with her."

"Celebrated?"

"Yeah, you interact far differently with her than with Dara. Listen, I'm old, I've had lots of friendships. A few I still have but most have fizzled away. Some are hard work. It's good to have a friend that's curious about you. That asks you questions and shares too. Your mother is like that. She always asks about my day, makes time to listen. And from what I've observed, Aggie is like that too. She's inquisitive."

"Yeah. Yeah, you're right. She tells me all sorts of things that I never even knew about. It's like . . . it's like she helps me to want to know more about me. She's been teaching me about feminism."

"Terrific! Spread it around!" Flor pulled me closer and hugged me. Then, I spent the rest of the bus ride reading from my new book. I love it already.

When we were almost home, I asked her why she thinks so many people are mean to gay people.

"That's a great question, Eleanor. There are too many reasons, but one is that sometimes our beliefs get in the way of our minds expanding. Sometimes what we don't know or don't think we are surrounded by makes us uncomfortable."

I thought about you, James. Your dad being a pastor and all. Maybe he said something to you to make you feel like being gay wasn't okay? I don't believe in all that, but if God existed, wouldn't he or she accept everyone? I think we are all this way because we just *are*. I don't think we choose it. I am not *choosing* to be gay, just like Shirley isn't *choosing* to be depressed. I mean, why would we?

Flor wants to take me to the library and get me some more books by gay writers. She wants me to read about the history. About *my* history because I guess it is mine now. Just like America's history is mine because I live here and should be ~~knowlegable~~ knowledgeable about it. She mentioned a lady named Dorothy Allison. And Leslie Feinberg. She told me to take my time in this. In being gay. I haven't really talked to her about the body things. That feeling of being not quite right. I'm not ready for that yet. I thought it would shift once I came out, but I still feel something. It's like I'm a video game and I really want to get to the next level, but I keep messing up or forgetting something on this one. So I just remain here. Waiting. Waiting for a clue or a hidden trap door to hoist myself out of this and into something different.

Dear Elinore,

I overheard my parents arguing tonight. I heard my name in there, so I think I must have had something to do with it. I'm failing math, yet I was able to keep count of all the times my dad called me a failure tonight: 8. If I had more money saved up, I'd run away, pack up my bookbag full of enough clothes to last, I don't know, a week? Bring my discman and some of my favorite albums: Bossanova (Pixies), Disintegration (the Cure), Bleach (Kurt), Sweet Oblivian (Screaming Trees) and probably another Nirvana one. Here's what I also want. I want to be an astronaut one day and then I can travel to a planet where it doesn't matter what I am. I've actually always wanted to be an astronaut. I think my folks see it as some sort of dumb dream, but I want to be just like Yuri Gagarin. You know, he was the first one to go to outer space? Imagine experiencing something no one else has. Today, I overheard you tell your friend that you think I'm the worst person on Earth. Yeah, I think you're right. I think I would do much better on Pluto. I heard you say something else too. You said Mrs. Butler was so beautiful and I noticed your face when you said it. Like you really really meant it. I don't know, like you like her. Like that. Or maybe girls can say that. Maybe girls can just go around saying other girls are pretty without people thinking things. I think Brian is cute, even though he's a dick. But I could never say that out loud.

79

Monday, November 15

Dear James,

I guess you're right—about things being different for girls—but I'm not sure why. We can be emotional and touchy-feely with each other, but boys can't. Aggie said that boys can be feminists too, but most feel like they aren't supposed to. But if a feminist is someone who believes in the equal rights of men and women, then what's the big deal? Shouldn't we all want that? Flor is a feminist. I think Shirley is too. Audre Lorde definitely was. Last night, I read that she changed the way her name was spelled because she didn't like the way the 'y' hung past the lines in her notebook. So she just removed it.

—

Tuesday, November 16

Dear James,

Dara once told me that no one really likes to hear about someone else's dreams unless they are in them. Well, you were in my dream last night. I was visiting Shirley in the mental hospital and even in my dream, all of the smells and sounds came back to me.

In my dream, I didn't think it was strange that you were in the same ward as Shirley (they usually separate adults from adolescents). You were walking around reading a book that I can't remember now, and I stopped you. I asked you why you were there, and you just shrugged. I told you I was visiting my mom and you just stared at me as though I was speaking a language you didn't know. Then I grabbed you, kind of forcefully. You just let me. You didn't pull away, you didn't scream. And then I hugged you. It was so strange, James. When I woke, I was crying because I realized it was just a dream and you weren't still alive. Did you want someone to stop you? ~~What were you thinking right before~~

I used to visit Shirley every Sunday when she was in the hospital. Greta came too, though there was one time that it was just me. It was the first time I'd been there, and I didn't really know what to expect. I imagined everyone to be kind of out of it, like in a weird, milky daze, everyone drooling and talking to themselves. I mean, I did read *One Flew Over the Cuckoo's Nest* freshman year, but it wasn't as scary as I thought it would be.

I remember I had to go to the bathroom, so she brought me into her room, which she shared with someone else. When I was going to the bathroom, I counted seventeen ants while I was peeing.

James, there are all sorts of new vocabulary words to be learned from being in a mental hospital, like contraband (I brought a bag full of crossword puzzle books and cans of diet soda, but the nurses had to check it first to make sure I didn't bring in any banned stuff). Also vitals (heart stuff), ~~psychomatic~~ psychosomatic (actually I can't remember this one), and intervention (like getting family and friends all together in the same room because someone drinks or takes drugs too much).

Each time I visited Shirley, we ate lunch in the cafeteria. It kind of smelled like ours at school, but way worse. It was always hard to locate my appetite when all the food looked pre-chewed and preserved into cardboard cutouts of artificial versions of the *real thing*. We'd wait in line and choose a sandwich with pink meat between slices of tomato, brown lettuce, and neon yellow cheese. Pink meat. Ham? Even after I took a few bites, I could never figure out what animal it belonged to.

When it was just us—no Greta—we ate in the solarium, which felt like a really warm hug with giant windows surrounding us. There was a bookshelf with tons of books. I remember Shirley telling me the story of how she met my dad without any prompting or anything.

"Your father and I met in a library. Did I ever tell you this story? I thought he was strange. But cute. I was writing an essay contrasting male and female photographers. I liked thinking about lenses separated by gender."

Shirley met my dad when she was a sophomore in college. She wanted to be a photographer. She still has some of her old photos in shoeboxes. None are up, even though they're good enough to display. Some are even great. After they started dating, Shirley stopped going to her classes. It's like she just couldn't do more than one thing. She told me she didn't know how to multi-task, which is odd, since Shirley used to be found smoking a cigarette, eating a meal, and doing a crossword puzzle all at the same time. I think love distracted her. Or maybe she felt like it was too late to go back to class and deal with her left-behind studies. I never really asked because I didn't want to make her feel bad.

"Your father was reading a cookbook. He had a notebook, one of those black-and-white compositions I buy you at the start of each school year. I remember watching this young man steal recipes. I thought it was extremely strange."

"It's not stealing."

"I know. I know," Shirley said, smiling.

"Do you still love him?"

"I'll always love him because he gave me you and Greta. But sometimes two people grow apart." Shirley let go of her "sandwich" and carefully pressed it back onto the plate.

On one of my last visits with her, while Greta was in the bathroom, I confided in her about how I was starting to feel in my body.

"The thing is that lately I feel like something is off with me, like that time you made macaroni and cheese with sour milk and we all just made these awful faces but still continued to eat it. That was terrible. Do you remember? Why did we do that? Why didn't we just say something? But it's like we were afraid to hurt your feelings, or maybe we were just so hungry and didn't want to stop and question if it was even good. I feel like that now. I feel like I'm eating this sour meal and just ignoring how it's making my body feel."

"Eleanor," Shirley said, "I don't . . . I don't understand what you mean."

She looked so confused, so I dropped it. I didn't know how to explain. I zipped up that part of me real tight.

But now I feel like I'm choking. I want to understand what this feeling is, James. I just wish I knew how to speak it.

~

Wednesday, November 17

Dear James,

I tried to actually *study* in study hall because I have a chemistry test that I feel pretty confident I'm going to fail. But instead, I obsessed over the right words to tell Aggie I'm gay. She couldn't possibly think differently of me, but then I think of what Flor said and how she lost a lot of friends when she came out. James, is that what you were afraid of?

As I was swimming in my thoughts, I noticed a tiny piece of paper on my desk. Aggie's beautiful handwriting was on the front with my name on it. I turned around and she smiled.

Want to come over after school? Circle YES or NO or just smile at me for YES and stand up and scream out loud for NO.

Of course, I turned around and smiled. Maybe that's a sign to just tell her and be done with it.

Right before heading into science class, I noticed Dara holding hands with Damian. I don't think Dara saw me stare at their interlocking hands. When did this happen? She never mentioned even thinking he was cute. This made me think about when I was younger, and I thought that if I turned off the radio, it would stop. The singers would hold their breaths, the DJs would halt their conversations, and they'd all just wait for me to turn the dial. But the thing is, James, nobody waits for you. Life continues to go on whether or not we are ready. Dara and I were best friends for so many years and she was always the first person I shared my news with. Now she seems to have a boyfriend and I didn't even know.

~

Thursday, November 18

Dear James,

Yesterday was incredible.

I was trying so hard to listen to Aggie's smoky voice—like how January would sound if it could speak—but the truth was it was hard not to stare at everything around us.

We sat on her bed!!! and listened to a singer called PJ Harvey, who I'd never heard of.

"Oh, Eleanor," Aggie said. "It's like she's ripping out her insides with every lyric!"

Being in her bedroom allowed me to peek into who Aggie is (without her telling me).

She had a poster of a really beautiful, skinny woman who I didn't recognize.

"Audrey Hepburn!" Aggie told me. "We must watch *Breakfast at Tiffany's* together, although . . . " she paused, "it's kind of racist in some parts. Actually, I wasn't thinking it until my mom and I watched it together and she got upset. But Audrey is just so beautiful in it."

Her carpet was green like summer grass and her walls were sponge-painted.

"They were like that when we moved in. I wasn't too sure of it in the beginning, but I kind of like it now," she told me.

She had a bookshelf between her two windows and I couldn't believe how many books she had.

"You can tell everything about a person based on what they read and listen to," she said.

"So what does all this say about you?"

"I like reading about other people's lives and listening to angry riot grrrls."

"Riot girls?" I asked.

"Oh yeah! L7, Bikini Kill, 7 Year Bitch. I like Sylvia Plath and Anne Sexton and Nikki Giovanni and Gwendolyn Brooks and Jane Austen. Henry Miller, Marge Piercy, Gloria Steinem. Do you know her? My mom bought me a *Ms.* subscription for my tenth birthday. I didn't understand a lot of the articles at first, but we'd read it together. I still get it in the mail."

"I've never heard of that," I said, bashfully. I loved being around Aggie, but I was often reminded of how much I didn't know.

"I'll give you a bunch to take home, if you want."

"Cool, I'd love that. I'm reading Audre Lorde right—"

"I love her! *Movement Song* is one of my favorite poems."

"Gosh, I haven't even read her poems yet. I'm reading *Zami*."

"Can I borrow when you're done?" Aggie asked, fondling the end of her braid as though each strand contained a tiny poem weaved in. "Oh, how was the Chem test?"

"Ugh, bombed. I wish I could just take English classes. An entire day of Ms. Raimondo."

"She's awesome. I'm still writing my letters. Are you?"

I blushed. James, if only she knew. I feel like my life has become composed of just letters to you. "Yeah."

"Hey, let's read one to each other!"

"Oh, uh, I don't—"

"I'll go first." I watched Aggie hop up and walk to her book bag. She lifted out a green notebook and started leafing through it.

"Dear Richard Brautigan," she looked up at me and smiled. Aggie's legs were bent like wings and she was fumbling with her braid like she always does when she's nervous. She took a deep breath and I watched it remain in her body. "How often did you think of guns? A boy in my old school stole a gun from his dad's never-locked cabinet and accidentally shot himself in the foot. When he went back to school, he bragged to all his friends about how macho he was, surviving a gunshot wound. But he never talked about how dumb he was to steal a gun he didn't know how to use and the stupidness of shooting himself. I never want to be anywhere near a gun. My mom told me about rallies where she marched against guns. Sometimes when I listen to music, I close my eyes and imagine what it would look like to replace all the weapons with something else. Dad says if we take guns away, people will just replace them with something worse. Maybe. If there weren't guns, would you still be here? Or would you have just found another way? I think—"

"Another way to what?" I interrupted.

Aggie took a loud, deep breath. "Kill himself."

"Oh."

"Sorry, did I . . . I never want to—"

"It's fine, I . . . I was thinking about something Dara said to me once. After my mom . . . after she tried. Dara was trying to make me feel better, but then she said that people who kill themselves— or try to—don't realize how selfish they are. And I get it, you know? Like for those of us who survive—like James's mom and dad—it's so hard to understand, to make sense of it. I understand that more and more from the support group. But I also feel like James was in such incredible pain. He was all alone, he felt like he had no other—"

"Wait. How do you know this? Did his mom say that?"

"No, James did."

And then I began to tell Aggie about your notebook. I didn't dare tell her what you wrote. I wouldn't betray you like that, James, even though you probably didn't mean for me to read it either. But I let her know how isolated you felt.

"But don't we all feel that way?" Aggie asked. "I mean, being a teenager is like a full-time job that no one prepares you for. Reminds me of the bagel shop. I worked there for like, three weeks last year. Thought it would be good to get out of the house and get my mind off things, make some money too. My dad was super supportive and eagerly signed my work permit, but it was terrible. We'd have lines out the door on the weekends and people acted as though it was a travesty if their favorite kind of bagel sold out. Customers would scream—actually flip out, Eleanor—and I just walked out one day during my lunch break. Never even went back to pick up my last paycheck. But we can't exactly walk out of being a teenager."

"Well, actually, we can," I said.

"Yeah, yeah, I guess. I just mean, we can't walk out and be something else."

For a while we just sat beside each other in silence. Each time I breathed, I inhaled Aggie's delicious scent of apricots and my grandmother's garden.

"Will you read me a letter *you* wrote?" she asked, flapping her eyelashes like extended spider's legs.

James, this was the moment.

"Uh," I stumbled. "Okay, let me grab my notebook."

I slowly walked to my book bag. With each tiny step, I tried to grow courage to speak the words I've been wanting to. Words which fell right out of me onto the page and into a letter to you.

"I don't want you to . . . " I paused, almost stopped entirely. " . . . think of me differently."

"Eleanor, you're the most awesome person I've ever met."

I guess that was what I needed because suddenly I was reading my words to you out loud for the first time. Could you hear it too, James?

"Dear James, I feel like my body is in a waiting room. I took a number just like we do when I go to the butcher shop with Shirley. But it's like my number keeps getting skipped. Usually I hate to wait on line, but I'm really in no rush. I remember when Dara got her period and she was so excited. Her mom actually took her out to dinner to celebrate. Can you believe it? When you started to grow hair on your body and your voice dropped, did your dad get like, all proud and stuff? Shirley said that it will happen soon. Greta got hers when she was twelve. Her breasts are huge, but I think she likes them like that. James, sometimes at night when I stare at the glow-in-the-dark stars on my ceiling, I whisper out loud: I'm gay and it feels so . . . "

James, have you ever rehearsed something so many times in your head it becomes all you can hear? Like even when you are saying something else, somehow that speech is like sewed in somehow? Here is what I wanted to say to Aggie:

It's not that I needed to meet you to realize I was gay. I think I knew for quite awhile, but I was waiting for the words to explain or describe this. That day in study hall when you noticed my fingers dropping crumbs on the floor, I felt something more than just understanding myself. I felt gurgles in my belly. My skin grew goosebumps and I felt the way Greta must have felt when she first met Vegetarian Todd. It's like I wanted to walk around the school and just say your name out loud. In fifth grade, Gene Fishman asked me to be his girlfriend. I said yes because I didn't really have a reason to say no. Every day, he brought an extra snack in his lunch just for me. Usually crackers with the fake cheese and a small, red stick that comes in the package, but it was the thought that counts, right? A few times he brought me pudding. Butterscotch, which is my favorite. For Valentine's Day—which was just a few days after he asked me out—he gave me his mother's honeymoon bracelet. I know this because I had to give it back. He hadn't really asked his mom's permission. At the very end of the week, we broke up. It wasn't exactly a dramatic end. We were boyfriend and girlfriend on Monday, and on Sunday, he called me up and said, "want to just be friends again?" and I said sure. There wasn't any love or kissing or stealing sneaky glances toward each other. It was kind of silly, actually. I've had crushes here and there, but I never felt like someone scooped out all my confusion, all my sadness, all the grey growing in my body. Scooped it all out and replaced it with neon rainbows, or the yummy sugar cereal that turns the milk into something so sweetly delicious, you slurp up every last drop in the bowl. That's you, Aggie. You are my sugar milk. And . . . I love you.

No, I didn't say any of that. Would *you* have been able to say all that, James? I couldn't possibly tell Aggie how I feel about her. She's really become my best friend. Dara and I barely make eye contact now, and when we do, it's all scrunched up as though our pupils have been sucking on lemons. Aggie accepts all of me: my strange haircut; my strange family life; my strange thoughts. I would just die if she stopped talking to me because I made her uncomfortable with my professed feelings. So, I left that part out, but it still screams inside me. And that's really okay because I'm lucky to be in love with someone I still get to see every day and have sleepovers with and help each other with homework and—

" . . . and I couldn't even imagine you saying anything to me, Eleanor, that would make me not want to be friends with you. I love you."

What? What? What? Why do I get so lost in my thoughts? Did Aggie just say she . . .

"Eleanor," Aggie spoke.

Oh gosh oh gosh. I was reading so fast that I thought maybe she wouldn't hear it, but also I hoped she would.

I looked up from my letter to you and tried to lift my eyes to Aggie's face, but I was terrified. I was terrified she'd react like Dara.

"Have you told anyone?" she asked.

"Only Flor and . . . James," I looked down at my notebook. "But I want to tell Shirley. And my dad and Greta. I was so nervous to tell you because . . . "

Aggie grabbed my hands and put them inside hers, even though her fingers were smaller than mine. She squeezed, and I wanted to stay like that forever.

Then Aggie's bedroom door opened, and her dad walked in.

"Hello, you must be the famous Eleanor," he said.

James, my face turned into a tomato. Bright, bright red.

"Uh, hi," I said.

Aggie's father had dark hair just like her and his smile was slightly crooked like hers too.

"Can I make you girls something to eat? How about some grilled cheese sandwiches?"

"Yum!" Aggie screamed.

The rest of the afternoon was a blur of music and laughter. It was a relief to come out to Aggie and still feel like nothing had changed between us. It just made me a little sad to be reminded of how different it was with Dara.

Dear Elinore,

Brian had two different kinds of socks on. I noticed this in the gym locker room and I couldn't help but smile. And I could see what side he sleeps on cause his hair was all flat on that side. It's hard to stare at someone so hard and still be invisible to them. I wish I didn't know what it was like to kiss him. I wish I didn't like it.

I'm reading The Catcher in the Rye, not cause I have to but because I want to and I read it last night instead of studying for my math test. Man, Holden Caulfield is the coolest. He does whatever he wants and no one seems to care. That's how I want to live, and he seems to be alone like me. Sometimes I wish that book had pictures because I want to know what he looked like. Maybe he and I could have been friends, or maybe more, or at least just listen to music together and swap records.

I will never have a boyfriend.

Friday, November 19

Dear James,

Last night in group, Peter reminded us that we weren't meeting next week because of Thanksgiving. Thanksgiving! I completely forgot. Usually we do it with Shirley and then go to Dad's for the weekend. I watched your mom's face drain when Peter mentioned the holiday. Afterwards, I talked to Flor and asked if it would be okay to invite her and your dad to our house. She figured Shirley would be fine with it.

"Honey, that's terribly sweet of you," your mom said. "But we'll just have a quiet, no- frills meal. I'm not abundantly grateful this year."

James, it took a little bit of convincing, but she eventually said yes. Finally, I'll get to meet your dad.

On the ride home, Flor said I did a real mitzvah.

"How do you know that word?" I asked.

"Honey, you don't need to be Jewish to know that word," she smiled. "I imagine every day is a difficult reminder of loss, but a holiday is even worse. And it's their first one."

―

Saturday, November 20

Dear James,

I've been keeping a list in the back of my notebook of songs to put on your mixtape. Here is the music I would have given to you:

> Groove is in the Heart (Dee-Light)
> Suedehead (Morrisey)
> Smells Like Teen Spirit (Nirvana)
> Nothing's Gonna Stop Us Now (Starship)
> Rhythm is Gonna Get You (Miami Sound Machine)
> Finally (CeCe Peniston)

Set Adrift on Memory's Bliss (P.M. Dawn)
Miss You Much (Janet Jackson)
Palace of the Brine (Pixies)
O Stella (PJ Harvey)
Behind the Wheel (Depeche Mode)
Here Comes Your Man (Pixies)

I was going to do only rock songs, songs I knew you'd like. But I had to put some dance ones in there too. Greta and I used to shake our entire beings to Gloria Estefan. I love that it sounds like there are wild animals harmonizing in "Rhythm is Gonna Get You". Dara used to say that the best mix tapes have at least two surprises. You know, like songs that go against the rest of the flow of the mix or songs that the person listening may never have heard of (or even wanted).

Anyway, if we had been friends, I'd have made you a ton of mixtapes.

Yesterday at school, Dara and I passed by each other in the hallway and she looked right past me. I would have talked to her, I would have listened to her try to explain how she was feeling. But then I thought about Flor. She said that she used to hide who she was, so her friends wouldn't be uncomfortable. So basically, she put her own comfort aside. No way. I am not doing that, even for Dara. So what if I'm gay? I bet there are other people in my school who are too. Why should straight couples be able to hold hands and kiss all over the place? Can you even imagine, James, if two girls or two guys kissed in the hallways of our school? Why do some people get to live however they want, while others have to hide? ~~Or kill themselves?~~

~~

Sunday, November 21

Dear James,

The view outside my bedroom window is of the back of the house of a family I used to babysit for. I think they're divorcing. I only know this because I overheard Flor and Shirley talk about it during book club one time. The parents—Aaron and Margaret— have two kids. A boy called Franklin or Frankly which *I* call him. And a girl called Susie. Frankly is nine and Susie is five.

Once, I was standing in front of my window at night and I could see into their house. I could see the neon reflection of their television screen and the shadows of their bodies going in and out of rooms. And I just watched.

Sometimes I use my plastic yellow binoculars (that are really just a toy) but they work just fine to see from small to big. They aren't anything special, like the expensive ones that can see from miles and miles away, but I feel like Harriet the Spy when I look through them. So, this particular time, which was before all the divorce stuff, I saw them naked. Aaron and Margaret. I remember feeling awful that I saw them, guilty to have been snooping. But I couldn't stop. I couldn't turn away. They were kissing and rubbing all over each other and then, I saw them have sex.

At the time I just thought it was their fault for leaving their curtains open. Afterwards, I had an extremely difficult time looking at them. Babysitting put me in a cold sweat. I remember Aaron paying me one night after they had gotten home, and all I could think was: I saw your penis!

James, if I can see into their room, they can definitely see into mine. So, what would they notice about me? What might they observe me doing?

Dear Elinore,

I can't remember how old I was, but my mom told me once that she tried having more kids after me but kept having miscarriages. I didn't ask her why or how it made her feel. But I always wished for a brother. Heck, I'd even take a sister. Maybe I'd feel less alone or something.

I almost said something to you today. Something not mean. Maybe even an apology. But what would that even matter? I see the way you look at me. Kinda scared. It's just easier that way. Making friends, letting people know me, only makes things worse.

Brian is in three of my classes this year. Every time I see him, it's like a punch in my gut. I feel like I'm underwater. I feel like every time I breathe there are razors against my lungs. When he smiles, when he laughs, I want to curl up and just die.

Monday, November 22

After school today, I helped Shirley plan the menu for Thanksgiving. I was only a little nervous that she'd be mad I invited your parents without asking her first, but Flor was right, she was fine with it.

"What do you think James's father is like?" Shirley asked me, as we began listing ingredients needed from the grocery store.

"I have this weird feeling that he's super strict. I really like Helaine though."

"How is school going?"

I told Shirley all about my classes, leaving out the daily awkwardness of seeing Dara and the thick silence growing between us. I wanted to ask Shirley if she has had any thoughts or feelings of hurting herself. In group, Peter said that it's okay to check in with our loved ones, even though it can be scary to hear the answer. It's all part of open communication and building back trust.

"How are . . . are you . . . have you had any . . . " Oh gosh, I guess it isn't so easy to ask your mom if she's thought of killing herself recently.

Shirley just looked at me blankly.

"Are you gonna try to kill yourself again?" Not quite how I imagined it coming out, but there it was.

Shirley put down the pen and faced me. "Eleanor, no. I am working hard each day to be here. To stay here."

"I really like the canned cranberry sauce with the ridges on it," I said. In group, Peter calls this deflecting.

"Honey, we can talk more about this if you'd like. I never want you to be afraid to ask me anything. Or . . . tell me anything."

Tell her anything? What's to tell? Oh, gosh. Did Flor tell her? No, she wouldn't. Would she?

"Nothing to tell," I said abruptly.

"I just know that this has been a challenging school year so far. Things are changing. Things are always changing, but—"

"Did Flor say something to you?"

"What? No. Is there something she should have told me?"

I stared at Shirley, trying to read her face. Maybe this was a sign to just tell her. I did feel kind of bad that I told Flor before Shirley, but it was different with Flor. She was gay, she understood.

"I guess maybe I do want to tell you something? I . . . " Deep breath, Eleanor. You can do this. And anyway, Flor said that the hardest part of coming out is the first time. It doesn't always get easier, but we grow stronger. I don't really understand that, but maybe I will later on.

"I'm." James, that was all that came out for at least five minutes. *Really.* Shirley stared at me, while I stared at my fingers, trying to locate a nail that was long enough to bite, but my nervousness these past months has really ~~abliterated~~ obliterated them.

"I'm . . . " I tried again, took a deep breath, then continued. "I'm gay."

My heart jumped out of my chest and flung itself out the window.

"Okay," Shirley said, plainly.

"Okay? Are you . . . are you mad? Are you disappointed? Are you . . . "

"Eleanor, you're my daughter. I can't fathom a world where you did or said anything that made me feel differently. Also, I . . . I had a sense."

"You had a sense that I was gay? You knew? How'd you know? Did I say something? Is it because I cut my hair?" James, it's like all of my thoughts were threaded together and I couldn't disconnect them.

"I can't really tell you what it was, but I just had a feeling. Regardless, it means a lot that you shared this with me. I imagine it's not easy."

"Not easy to tell or . . . "

"Flor and I have had so many conversations about this. Not about *you* being . . . just about her experiences in this world being gay. Not being gay myself, I can't even imagine what it's like to experience such hate from people for something that you can't help."

"You make it sound like it's a terrible thing to be."

"Oh, honey, no. I just . . . never want anyone to hurt you or make you feel anything but loved and some of the stories Flor has shared with me helped me to see that it's not always easy to be different."

James, is this what stopped you from living? I hate thinking about you holding all of this in. Having no one to tell. Your letters . . . what you've written about Brian and how he just tried to ignore you away. I've thought about saying something to him. I've seen him in the halls. Or at least, the Brian I assume you are talking about. We have a bunch in our grade.

"Eleanor?"

I shook my head and realized that Shirley was still talking.

"Sorry. What?"

"Have you told anyone else?"

"Just you and Flor. I want to tell Gret and Dad, of course."

"Is this . . . is this the reason you and Dara aren't talking anymore? You've been friends for so long, I just don't—"

Suddenly, we heard the front door open. We watched as Flor walked in with a giant turkey still in its plastic packaging. Not like covered in feathers or anything like that.

"Hiya! I earned this bad boy. Eighteen pounds."

Shirley grabbed the turkey from Flor. "Thanks so much. I knew I wasn't going to make it this month."

I was confused. "What do you mean . . . make it?"

"Oh," said Flor. "At Food Town. Spend two hundred and fifty dollars or more in a month and you get this turkey for free."

"They're just giving away turkeys?" I asked.

"Well, I wound up spending more last month than I probably would have, so I basically bought it," she smiled. "Did I . . . did I interrupt something?"

Shirley and I awkwardly smiled at each other.

"I just came out to Shirley," I said.

"Oh, Eleanor! I'm so proud of you!" Then, Flor looked at Shirley and said, "And? May I ask?"

"Did you expect anything else but a warm response?" Shirley said to both of us.

"Well, maybe a few dishes flying, but that's probably because I watch a lot of TV and everything is pretty dramatic," I said.

I looked at Flor. "Is there a difference between a lesbian and a dyke? Not every lesbian has short hair, right?"

"Right. Although, we're much easier to find for some reason when there is less hair attached," Flor laughed.

"The thing is . . . I don't know *what* I am. I said what I said because I know that I'm attracted to girls. I like girls. I . . . it's not like I've *done* anything. Oh, gosh. This is weird."

"Eleanor, it's all right," Flor smiled.

"But the thing is that it's more than that. I'm more than a lesbian. I'm . . . maybe . . . maybe I just haven't found my word yet. Could that be it? But I didn't cut off all my hair to make a big statement."

"Audre Lorde said something really beautiful about that," Flor said. "A different book than what you're reading. I'll have to give to you. She talked about the words we don't yet have and the power of what happens when we find them."

"So how do I find my words?"

"Keep reading. Keep searching. You and your words will find one another," Flor said.

"Is Dara not being accepting?" Shirley asked. "Was she mean to you about this?"

"She hates my hair. She is definitely not comfortable with me being . . . gay. She's just being super weird about it all. And now she's dating someone and completely ignoring me. It's like she's become someone else. I guess we both are. I don't know. It's really disappointing, but I'm trying to be okay with it. I just don't understand what the big deal is that I'm gay. There's probably a lot more in my school . . . gays, I mean . . . and maybe if I said something, more people would—"

"Eleanor," Flor interrupted, "I understand what you're saying and it's my age that reacts more realistically than idealistically, but—"

"What do you mean?"

"I mean, we just want you to always feel safe. I would never, ever want to stand in the way of you coming out and being yourself, but. Not everyone is going to be as accepting as we are."

The thing is, I know that Flor is right. I don't really know what kind of reaction I am going to get from other people at school, and even if there are dozens more people in my school just waiting to come out or maybe just one, I could be risking my safety. If classmates couldn't handle my hair, what would they say if they found out I liked girls?

James, remember when Jackie came out as bisexual? Some people taunted her, made kissing noises each time she walked down the hall. I always thought it was so strange that people reacted in this kind of way. Who really cares?

Two people in our grade have already gotten pregnant— one had an abortion (I think) and the other actually gave birth. I think her mother or grandmother babysits when she's at school. When we were in seventh grade, Mark Culiano, who was in my math class, supposedly raped a girl. Did you hear that one, James? After that rumor went around, he kind of just disappeared. There's a rumor going around now about this girl who's a junior who slept with Mr. Fiorentino, the English teacher.

I feel like rumors are like pimples. For like a day or so, they are huge. It's all anyone can talk about and then, without any notice, they just go away. Eventually, of course, they are just replaced by another. And another. Some pimples, I mean *rumors*, explode. Pick at them enough and they pop, causing a fight of some sort.

In eighth grade, Tiana Ruiz and Kelli Johns started fighting over some rumor, which included a boy, a look, and kissing behind the bleachers. Tiana pulled out Kelli's weave—I only know this from the thick clumps left in the hallways afterwards. Kelli, in turn, ripped out Tiana's giant gold hoop earring with her name on it. Tore it right out of her ear, slit it open. There must have been blood, but only hair remained as evidence of the ripped-apart rumor.

The thing is, if I announce it myself, if I don't wait for someone to do it, but instead take the control, it's not a rumor. I'm claiming it. I'm—

"What makes you want to tell all your schoolmates?" Flor interrupted.

"I don't know. Because they probably think it already. Because maybe others will want to say it too."

"Eleanor, you can't expect that. And you certainly can't force it."

"I know, I know. I just feel like I've kept a lot in. I've kept all of this in. Until now. And it feels really good to say it out loud. To be heard. I think . . . I think if someone else in my school announced they were gay, maybe I'd . . . well, maybe I'd want to say something too, since I'm already feeling it. No one ever admits to things. No one ever wants to be the first on the dance floor, you know?"

"I don't—"

"You know, like the music is playing and it's playing for people to dance, but everyone is so shy to be the first one. Then, someone makes the first move and suddenly everyone is doing it. I saw it at Heather's birthday party last year. We were all in her basement and she made this really great mixtape of all our favorite songs. Even asked everyone ahead of time what songs they liked best. But as each song came on, everyone kind of just stood there—talking and eating—but never dancing. I wish I had been the one to just start moving."

"Are you expecting everyone to follow you, Eleanor?" Shirley asked.

"No, though that'd be pretty amazing. Like some sort of movie."

"Eleanor, this isn't a movie," said Shirley.

"I know. It's just that . . . we all talk behind each other's backs and everyone knows. Everyone hears. But no one ever says: 'You know what? You're right.' People have called me dyke so many times since I cut my hair. And you know what I say? Nothing. It's like afterward, I've got all these things in my mind that I could have said. But in the moment, I'm just speechless. Kind of shaking. Kind of angry. Part of me just wants to be like, *yeah, I'm a dyke. So what?* I looked up that word. Dyke. It's like this wall that stops places from flooding. So, basically, they are calling me . . . a . . . a solution. Something that fixes a problem! And you know fag is a cigarette. Like, where do they come up with these words, which are fine by themselves, but then kind of ruined." I felt myself getting angry, just thinking about the words suddenly replacing my name at school.

"You can't be expected to stand up when you aren't ready to," Flor said.

"I know. But that's what I'm trying to say, Flor. I'm ready."

DEAR ELINORE,

LAST YEAR FOR MY BIRTHDAY, MY UNCLE (THE ONE I LIKE, NOT
THE ONE I HATE WHO ALWAYS MAKES ME FEEL UNCOMFORTABLE)
GAVE ME A ~~PRESCRIPTION~~ SUBSCRIPTION FOR <u>ROLLING STONE</u>. IT'S
AWESOME BECAUSE I CAN LEARN ABOUT NEW MUSIC AND SEE
PICTURES OF MY FAVORITE BANDS. KURT WAS ON THE COVER LAST
YEAR WITH THE REST OF NIRVANA. I LIKED HOW HE INSULTED
THE MAGAZINE BECAUSE IT'S SO CORPORATE BUT ALSO LIKED
BEING IN IT AS WELL. HE DOESN'T TRY TO BE COOL, HE JUST
TALKS AND EVERYTHING COMES OUT LIKE A SONG. SOME PEOPLE
SAY HE DOES DRUGS, BUT I DON'T WANT TO BELIEVE THAT. I TRIED
WEED ONCE BUT I COUGHED SO MUCH I THOUGHT MY INSIDES WERE
GONNA COME OUT. I DIDN'T LIKE THAT IT MADE ME FEEL ALL
BLURRY AND TIRED. I FEEL THAT WAY WITHOUT DRUGS. KURT JUST
WANTS TO MAKE MUSIC. HE DOESN'T WANT THE FANCY STUFF.
BUT I GUESS ONCE PEOPLE CALL YOU FAMOUS, IT'S DIFFICULT TO
ESCAPE. I NEVER WANT TO BE KNOWN. I'D RATHER BE ALONE
THAN HAVE EVERYONE TALK ABOUT ME AND BOTHER ABOUT MY
LIFE. THAT'S WHY I WANT TO BE AN ASTRONAUT. I JUST WANT
TO TRAVEL INTO SPACE AND STAY THERE. BE SOMEWHERE WHERE
NO ONE ELSE GOES.

Wednesday, November 24

Dear James,

In homeroom, Aggie and I talked about Thanksgiving plans.

"My dad and I go to my aunt and uncle's in Long Island. Uncle Filip and Aunt Aurora. My cousins are younger, but we get along pretty well. The food's always good because my aunt is Italian and, mixed with Polish food from my dad's side, it's all my favorite things! Pasta and eggplant parmesan and kielbasa with sauerkraut."

"Do you still have turkey?"

"Yeah, and my dad makes my mom's potato bread that she always used to make. We also have a dumpling-off."

"What do you mean?" I asked.

"We make kopytka and Aunt Aurora makes gnocchi," I watched as Aggie licked her tiny lips. "How about you?"

"All the regular stuff. Plus Shirley's chicken soup with matzo balls. Gret's coming home. Flor will be there, and did I tell you James's parents are coming too?"

"Wow, that's crazy. So you'll finally get to see what his dad is like."

In English class today, we read a poem by June Jordan that was really intense. I didn't understand all of it, but she basically talked about how her rights had been taken away, and the importance of naming herself.

I wonder what kind of student you were, James. Were you failing? Did you get As?

Then math class happened and everything went downhill. We had a sub, so of course everyone was acting like idiots. We were given a packet of equations to work on. The teacher said we could work in groups, and most people took advantage of that. I don't think anyone was really doing any math and the teacher didn't even seem to care. He just sat behind the desk and read some book he brought with him. I couldn't see the title, but he looked really into it.

I don't know what compelled me to do this, James, but I decided to approach Dara.

"Want to work together?" I asked, nervously.

Dara looked at me as though I asked her to inspect a rash on my body.

"Uh, no thanks," she said.

"Is this really how we're gonna be with each other?" I asked. "I'm willing to be the bigger person and just forget everything. This has become so ridiculous. Why are we even fighting?"

Just then, Damian walked in and went right up to Dara. He's not even in our class, James. He looked at me and said, "Fuck off, lesbo."

It was like the night you pushed me. All of my words were frozen. I couldn't move. Every possible comeback I could have possibly said was tangled up inside me.

Damian whispered something to Dara, which I couldn't hear, and she laughed.

"You're not even in this class," I finally said.

"Eleanor, just forget it, okay?" Dara said.

"You friends with this weirdo?" Damian said to her.

And she just looked at me and stared. I used to be able to read her thoughts. It's like we spoke a silent language to each other. But all of that has changed.

"No, definitely not," was all she could say.

I worked by myself and finished only three equations. I couldn't concentrate. What's more important, James? Being yourself or having friends? Do we have to choose one or the other? Can't we have both? I am myself with Aggie. I don't have to pretend away any of my parts. It was in that moment where I realized my friendship with Dara was over.

~

Thursday, November 25

Dear James,

Thanksgiving used to be my favorite holiday because it was all about eating and being loud with family. Aunts and uncles and more cousins than I ever knew I had all around the table eating food that Shirley took days to prepare yet took us minutes to gobble up. Enough social studies classes and I started to change my mind about things. I started to realize that it was just about people stealing land that didn't belong to them and spreading diseases and how did turkey carving and cranberry sauce come from all that?

When Shirley and my dad split up, it just wasn't the same. We started having two Thanksgivings and it wasn't as loud or crowded. I always felt bad because we were already tired of turkey and leftovers by the time we went to my dad's, yet Gret and I had to do it all over again. I guess nothing is quite the same when you start to understand the meaning of it.

This year, of course, was different because your parents came. They left about an hour ago and I think they had a good time. Your dad is definitely hard to read. I could tell that Shirley ran out of ways to try and engage him. For a pastor, he doesn't really talk much, does he?

When they arrived, Shirley was still in the kitchen cooking, so Shirley suggested I give your parents a tour of our house. I thought that was kind of weird, since our house isn't anything special, but it did give me some time alone with Helaine. Your dad was uninterested, so he just stayed behind in the kitchen.

"How are you doing, dear?" your mom asked as I introduced her to the family room.

"Alright. I did better on a chemistry test than I expected. And my best friend—*ex-best friend*—and I are no longer talking."

We walked into the dining room and Helaine complimented the china Shirley had put out on the table.

"I'm sorry to hear that. Any chance for reconciliation?"

"Probably not. Turns out she's a homophobe."

James, I wasn't exactly planning on coming out to your mom, but it just popped out. I immediately panicked because your dad is super religious and what if they up and leave because they don't want to eat food prepared by someone with a gay kid?

But Helaine just looked at me and said, "That's a real shame." Then, she took a deep breath and I watched her necklace rise from the inhale of her chest. "I imagine you've read James's journal."

I knew it! I knew she knew!

"Yes, but I'm trying to treat it like Halloween candy and make it last. I limit myself to only a few pages at a time. Sometimes only one."

"I found it the day after he . . . and I'd like to tell you that I thought long and hard about opening it, but I didn't. I sat on his bed and read it straight through. I had no idea who Eleanor was, thought maybe it was just a made-up person. He never mentioned anyone by that name. But after reading it, I knew I couldn't show Burt. He does not approve. He . . . he's a . . . he's a homophobe too."

"How did you know it was me?"

"Well, I had a sense after the second week of group. I didn't initially make the connection, but then I started to think that it might be you. So, the night you and your mom came over for supper, I moved it to an obvious spot in his bedroom and hoped you'd grab it. Maybe he didn't intend for you to read it, Eleanor, but he *was* writing to you. Reaching out somehow. I just wish he could have been a little louder about it."

Suddenly, your mom started to cry. By now, we were upstairs, stopped in the bathroom. I ripped off some toilet paper and handed it to her.

"Yeah, but the thing is he couldn't. Or he felt like he couldn't. His only way was writing, I guess. I'm so glad you shared his journal with me. Helaine, the thing is that I really thought he was awful. I mean, he bullied me pretty bad. But reading his notebook, I realize that we weren't so different. We could have been friends. We could have been really good friends."

By then, we were both crying. She hugged me and we both got a glimpse of ourselves in the mirror and started to laugh.

"Yup, typical Thanksgiving," I said. "Tears and over-sharing," I smiled.

After dinner of homemade chicken soup, turkey, roast beef (Greta insisted), cranberry sauce, mashed potatoes, stuffing, green beans with fried onions spread on top, and some kind of black bean dish that Flor brought that tasted so good I almost forgot about all that meat, we found ourselves in the family room. My stomach looked and felt as though a fully inflated balloon was living inside of it.

I felt overly aware of wanting to make your dad comfortable, I'm not sure why. Maybe I felt a little guilty that I already didn't like him even before we met, based on some things you had written in your journal. Conversation flowed throughout dinner, until the moment Shirley pushed it in a dangerous direction.

"What made you want to be a pastor, Mr. Bianchi?" Shirley asked.

He slowly put down his fork and grabbed the napkin from his lap to wipe his mouth.

"When I realized how important it is spread the word of God," he said, plainly.

"Burt writes the most beautiful sermons," Helaine said.

"I grew up Catholic, but don't practice too much these days," Flor said.

"You said it right. It's all about practicing. I like being part of something that reminds me that the work is never done," your dad said.

As I sat, cutting the gristle away from the roast beef, I glared at Greta, trying to silently scream at her to change the subject. Dad always said two things that should never be discussed with mixed company: religion and politics.

" . . . and that's why I believe we were in a much better place with Bush. I just don't trust these Democrats. And what these kids are being taught in school? Health class should be about just that: *health*. Sex talk should come from the parents. And don't get me started on this epidemic of homosexuality in . . . "

Oh no, oh no! James, I almost started screaming. Anything to get us off the do-not-discuss topics. Luckily, Shirley saved us all.

"Well, I must confess I cannot wait to try your coconut cream pie, Helaine. Is it a family recipe?"

And then, we were onto dessert and recipe-swapping and goodbyes.

James, even though I'm an atheist, I do think religion is cool. I mean, all these different traditions and wardrobes people wear to celebrate their God and prayers and songs. I think it's beautiful, actually. Stained glass and organ music and the smell of polished wood from the pews (when I was a kid, I called them pee-ews because I hated the way the polish smelled, but now I really like it). But what I don't like is when a religion tries to exclude someone because of what *they* believe or how they are. It made me think of one of your journal entries I just read.

DEAR ELINORE,

I'VE STOPPED GOING TO CHURCH. I USED TO BE ABLE TO GO AND JUST IGNORE HOW IT MADE ME FEEL. I DON'T BELIEVE IN HELL, IN A PLACE WHERE PEOPLE ARE PUNISHED. I MEAN, WE DON'T REALLY HAVE TO WAIT FOR DEATH FOR THAT. I BELIEVE DEATH IS DARK AND QUIET AND THERE IS NO FLOATING OR VISITING PEOPLE WE LEFT BEHIND. IT'S JUST THE END. I'M PLENTY READY FOR THAT. I USED TO LISTEN TO NIRVANA IN MY HEAD DURING THE SERVICE. I KNOW ALL THE SONGS SO WELL, THAT I CAN JUST IMAGINE THEM AND THEY PLAY AUTOMATICALLY.

SO WHEN EVERYONE ELSE WAS SINGING "O FOR A THOUSAND TONGUES TO SING", I WAS SECRETLY LISTENING TO "HAIRSPRAY QUEEN". THE ONE THING MY DAD CAN'T CONTROL: WHAT I THINK ABOUT. HERE'S ANOTHER THING. SOMETIMES I'D IMAGINE BRIAN'S TONGUE IN MY MOUTH WHILE DAD WAS DOING HIS LONG-WINDED SERMON. THE SMELL OF BRIAN'S BREATH, A LITTLE LIKE ~~SLAMI~~ SALAMI AND SWISS CHEESE, BUT PROBABLY BECAUSE THAT'S WHAT HE ATE BEFORE WE KISSED.

I BELIEVE IN GOD. BUT I BELIEVE IN A GOD THAT BELIEVES IN EVERYONE. MY GOD IS DEFINITELY DIFFERENT FROM MY DAD'S.

Friday, November 26

Dear James,

Greta came into my room before I even had the chance to rub
the sleep out of my eyes.

"You up? I can't believe how full I still am. Hey, scooch
over." Greta slid beneath the covers and I could smell coffee
on her breath.

"You know, I miss you," she said.

I smiled. "Are you . . . are you okay?" I asked.

"The truth is, I kind of almost dropped out this semester."

I just stared, waiting for her to go on. The way the early
morning sun was streaming through my window was cinematic.
Beams of sunshine bursting through the glass, creating shadows all
over my room. It was difficult not to immediately think about
Aggie. I just know that she would have not only noticed the light,
but she'd stop everything to grab her notebook and write its
description down.

"I didn't. I mean, I'm still there. I'm going to classes, but I
wound up dropping two of them: Philosophy and Intro to
Sociology. Eleanor . . . " She paused, grabbing at her hair and
swinging all of it to the side. She let it rest on her right shoulder
and I watched her study the ends as though someone had written
messages on them or something.

"Ugh, I need a haircut. I should have asked Mom to make me an
appointment."

"Greta?"

"I . . . I wasn't going to tell you. I don't know. Maybe . . . maybe
it's not necessary for you to know. I guess, I . . . "

"I don't understand."

"That guy I told you about. The one I was dating, you know?
Well, it started to get kind of serious. And umm . . . well, I know
you know I've been on birth control."

"Uhh—"

"El, I know you used to snoop in my drawers." She laughed, clearly finding some sense of humor over my invasion of her privacy. She grabbed my knee and squeezed it. "I love you. Even though you're the biggest snooper in the world! Anyway, last month, I . . . I got an abortion."

We sat inside that sentence for a really long time. I didn't know what to say and I didn't know if I should hug her or cry.

"Jenné came with me. She's in my Lit class and she's like my best friend there. She understood. I mean, she actually got an abortion when she was a senior in high school. Believe it or not, her *mom* took her. Can you even imagine Mom doing such a thing? I could never, ever tell her. It all kind of happened like a dream. A fog or whatever. I was late, which I never am. And I hated myself so much because I stopped taking my birth control—"

"Why?"

"It was making my skin break out all the time and I just hated all the side effects, you know? I feel like I gained so much weight from it. I mean, I know there's that freshman fifteen thing, but it's not like I eat all the time. Mom hasn't put you on it, has she?"

I looked at her, unclear as to what she was asking me.

"I mean, you are *too* young to be having sex, Eleanor, but it's about precaution. Also, plenty of girls go on birth control just because their periods are awful. Remember Heather? She would bleed out through her under—"

"Yuck. Enough said."

"Well, when you're ready, just know that Mom will take you. Anyway, we used condoms. Most of the time. And I guess this particular time . . . " Greta's voice trailed off and I watched her mouth still move a little, but it was as though someone turned her sound off. I wasn't used to her being so open and free with me. I liked it.

"It's weird. I knew almost right away. I know that sounds strange, but really I did." Greta stopped and I watched her move her eyes around, as if searching for a translation.

"I remember the first time I went to the store to pick up tampons. What a nightmare. Usually Mom bought them for me, but I really needed some and none of my friends had any. So, I went to CVS and of course Kurt Ettinger was working there, who I had a major crush on at the time! Why is it so embarrassing, you know? It's like a necessary thing. And boys must know that we wear them. But at the time, I was mortified. I was probably sweating a lot and made absolutely no eye contact. I think I threw in a pack of gum or something, thinking he'd focus on *that* over the super-super-absorbent tampons. Nightmare! Anyway, I kind of felt that shame when I had to buy a pregnancy test. It's like such a strange thing because I felt totally judged.

"Weeks earlier, I went to the store and bought a ton of junk food. Just a buffet of sugar, you know? And the girl behind the counter couldn't care less that I was feeding my body toxins. But a pregnancy test! It's like I could feel her bury me in judgment!"

I laughed, secretly wishing that she was still living here or that I was living closer to her so that I could have gone with her. I would have even bought the pregnancy test for her myself. Of course, I didn't tell her this. Instead I remained silent.

"Would you believe that the lady behind the counter actually said, 'good luck' to me right before I left?! But her tone, El. Like pity. Like such fear that a young person would dare bring another baby into this world. And who knew pregnancy tests were so expensive!"

"So . . . "

"So, I went back to the dorm and luckily it was the middle of the day. I totally skipped classes. I *had* to. It's all just a bunch of stalls, but I was the only one there. I waited five minutes and then . . . two lines."

"Two lines?"

"Pregnant. What does it say about me that I didn't even think for a moment that I'd keep it? I just knew I'd get an abortion.

There was no other option. I mean, I know in theory I could have done the adoption thing or even keep it. No, no. I just couldn't. I mean, I barely know how to do my own laundry. I always shrink things. My life would be . . . "

Greta stopped again. No words, though her lips continued to quiver as though sound was echoing out. I waited.

"Jenné had confided in me that she'd had an abortion. I knew I could tell her and she could help me out. So, I went to Planned Parenthood. This place where women can—"

"Yeah, I've heard of it. You can get abortions there?"

"Well, yeah, but at first I just spoke with someone. This really nice lady who was super kind to me. And she told me about my options. I learned about what really happens during an abortion and how my body might feel afterwards. She told me to think it over for at least a week. Actually she said, 'Make a decision in your mind and then live inside that decision for a week. Think about your body and mind. Think about regret and acceptance.' Then, she told me that when I was ready, I could make an appointment. So, I thought. And thought. And then I made my appointment."

"Did it hurt?"

"Mostly afterwards. It was such an intense decision to make and I was just really in a bad place. It made me scared that I would lose it like Mom did. Because it's in us, you know? That *crazy*. I mean, I got really sad *afterwards*. Not from regret, but just that I had sucked this part of me—that I never even got to see—out of my body."

"What about the guy? Did you tell him?"

"I wasn't going to, but then Jenné said I should. That it was *his* right to know. I told him before I made the appointment. He was glad I decided to get an abortion but made no effort to come with me or call to see if I was even okay afterwards. He didn't even offer to help pay for it. I hate him now. Anyway, I am telling you this because I don't want you to make the same mistake. Of getting pregnant, you know?"

"I'm not too worried about that."

"Well, good. But also, you never know."

"I'm pretty sure I won't be getting pregnant accidentally," I smiled.

"El, you know I started having sex in high school."

"Yeah, I know. I almost lost the ability to eat that time I overheard you and Vegetarian Todd."

Greta laughed so hard that the bed shook.

"Greta . . . "

"Do you think differently of me now? Are you disappointed in me?"

"I'm definitely not disappointed in you," I said. "I can't . . . actually I'm just really surprised that you told me. It means a lot to me."

Great smiled slowly. A hesitant spread of her lips. And then she leaned over and hugged me.

James, I felt you beside me, nudging me not to wimp out. I know I've created a version of you in my head that may not be so accurate.

"And El, I've wanted to reach out about James. I'm really sorry about that."

"It's okay. I didn't . . . we barely . . . it was more upsetting because of just, you know, it didn't have to happen. But I feel lucky that I got to meet Helaine. I actually feel helpful, being able to talk with her and listen too."

"Definitely. I'm glad you're still going to the support group. And mom said she's been going to one too? How's she really been? She seems in good spirits, but she does love cooking for people. Actually, it was cool to have some more people here. Without Dad, it's quiet. Emptier, you know?"

"Yeah, she's been okay. I think she's making friends. She's mentioned a few names. Gret, do you ever feel like it could happen again?"

"It?"

"Shirley . . . trying to . . . kill herself again," I said.

"I don't know. Maybe? I try not to think about it. If I do, I'll just obsess. We need to keep living life. That's what Peter said, remember? He said living is contagious."

"Yeah, I guess. I'm trying."

"Tell me more. How's Dara?"

When Gret still lived at home, we barely spoke to each other. It's like we were strangers with the same last name. But now with her being away at college, it's like suddenly we were more interested in each other's lives.

"We hate each other," I said. Then, I realized, that to tell her why we were fighting, I needed to come out to Greta.

Coming out: Take three!

James, have you ever accidentally swallowed a piece of celery without chewing? The feeling of its weight lodged in your throat, scraping its way down. You think you're gonna choke, but your throat takes over and digests it, and it takes all the wind out of you. You need to lie down, catch your breath, maybe even take a nap. That's how it feels to come out each time.

"Actually the reason we aren't talking anymore is I guess she's kinda homophobic."

"Really? She was always cool to Flor. Did she say something mean about her?"

"No, not Flor." Deep breath, Eleanor, you can do this. "Me."

I looked at Greta and watched her consume my syllable, slowly figuring out what I was actually telling her.

"Wait, are you . . . did she . . . El, you're . . . "

"Gay," I said.

Every time we meet someone new, we have to tell them our names. It helps them identify us, give them a way to address us. But no one ever hears someone's name and then says: *nope, that name is disgusting, can't be your friend now*. I was thinking about this as I stared at Gret taking in my news because being gay is really just the same thing. It's just a part of me. Like my name because I didn't choose that either. Yet, unlike my name, someone may stop talking to me because of it. That part scares me. Kinda makes me angry too.

"Have you told Mom?"

"Yeah, and Flor too. They're cool with it. I guess I wasn't too worried. Are you . . . "

"Cool with it? Eleanor, I'm amazed by you. For you to be so bold already. Doesn't change how I feel about you at all. Wait till you get to college. So many people are gay and no one cares!"

My heart sunk. James, a few more years and you could have been out, maybe even in another state. Far away from your dad. But you couldn't wait, I guess.

"I'm disappointed by Dara. What did she say exactly?"

"It's more like what she didn't say. I mean, actually, she kinda outed me to myself. Just because I cut all my hair off. And then when I said that I was a lesbian, she was weirded out. Worse, her stupid boyfriend made fun of me in front of her and she didn't even say anything. But I've made a new friend this year and she's really wonderful. She totally accepts me."

"You gonna tell Dad?" Greta asked.

"Of course, just maybe not this weekend. I don't know. You're lucky. You don't have to make some grand announcements that you're straight. Everyone just assumes it already."

Dear Elinore.

I share a birthday with William Pailes. You probably don't know who he is, but when I did a report in sixth grade about famous people from New Jersey, I learned about him. He's an astronaut and we were both born June 26th, just many, many years apart. Will I ever be important enough to be mentioned in someone's school report? Part of me hopes so, but at the end of each day I wonder how I'll make it to the next.

—

Saturday, November 27

Dear James,

I may need to get a new notebook because so much happened yesterday, I can barely believe it all fit inside one day!

After a restless sleep full of dreams about dancing turkeys and oceans full of cornstarch and chicken bouillon, Shirley announced that she wanted to take me clothes shopping.

"You wear the same thing every day," she said. "You're beginning to smell."

To say that I hate shopping is not strong enough. Is loathe meaner than hate? I would rather dig beneath my fingernails and pull them up. Then eat them. Then regurgitate them. Then eat that.

My List of Things I Hate
(Dad says it's not nice to hate, but don't you think some things are deserving of it?)

1. **Shopping of all sorts** (clothes, shoes, household stuff).
   Wait, actually I do like food shopping, but that's because sometimes there are free samples.

2. ~~**Elvis music.** Flor once told me that you are either a Beatles or an Elvis fan. Obviously, Beatles for me. They are just the coolest. I guess I feel like you shouldn't have to move your hips all weird and wear sparkles to get your point across. I don't <u>hate</u> hate him, maybe it's more dislike. Okay, I guess Elvis comes off.~~

3. **Mushrooms.** Slippery, smelly, and they're a fungus!

4. **Homophobes.** No need to really explain that one.

5. **When it snows on a school day, but we don't get off.**
   Not fair!

6. **Elevator music.** I don't know, I guess it's just kinda depressing.

7. **Math.**

8. You used to be on this list, James, but I'm retiring your name. I just can't hate you anymore.

9. **Music where the singer screams at me.** Minus Kurt. His screams are like necessary. And beautiful.

10. **Pop quizzes.**

After finally finding a parking spot, Shirley and I entered through the double doors of Macy's at the Freehold Raceway mall. It smelled of old lady perfume and cigarette smoke. Even though there is a designated smoking section, the scent of burnt tobacco wafted throughout each floor. I think that if they ever ban smoking from this place, it will forever smell like Marlboro Reds or Shirley's Salems. Luckily, we don't have to go to the smoking section anymore, since Shirley pretty much quit.

We headed to the junior's section—I hate that it's called that, though I'm not sure why. I'll have to add that to my list too.

Shirley and I do not share the same taste for clothing. She likes turtlenecks and jeans that strangle ankles. She wears sweaters with unidentified animals on them. I prefer my clothes to barely touch my skin. Loose. Comfortable. I don't waste time on patterns or matching tops to bottoms. I just like to be covered. Oftentimes, I get Gret's hand-me-downs, which I really don't mind. The only catch is by the time I get her clothes, what once was cool and fashionable, suddenly becomes passé: Z Cavariccis, her favorite tie-dyed Champion sweatshirt, and a powder-blue hypercolor shirt that, by the time I got it, no longer changed its color.

She handed me a few of her chosen pieces for me—completely ignoring my desired style—and I entered into the dreaded dressing room.

Shirley was close behind and I stopped her before I opened the curtain.

"Can you wait outside?" I asked.

"Promise to come out and show me?"

I smiled, realizing that to Shirley, *this* was a good time. I tried to lighten up. The thing is, I love Shirley. A lot. Sometimes it's just difficult to be around her.

I stood naked in front of three mirrors broadcasting every inch of me. I tried not to look but couldn't help seeing parts of me I could never reach with my eyes. It felt like a warped version of Alice in Wonderland through the looking glass, but the more I peered in, the blurrier I became. *Are those really* my *legs and why must my breasts jut out like that?* This should be illegal.

With just my underwear on, I became very aware of something. Like a wetness. Also, a slight smell. Kind of like wet pennies or the scent of my metal roller skates when I left them outside after it rained. Rusty. I peered into my underwear and knew immediately.

Sometime this past summer—July maybe?—Shirley said that if I didn't get my period by my sixteenth birthday, we'd have to go to the doctor because maybe something was wrong. A part of me wished my period was like a package sent to the wrong address. And with no return address, it would just float in the air or attach itself to someone else or . . . I know, I know, this was weird to think. But I really didn't want it.

James, I would never, ever normally tell you about this. But I guess I'm writing this because after it happened, nothing was the same. Funny how little we can control over our bodies. Hair grows even when we cut it, and bits of us get bigger or change shape whether or not we want it to.

"Oh, Eleanor. This is so exciting. Are you excited? How about we go to the food court to celebrate."

You are probably wondering why I even told Shirley, when I could have easily kept it secret and just told you and *you* certainly aren't going to blab. Well, I may appear morose (hello, vocab word), but I knew how happy she'd be. I've learned through many of my friends that menstruation is like a powerful drug.

The other thing is I wanted to be as excited as Shirley. I really did. Most girls I know wear bras and already memorized the best brand of tampons to buy. So, it should feel good to be part of "the club" or whatever. But what I was feeling at this moment was definitely not joy, but remorse. Unfortunately, we were at the mall and there was no time for sadness when my underwear was stained and Shirley was crying menstruation-inspired tears.

"How about we go bra shopping and then I take you for lunch? You aren't going to need to wear undershirts any longer, Eleanor! Eventually, you are going to want to wear underwire, which just lifts and gives you more support, but they don't put wires in your size," Shirley told me.

"I don't have a size. I barely have breasts." Even as I said this out loud, I knew it wasn't true. Many times, Dara told me that she thought it was embarrassing that I wasn't wearing a bra yet because it was pretty obvious I needed one. I noticed boys noticing and I tried not to notice them.

I tried on several varieties of bras, none of which felt natural. "I'd really prefer to keep wearing my undershirts. They're a lot more comfortable," I told Shirley.

"You really should have been wearing one already to cover your buds."

My buds?

"You're a *woman* now, Eleanor."

Oh my God, is *that* what I am now?

James, what is the equivalent of this for guys? I mean, I know your voice changes, and maybe that can be annoying, but you don't all of a sudden wake up to blood in your underwear.

When we got home, I rushed upstairs to my bedroom and emptied the bag of clothes—including two highly uncomfortable bras—onto my bed. I grabbed the pair of jeans and striped sweater, neatly folded by name-tagged Sharon, and hid them inside the third drawer of my dresser. The bras remained on my bed, taunting me. I removed my shirt and put one of them on. The color was called nude, though it looked nothing like my skin or any skin color I've seen on real flesh. Whose nude *is* this? I turned to the side, adjusted the straps, pulled at the cotton trying to befriend my breasts. And then—

"Eleanor!" Greta walked in with a friend I didn't recognize and I was beyond mortified.

"Get out! Get out! Get out!" I bellowed.

"Hey, meet me in my bedroom," Gret motioned to her blond-haired friend. "I'm sorry, El. I didn't realize—"

"Yeah, right. I know Shirley told you about this." I motioned to the bra. "And are you going to tease me about getting my period too?"

"What? You . . . no! I didn't know! When did you—"

"At the mall. I became a woman at the Freehold Raceway Mall. Can my life get any more humiliating?"

Greta walked further in and sat on my bed. The remaining bra bounced from the weight of her body. "You want to talk about it? I promise not to be weird."

"What do you want me to say? It's a lot grosser than I thought it would be. Shirley gave me a pad *with wings*. How is that supposed to feel natural? It's like putting a Barbie bed in my underwear."

"Well, I'm sure when you're ready, you can wear tampons. They're much better. And you forget they're in there."

"All my friends have had it for a while now. I'm the last one to get it. I guess I thought I'd be so excited or feel different. Feel more . . . I don't know . . . more like a—"

"Woman?"

I shrugged.

"El, it's okay to feel a little weirded out. I mean, I definitely did. It's like before my period, I was totally invisible to boys, and then suddenly I got it and my boobs got bigger and my body changed. I wasn't cool with it at first either."

"But you liked the attention, right? I mean, I've seen you in the mirror or . . . I used to see you pressing them together and pushing them up. It's like you want people to see them."

"I do," Greta smiled, touching her breasts, which seemed even bigger.

"Well, I don't want that. I don't want them. And I definitely don't want boys noticing. This really sucks."

After Greta left, I took off the bra and put my shirt back on. I announced to Shirley that I was going on a bike ride. I just needed to get out of the house. It wasn't too cold out and maybe the fresh air would help me to forget what was happening.

My bike is purple and green with a white basket. I remember when Dad got it for me. I may have gotten a little big for it, but I love the speed it gives me.

We don't really walk places. We drive to where we need to go—Jamesway or the movie theater or the mall. There's nothing just around the corner to pick up things. Wheels, of some variety, are always required.

Flor has told me stories about walking to and from school in New York, a mile or so walk but she never paid much mind to it. For her, there were tons of things to distract her: graffiti on buildings, places to eat and lots of noise from cars and people. In New Jersey, the only thing that grows is boredom. Outside noise comes from the tiny ticking sounds of sprinklers tricking the grass into thinking it's raining. Or dogs behind fences. Cars don't really honk much here; I notice this each time I go to New York where everyone likes to show off with all the sounds their automobiles can make.

When I was younger and I'd go on my bike ride, I loved stopping at the tiny strip mall with pizza and a great gift shop where I'd buy fancy paper to write letters on. The gift store went out of business two years ago and now it's a jewelry shop (boring). I decided to stop at the WaWa to get something to drink and eat.

Shirley doesn't keep sugary items in the house, so in moments like this when I'm in a convenience store full of Little Debbie's and pre-packaged treats made of sweetened preservatives, I tend to get a little crazy. I don't even think I like Twinkies or those other cake-type things, but I like that I'm not supposed to be eating them, so, in turn, they somehow become more delicious.

When Flor took me to New York, she told me that she could peg every tourist because they are the ones who look around. They look up and stare at everything. Flor calls them giraffes, stretching their necks as far as they can to see the tops of the skyscrapers. As I perused (vocabulary word) the plastic-wrapped snacks, I happened to look up and see the most beautiful woman I've ever seen. Even more beautiful than Madonna and Drew Barrymore combined. She definitely looked like she wasn't from here. Ripped ~~criss-cross stockings~~ fishnets. Wild blond, wavy hair. She sparkled. Like Heather Locklear, but maybe a little older.

I have never felt like a tourist before. I have lived in New Jersey my whole life and my surroundings have always been familiar and boring and not much to write about. Were you born in New Jersey, James? Did you ever get to live somewhere else? I feel like the New Jersey I've seen is just trees interrupted by stupid strip malls repeating the same places: shoe store, chain restaurant, curtain shop or lighting store or some kind of place selling *home goods*. What are home goods, anyway? Bank. Grocery store. Walmart or some store that seems to sell everything you think you need but really don't.

"Oh, am I in your way?" She looked at me and I had that same feeling in my body like when I first saw Aggie.

"No," I utter. I admit that I was staring, but you would have too, James.

"Uh, sorry," I dribbled out.

"Damn, this place has everything and nothing at the same time." Her voice was deep, with like other higher-pitched instruments in there too. Hard to explain, I guess.

"Their subs are pretty good."

"Something about you reminds me of me when I was your age. What are you . . . fourteen?"

"Fifteen," I blushed. James, I know what you are thinking, if you were thinking, if you were still alive and could read these letters. But it wasn't like *that*. I mean, she wasn't some creepy older stranger, there was something familiar about her.

"Well, I'm just passing through, killing time before I see my mother. I'm Reigh, by the way. Spelled like sleigh."

"I'm Eleanor. Spelled like . . . well, just the regular way. Not sure if there is another."

"Eleanor, huh? Doesn't look to me like there's much regular about you," Reigh smiled. "Dig the hair."

I suddenly stopped breathing.

Reigh's lips were painted stop-sign red. I remember the first time I saw Greta in red lipstick and I thought she was bleeding. I started to scream. I can't remember how old I was, but embarrassingly old enough to know better.

"They don't make people like *me* around here," Reigh interrupted my thoughts.

"Like . . . what do you mean?"

"Sweetie, I can spell it out for you, but something in me tells me you have some idea. Uh, I'm starving! How can a place be filled with so much food and yet, nothing of actual substance?"

Reigh looked at the plastic-wrapped cupcake I was holding in my hand and raised her eyebrows.

"You look young enough to not be bothered by the shit in that, but how about I find something with at least one ingredient that grew outta this earth and wasn't made in a lab?"

Reigh smiled and I noticed a gap between her two front teeth like Madonna's or my cousin Tiffany who can slide her tongue between her teeth like a credit card.

I found myself mesmerized by Reigh's voice. It had a tone I never heard before. There was a softness to it, but it also sounded rehearsed.

"Hey daydreamer, want to sit outside with me?"

"Uh..."

Reigh threw up her hands. "Oh, right. I'm a stranger. You should be leery. I mean, if some old broad approached *me* in a convenience store when I was your age, I'd have . . . what am I saying . . . I'd have loved it. I'd have said, 'please, take me with you!' You should ask me something."

"What?"

"Strangers are only strangers until they're familiar. So, ask me a question, *anything*, I'll answer and then I won't be a stranger."

I looked around. I know I should have thought all of this was really weird. I mean, it *was*. She was right. There just aren't people like *her* in New Jersey. Like *her*. What do I even mean by that?

"Sorry, sweetie. Am I putting you on the spot?" I looked at Reigh as she shifted her weight to the left side of her body. I stared at her hips, mesmerized by her angles. Then, suddenly, I felt guilty that I was looking at her like that.

"No, no," I muttered. "I just, I guess . . . I don't know what to ask."

"Anything."

"Well, umm . . . were you born with the name Reigh?"

"Yes, but I spell it differently now." She looked at me as though wanting me to dig further.

"Oh," I said.

"Next!"

"Uh, what were you like when you were my age?"

"Smarter than my brain could handle at the time. Hungry to get out of my house, my body. And annoyed that everyone kept calling me by the wrong pronoun." Reigh laughed and her curls jiggled a little.

Suddenly, I had a million questions I wanted to ask Reigh. "Okay, I'll sit outside with you."

Reigh generously purchased snacks for both of us. I was so wrapped up in staring at her that I completely forgot that I was still holding that cupcake in my hand. We took a seat on a bench right outside the store. Reigh looked at me and laughed.

"Well, I've stolen far worse in my lifetime."

"No, I . . . I didn't mean to steal this. I just—"

"No matter. One less toxic cupcake haunting the shelves. How about you leave that here on this bench for someone in need of a non-nutritious snack. Oh, I got you *this*."

Reigh handed me a granola bar. I tried to hide my disappointment.

"Don't think that's all there is. *Here*."

Reigh pulled out a small jar of Skippy peanut butter from the plastic bag, untwisted the cap and pulled off the paper seal.

"I love dipping my granola bars in peanut butter. Makes it a hearty snack. Oh, jeez, I must sound so hippie dippy. But it is really good. Try it."

I unwrapped the bar and dipped it in. Then, I brought it to my mouth and took a big bite. It was really delicious.

"My spirit guide tells me that we were supposed to meet."

"Your spirit guide?" I barely uttered, my tongue caught on the thickness of peanut butter.

"Oh, that's what I call my intuition."

"Where are you from?"

"Oh, sweetie, I have been on the move my whole life. It's hard to remember where it all began. My first birth was in New Mexico."

"Your first birth?"

"We arrive many times in life, Eleanor. The first time was out of my mother, but I was birthed again when I came out."

My granola bar plunged into the peanut butter and I stuffed the rest of it into my mouth. I barely had room for my tongue with all the oats crunching around between my teeth.

"Do you know what a transsexual is?"

I swallowed the mass of food in my mouth and could feel the hard bits dig into my throat. I almost choked on the persistent oats refusing to make their way down. Reigh looked at me and I noticed that she had a bit of peanut butter stuck to her lip, but I was too nervous to tell her. Then, as if she could read my mind, she stuck her tongue out, light pink like her fingernails, and licked it away with one quick swoop.

"I'm sorry. This is why my mother and I have a difficult time getting on. She hates the way I just blurt out my truths. Or *any* truths, for that matter. In my circle of friends, we always check in with each other in case we ever go too far. So, this is me checking in. Too far?"

"Yeah . . . I . . . no," I said. I liked the bluntness of Reigh. How easy her words just floated out. I immediately made a thousand wishes that I would be like that when I get older.

"I watched that movie, *Rocky Horror Picture Show* and the guy from Clue called himself . . . *herself?* . . . a transvestite," I said. "I remember because I asked my sister what that meant and she just kind of laughed. But he dressed like a woman. Like you. I mean—"

"Yeah, like *that*, only my taste in clothing is a bit more . . . demure. And this doesn't stop when the credits roll," Reigh signaled to her outfit. "My gender is not just an article of clothing. It's *in* me. Sometimes the people around us are wrong. And it takes some time to make our own realizations."

I took the deepest breath of my life. I wanted to say so many things, and they all ran into each other like a mosh pit of sounds. I felt the weight of what she said stick to my chest and I just left it there.

"Thanks . . . for this, Reigh." I pointed to the empty wrapper of the granola bar.

"Of course. You looked like a lost puppy in there. You live around here?"

"My entire life!" I exhaled.

"Well, I was in Denver for a bit. Eleven years actually. Then went to Portland for a few years to stay with a friend. Could write an entire novel about *that* rollercoaster ride. Spent a spring in Vancouver. Gorgeous. Ever been to Canada?"

I shook my head.

"Worth checking out. Let's see . . . a few weeks in Montana. Realized I'm not much for camping. Two years in a small town in Minnesota. Then Chicago. Really liked Indiana. Stayed with some lesbians in South Carolina at an artist's haven. Found my soul there," Reigh paused and I watched the slow-motion stretch of her lips form into a smile. "And now I'm making my way to New York."

"Wow. You're a walking postcard," I said.

This made Reigh burst out in laughter. Each time she laughed, her eyes squinted and I could almost count all of her teeth.

"Where does your mom live? Is she cool that you're—"

"Freehold. No, she's not cool. In fact, she hasn't seen me like *this* yet." Reigh took her hand and motioned toward her entire body. She slowed down at her breasts. "These are just a few years old now, but it's been about six since I last saw her."

There was something about Reigh that made me feel like I had known her for years. It's almost like she was planted in that WaWa, waiting for me to arrive with hunger and deep thoughts, in search of some sort of sign. A sign in the form of a tall transsexual with beautiful skin and cherry red lips and hair like a bleached forest. She was far more of a woman than I think I could ever be.

"Reigh . . . " I knew what I wanted to say, but I was feeling so nervous to speak it out loud. "When did you know?"

"Oh, Eleanor, if I could remember as far back as the womb, I might say *then*. But the truth is I knew quite early on. I was an only child, so I didn't have any siblings to play with or a sister to steal clothes from. You have any siblings?"

"One. Greta. She's in college."

"College," Reigh repeated. "I tried that out. Maybe I'm just too restless to stay in one place for too long. Those desks always felt . . . constricting. Anyway, I always loved to dress up. I had a trunk my dad built out of wood scraps and my mom would keep her old clothes in there. I loved making forts and little caves as a kid. I guess I was building something to come out of," Reigh giggled. "She probably thought I'd rip up the fabric and use it as some sort of tarp. But instead, I'd wear them. I have this crisp memory of being four or five years old, taking my mom's lipstick, and painting my nails with it."

"Your nails?" I laughed.

"My mother is . . . how can I describe her?" Reigh puffed up her chest with a deep inhale. "A classically-trained narcissist."

"What's that?"

"My mother will walk into a room and think that all the walls have been placed there for her to lean on. She was very private about her beauty routine, so when I'd wake up each morning, she already had all her paint on. Lipstick. Rouge. Eye shadow and mascara. A regular Joan Crawford without the wire hangers and talent. Her nails were always coated in smooth strokes. Her hair . . . perfectly curled from giant rollers she'd sleep in every night. God only knows how uncomfortable that must have been. And a chin strap! She refused to get a jowl, she'd say. She thought she could train her skin to remain intact.

"I never knew *how* all this color got on her skin, so when I was able to storm her vanity full of perfumes and every kind of make-up imaginable, I just covered myself. Put blush all over my arms. Lipstick on my nails. Eye shadow on my lips. I was quite a sight!"

Reigh's eyes squinted as she burst out in laughter. I began to lose it as well, as I pictured her covered in mismatched make-up.

"Did you like the way you looked?" I asked.

"You know what? I can remember how I felt, even then. Something just felt *right*."

James, I felt myself locating every cell of my skin. *Really*, I could *feel* my cells. In that moment, talking to Reigh, every sensation and swallow and itch were magnified. It's like parts of me were awakening in this weird and wonderful way. It was all so strange.

"How long will you stay here?" I blurted.

"Well, I've been here two days and I haven't gotten very far. I keep thinking I'll wake up with the right words to say to her when I finally see her. All that ever comes to mind is . . . *I'm not dead, Mom.*"

"Does she think you are?"

"Ha, wouldn't be surprised. But part of me *is*. The me she birthed isn't the me now, but this me is much better. Far more improved, I'd say. I was . . . I was dead before I ever even knew I was."

"What do you . . . "

"I didn't even know that there were bits of me that had yet to be birthed, I guess. It's complicated and yet, not really. The thing is, Eleanor . . . " Reigh moved in closer. I could smell the peanut butter on her breath and it was a comforting aroma, perhaps because it matched mine.

"I was always living outside of myself. It took a while to finally be *the me* that I longingly saw in others. Jeez, I must be talking your ear off, honey."

"No, no, not at all," I said. "I had a . . . difficult day, so I just hopped on my bike and came here and found you and this is all so strange, but also pretty wonderful and—"

"What made your day difficult?"

"I . . . I'm kind of embarrassed to say."

"No worries. I won't pry," she said.

"I got my period at the mall with my mother while trying on clothes, which I hate doing to begin with."

Reigh laughed, then looked at me. "Sorry."

"It was my first time," I added.

"Going to the mall?"

"Getting my period."

"Oh!"

"And I'm not one of those people who is all excited about getting it. Shirley—my mom—took me bra shopping afterward. It was a nightmare. I don't want this. But I don't know how to make it go away. And . . . " I paused, trying to decide what to say, knowing what I wanted to say, knowing Reigh wouldn't run or make fun of me or make me feel any sort of bad. "I just came out actually. As a lesbian, I mean. But . . . I don't know, sometimes I think there's more that wants out. I just don't know . . . how to . . . say it."

"Fifteen, aye? You are quite perceptive. Mighty, I'd even say. Listen, the words come when they're ready."

"I know, but right now it feels unbearable."

James, being next to Reigh felt like reading a thousand books at once. Gaining new vocabulary and insight, it was amazing. We talked for a little while more and then I realized how much time had passed. We said goodbye, but not before exchanging phone numbers. Reigh said that it's important to collect good people, especially ones that are a part of the letters. I didn't understand what she meant until she explained that she was the T and Flor (I told her all about her) was my L and all I needed was a G and a B. Maybe you could have been my G, my gay friend. My *friend*.

Monday, November 29

Dear James,

Gret and I spent the weekend at my Dad's and then she headed back to Massachusetts for school. I couldn't stop thinking about Reigh all weekend.

On Saturday night, Gret and Dad went to the China Bowl to pick up dinner, while I waited at Dad's house and snooped around a bit. When Dad got his apartment, it was so strange in the beginning, seeing just *his* things around. Growing up, all our stuff was ~~entigraded~~ integrated. I walked into his bedroom, which was pretty bland. Tan comforter. Nothing on the walls. A photo of Gret and I on his dresser.

He had one closet in his room. It was small but neatly organized. Everything was hung, even his ties. I took one—green with tiny yellow dots—and put it around my neck. I used to sit on the bathroom counter beside the sink and watch him put on a tie before work. At that time, I was in love with origami and I loved folding anything that would turn into something else. I remember asking him to show me, and he did. But with any learned task, if you don't practice you forget. So, I forgot.

I twisted the tie around my neck, trying to remember what goes over and under and how does it loop? I walked toward the mirror and took a look. It was messy and definitely not twisted correctly, but I liked the way it looked on me.

Dinner was our usual favorites: chicken with broccoli, shrimp with lobster sauce, vegetable lo mein, steamed dumplings. Different textures and smells and everything was so delicious, it was difficult to stop even when I was so full.

"This is way better than turkey," I said.

Dad smiled and Gret laughed. "Well, you'll still be eating it all week," Gret teased.

After dinner, Gret sat on the couch watching TV, while Dad and I played Uno at the kitchen table. I told him that I tried on one of his ties while they were getting the food.

"Yeah? Do you remember me teaching you how to tie it?"

I nodded.

"Do you want one to take back home with you?"

Thursday, December 2

Dear James,

I'm only writing less because some days I come home and just want my thoughts to stay inside me. Like they are pieces of fruit that still need ripening. Tonight is group and earlier today in English, Aggie and I kept passing notes about Reigh. She kept saying that it all sounded like a movie.

AGGIE: Has she called you yet?

ME: Nope, and I feel too shy to call her. But I definitely want to see her again.

AGGIE: You think your mom will be OK with that?

ME: Sure, why not?

AGGIE: Didn't you say she was old? I mean, an adult?

ME: Yeah, but she's not creepy or anything like that. ~~She's~~

James, I haven't told Aggie that Reigh is a transsexual. It feels weird to say it. I kind of just want Reigh to exist as just a person. Not be defined by anything else but *who* she is, not *what* she is.

Thursday, December 2

Dear James,

In English class, Ms. Raimondo had us write haikus. It's hard to write much in just three lines with only seventeen syllables. Aggie said that is the best part: restraint. So I thought my letter to you could be a collection of haikus:

In group therapy,
Peter reminds us living's
a constant action

But Maeve kept saying
how easier it is to
do nothing but sleep

She is having a
difficult time moving on
stuck in a pothole.

Reigh called! We talked for
two hours! She wants to take
me to an open mic

(went one syllable over, see how hard it is!)

Okay, my fingers hurt from counting syllables. It was awesome to hear Reigh's voice. I thought I'd be shy on the phone or we wouldn't have anything to talk about, but the only reason we got off the phone was because it was a school night and Shirley said it was getting late. Things we talked about: Reigh's beloved (her words) cat, which she had to put down right before she came to New Jersey. His name was Kathy Acker, who Reigh told me was her favorite writer. We also talked about our favorite foods (me: potatoes of all kinds and Reigh: sushi). And music and school assignments and her mother and my mother and tomorrow night, I get to see her again!

Of course, Shirley asked who I was talking to for so long.

"Just this person I recently met," I said, hoping she wouldn't ask more about it.

But Shirley wanted to know everything, so I told her because I'm trying to not keep things from her, even though secretly I always worry that I will say something to upset her and cause her to try and kill herself again.

Shirley insisted that she meet Reigh first before we go out, which I felt was fair. I really wanted Reigh to meet Flor too.

So, Reigh is coming over for dinner tomorrow night and then we are going to an open mic!

～

Friday, December 3

Dear James,

I am so tired, but I don't want to forget anything about this day, so I am going to do my best to get all of it out before I fall asleep.

Reigh came over and she looked beautiful. Shirley was very welcoming, although I could tell she was a bit ~~leary~~ leery about it all. Reigh had her hair up and it looked like a waterfall of curls. During dinner, she talked about places she's lived, the band she used to play bass in (The Scraped Knees), and her nervousness to see her mom after all these years. I mainly just listened, amazed at how free and open Reigh is. I guess that's what happens when you become an adult.

"Before I became my true self," Reigh said, "I lived in books and music. I'd put Diana Ross on the turntable, close my eyes and imagine myself as one of the Supremes. My mother used to wear wigs because she was very self-conscious of her thinning hair, so I'd put them on when she was out. When I started existing on the outside how I felt on the inside, I *became* Diana Ross. I was no longer the back-up singer, if that makes any sense. I guess . . . I started to feel like the star of my life, rather than the over-shadowed version of what was being prescribed to me."

And that's all she had to say, James. I watched as Flor and then eventually Shirley started to understand. We laughed so much our food got cold. And then, Reigh drove us to Freehold for the open mic.

As we were getting out of Reigh's car, Reigh said, "I haven't even asked if you were planning on reading anything. It is an open mic after all. I've got my bass in the trunk. I could play alongside you, if you were interested. What do you think, Eler?"

"Huh?" My thoughts had traveled me away and I was awoken by Reigh's last word.

"Is it cool if I call you that? Eleanor's a great name, it's just that it's a bit . . . " Reigh turned her mouth into a curious smirk. " . . . limiting, don't you think?"

"Eler," I repeated. "I like that. Yeah, cool. Sure. You can call me that."

I felt so cool being in the café with Reigh because she is so beautiful and I'm just plain, plain, plain.

"Here alright?" Reigh motioned at a small circular table off to the side, but not far from the stage.

"Yeah, sure. You gonna get something?"

"I never oppose caffeine. Do you drink coffee? I can't remember how old I was my first time. *That* first time," she chuckled.

Reigh steals my breath each time she smiles. She's like a giant spotlight in a dark room, shining her light everywhere she walks. I want *that* to be contagious.

"It's okay. Shirley used to let me take sips of hers. Now she's cool if I drink a cup of my own. But I'll have a root beer or ginger ale."

"Got it. I'll go grab us something. You hold down the fort."

I hung my backpack on the back of the chair, took my coat off and breathed in the room and all its inhabitants. I grabbed my notebook from my bag and leafed through my letters to you. Could I possibly read one out loud?

When Reigh sat down, I asked her how long she's been playing bass.

"I feel like I came out of my mother playing it," she laughed. "But I played professionally for many years. Went on tour and everything. The bright lights. Backrooms. Screaming audiences with wild hair, rocking out. Gosh, that feels like a lifetime ago. During much of my twenties and a little in my thirties."

"What kind of music did you play?"

"Let's see, we called it tie-dye rock back then. Electrophonic, metallic, throw-back."

I laughed. "I have no idea what any of that means, but it sounds really cool. Did you record any albums?"

"Oh sure! I'll send you off with a few tapes before we part tonight. I've got a bunch in my trunk."

"I'd love that!"

Reigh took a bite of the almond croissant she bought for us to share. I watched a few flakes of the buttery dough stick to her faded red lips.

"Umm . . . " I motioned at her mouth. "You've got some . . . "

She lifted her fingers toward her lips, gracefully swatting, but the crumbs were persistent.

"It's . . . it's still there."

Reigh gently grabbed my hand. "Can you?"

I hesitantly rubbed at her bottom lip, which was soft and sticky. I removed the pastry and could feel something happen inside my body. Between my legs. It's kind of how I feel when I'm around Aggie.

"I think your face just about matches my lips. Or at least what my lips looked like at the start of this day. Did I embarrass you?"

"Perhaps just a little. You're really beautiful." James, I couldn't believe I had said that!

"Why thank you, Eler. And you are quite handsome."

Handsome? I'd never been called this. Pretty. Cute. Dad has called me beautiful, but parents don't count. Handsome. Eler. Handsome Eler.

"Uh, speaking of blush-worthy humans," Reigh said. "One just walked in and seems to have noticed you."

I clumsily turned around.

"Who?"

"Who?! Obviously that one in the purple crushed velvet sweater. Tight black pants. Looks like a female Prince. What am I saying? *Prince* looks like a female Prince." Reigh chuckled and her eyes pressed together.

I noticed Prince. She was with two others and they were laughing about something inaudible. I tried not to be too obvious as I took in her outfit and style. Reigh was right; she was definitely blush-worthy. Her skin looked just like a London fog, my favorite hot beverage.

"You gonna make a move, darling?"

I turned back toward Reigh and froze. "What? A move? No, I'm definitely not cool enough for . . . *her*. I mean, she's . . . she's *Prince*."

Reigh started talking about this person she used to be in love with called G. I was a little confused because Reigh kept skipping over the pronoun, so I couldn't tell if G was a girl or a boy and then I decided it didn't matter.

"G was definitely out of my league. I mean, a drummer *and* a mountain climber?! G was fearless, dropping beats everywhere. I spent months just trying to be anywhere I thought G was and then."

Reigh stopped talking and smiled. I waited.

"And then, I realized that G was everywhere *I* went. We finally had a conversation and realized we were each other's . . . stalkers." Reigh busted out laughing as though she just heard the most fantastic joke. "Five years of my life. Five . . . tumultuous years together. But that's another story for another day. Quite. A. Doozy."

"So . . . you're telling me I should say something to Prince?"

"Hell yeah! Look, she just got in line for the bathroom. Perfect. *That* is where many love affairs begin."

"Waiting to use the bathroom?"

"Sure. Waiting on line is the best time to strike up a conversation. Trust me, Eler. My intuition is signaling me to push you on this!"

I took a sip of my root beer and swirled the spice around against my teeth. The sugar was strong and thick, creating a film over my tongue. I stood up, headed toward the back where the line was, and walked behind Prince.

Prince smelled like Gret's high school friend, Farrah, who wound up choosing The Grateful Dead over college. She now drives all over the country, going to Dead shows, shaking her long brown hair, dancing in various indoor and outdoor venues. I remember Farrah coming over a few times, imprinting her scent all over our house. I lusted after her way before I admitted to myself what that even meant.

"Ugh, there's always a line."

What? Huh? Prince is talking to me! *Play. It. Cool. Eleanor.*

"Yeah," I dripped out of my nervous lips.

"You here for the open mic? I haven't seen you before."

"Oh, yeah, I'm just here with a . . . a friend she took me here I've never been to a . . . " *Breathe, Eleanor!* "Are you performing?" I asked.

"Yeah, still need to sign up. I play bass. I'm still working up the courage to sing. Until then, I just play instrumental for now."

"Hey, that's cool. Actually, my friend used to tour in a band. She plays bass too!"

"It's a fuckin' cool instrument. Got calluses on pretty much all my fingers to prove it."

I glanced at her fingers, which I suddenly wanted to sip from as though they were straws.

"Yeah, anyway, I'm T'nea."

"T*i*nea, hi, I'm—"

"No, T'*nea*. No 'I'."

"Got it. T'nea. I'm Ele . . . Eler."

"Awesome. Ah, shit, it's my turn. Nice to meet ya."

T'nea disappeared into the bathroom and I just stood there, drenched in amorous thoughts. I peeked my head around and looked at Reigh. She caught my stare and smiled.

When T'nea walked out, I told her I didn't really have to go to the bathroom.

"Oh? You just like hanging around bathrooms?"

"You know," I said. "I hope you don't take this the wrong way, but you . . . you kind of look like Prince. In the best way. I mean, the *girl* version, but—"

"I fuckin' love Prince. No bad way to take that. Thanks, Eler."

T'nea moved closer and sniffed me.

"Then, uh . . . don't take *this* the wrong way, but you smell like a boy."

"What? What do you mean? Like dirty laundry or sweaty sneakers?"

"Shit, what kind of boys you got hanging around you? No, like . . . I don't know. Musk. You smell good. I just mean, you don't smell all florally like most girls. You smell . . . good. Damn, I don't know. You got me all stuttery now."

Perhaps we were both blushing.

The bathroom door opened. T'nea grabbed my hand and without exchanging any words, lead me in and asked me a thousand questions in the span of seconds just with her eyes. Suddenly, we were inside this single-serving room with a toilet and sink. Door closed, locked. Did anyone see us walk in together?

"Hi," she smiled.

"Hi," I smiled.

"You queer?"

"W-what?" I choked out.

"I don't know. I just get a sense from you that you are, but I definitely have been wrong. Are you?"

"Uh, y-yeah," I blurted. "I mean, I just started calling myself a lesbian, but . . . "

T'nea held my hand. Her fingers wrapped around mine, pressing against my knuckles. Her tea leaf skin against my apple juice flesh.

"I really wanna kiss you. How old are you anyway?"

"I'm . . . I'm fifteen," I embarrassingly stuttered.

"I'm sixteen. You cool with that?"

"With your age or . . . with you—"

And suddenly, T'nea's mouth was on mine. Her tongue was hot like an electric blanket. We were circling our tongues around each other, lips moistened by our combined spit. I could feel her breasts, pillowy and soft, press against my chest. Her hands in my short, choppy hair. My hands in her hair, a mass of twists like fireworks thrust from her scalp. How was this happening?

James, I want to report to you that our kissing lasted for seven days and six nights. I want to tell you that we celebrated a new year within the span of our kissing. Perhaps I celebrated two birthdays as our mouths mashed together and hands explored places I barely like to acknowledge on myself. Or it could have just been a few minutes. Or maybe less than that.

T'nea touched her mouth with her hand. Was she wiping me away?

"My lips feel like they are on fire!"

"They do? Are you okay?" I asked.

"Ha, ha, yeah! You're a fuckin' amazing kisser, Eler. My thighs are all rubbery and shit."

If only she knew this was my first real, *real* kiss. Wow. I thought it would be with Aggie. Oh, Aggie.

"We should give back the bathroom, what do ya think?"

"Yeah, probably should. Umm . . . do you wanna sit with my friend and I? I mean, I saw that you came in with some others. You're all welcome to—"

"Cool. Yeah. Let me put some liquid in me. That is, besides just your sweet spit. And then I'll come and join you."

We exited the bathroom and walked in our separate directions.

"Well, there you are," Reigh greeted me loudly. "Thought you ditched me, sweet one!"

"Reigh, I'm so sorry, I—"

"Are you kidding? I'm fine. I'm just hoping you got a story for me!"

"Reigh, I . . . "

"Let me guess . . . you're in *loooooooove!*"

"Well, I don't know about that, but . . . oh my gosh, we made out!"

"Well, aren't *you* a surprise, Eler! How was it to kiss Prince?"

"I feel like I stopped breathing. Her name is T'nea. And I told her that she looks just like Prince. And Reigh?"

"What, doll?"

"She said that I smell like a boy. But like, in a good way. It confused me at first, but then I started to feel really . . . uh . . . " I whispered, "*Turned on* by it."

"Yeah, I can wrap my mind around that."

"I invited her and her friends to sit with us. Is that okay?"

"Hell yeah!"

⌇

Sunday, December 5

Dear James,

I've been in such an Aggie haze that I am still processing (therapy word) these past few days. It's like when I switched my crush from Michael Jackson to Janet. Michael was all over my bedroom. Pictures ripped out from every magazine ~~colleged~~ collaged on my walls. I still love his music, but Janet owns my heart now. I know that Aggie will always just be my friend. I get that. I still cannot believe T'nea kissed me!

I definitely didn't expect T'nea to call me so soon. We exchanged phone numbers right before Reigh and I left. I was shy, at first, on the phone. Luckily, T'nea filled in all the gaps of my nervous silence.

First, she walked me through her entire Saturday.

"I had soccer practice, almost got hit by the ball twice, because you kept swirling in my head, thought about doing homework when I got home but then decided to listen to music instead, dinner at my Dad's, fight with my brother, fell asleep thinking of you."

James, my entire face caught on fire from blushing so much.

"What kind of music do you like?" I asked.

"SWV, Mary of course, Whitney, Salt-N-Pepa, Tupac, and Pearl Jam."

"Pearl Jam? Do you like any other rock?"

"Mainly I like music I can dance to. How 'bout you?"

I told her all about my love for Nirvana, Pixies, she'd never even heard of The Velvet Underground or even Bob Dylan! I like that we have different tastes. It means we can teach each other new stuff.

~

Monday, December 6

Dear James,

Today in English class, Ms. Raimondo soaked us all in a noise bath. I know that sounds weird and it kind of was, but also really cool too. You would have loved this, James, or at least I think you might have. She said that it's important to be aware of every sense around us. To smell the air and hear the wind and taste the words floating all around. Isn't that beautiful? She said that to really hear creates an opening for more, to understand the ideas and words we read. She said it can even help us be better readers and writers.

So she had us close our eyes. I peeked a few times to see if everyone else was doing it and I was amazed that they were. She librarian'd into the air. Dara and I used to say that anytime we were shushed. Then she said, "listen."

First, all I could hear was my own breathing. Then, I noticed people shifting in their seats. I felt like I could hear Aggie's braid in front of me. The gathered hairs gasping because maybe her twists were just a little too tight today. Someone sneezed. Then a cough. Another sneeze. A giggle. Then, suddenly the quiet was gone.

Then, Ms. Raimondo reminded us to keep listening as she introduced new sounds into the classroom. Sounds she recorded like cars on the road and rain against windows. Some sounds I couldn't quite understand, but it's like they were all musical instruments creating momentary songs.

Ms. Raimondo had us write in our notebooks about what we noticed. What was uncomfortable. What happened for us.

Here is what I wrote:

I remember visiting Shirley for the first time in the hospital. The smells were really overwhelming at first. Rust and aged sweat and wet dog (though there were no dogs in sight) and sadness. Then I thought about how emotions could have a smell. What does sad smell like? I don't know, I guess like instant mashed potatoes from the box, salt free, no butter. I've never kept my eyes closed for this long while in class. Normally, we'd get yelled at. But Ms. Raimondo is encouraging us. I want to whisper to Aggie all about Reigh and T'nea. I called Aggie this weekend, but she was out and I figured we'd catch up at lunch. I hear Reggie snickering. I can tell it's him. Someone coughed, though it sounded made-up. What does a made-up sound sound like? I can hear my stomach wishing I had eaten breakfast. I somehow forgot because I was in a T'nea cloud. We talked on the phone yesterday for almost an hour! Her voice sounded even better through the tiny holes of the telephone. I wonder if Ms. Raimondo's eyes ever checked in on us during our sound bath? James, I wonder what you'd write if you were here.

In the cafeteria, I finally told Aggie all about my weekend. As I spoke, I watched her grab at her thick, black braid. James, I have spent hours, no, *days*, fantasizing about that braid against my skin. I have thought about undoing her elastic and watching her hair unravel from its twists. I've imagined Aggie's lips, which are kind of diamond shaped, pressed against mine. But it's just a little bit different because I was also fantasizing about T'nea.

I described the beauty and mystery of Reigh and being at the open mic, promising I'd take her next time.

"Aggie, this weekend I had my first *real* kiss."

"What?" Aggie grabbed my shoulders and shook them.

This is when I gave up all the details, trying to make her feel like she was there. Though secretly, I knew that if she *were* there, it wouldn't have happened. Usually when Aggie is around, I don't notice anyone else.

"Did you like it, El? I mean, was she a good kisser or what?"

"It was . . . I don't know . . . like warm and kind of sloppy but in a good way. She's really soft."

"Girls tend to be," Aggie smiled.

As I went about my day, I kept thinking about yesterday. I've been living in New Jersey my whole life and suddenly now, I'm meeting people who are helping me to find bits of myself which have been waiting to be defined. It's like I've been puzzled. No, it's like I've been this puzzle, all intricate and jagged pieces but unfinished.

I remember driving to Nebraska once with Shirley, Dad and Greta when we all got along. It was a long car ride, about three or four days, I think. We exhausted all the car games we could think of. We played all our chosen tapes enough times to have each song memorized and no longer liked. I remember it was during that car ride, that we were listening to the radio and the DJ announced that Lucille Ball had died. In the backseat, I quietly cried because I loved her so much and had assumed she was already dead. I watched reruns of *I Love Lucy* and *The Lucy Show*, where I got to actually see the red red red of her hair. I cried because in that moment, I realized she had existed somewhere. I probably wouldn't have met her, but maybe I could have written her a letter. There are those books that publish stars' addresses. And maybe she would have gotten it and written back. But now, she was really dead. I let each tear slowly travel down my face. I remember not wanting to wipe them away, hoping they'd form some sort of puddle on my knees. A pool of salt for Lucy.

When we finally reached Aunt Wenda and Uncle Yurick's house in Aurora, we were all so tired. And maybe I am remembering this wrong, but after we put our bags away, Aunt Wenda—whose teeth were always covered in layers of bright pinkish-orange lipstick—grabbed a puzzle and encouraged us all to take part in putting it together. Maybe I am forgetting something. Maybe I am forgetting that we ate first or drank lemonade in their screened-in porch. Maybe we puzzled the next day, but I really feel like there was this strange urgency to stand around their dining room table to create this cardboard cutout picture together. I've always hated puzzles, but it didn't seem like we (Gret and I) had much of a choice. Shirley didn't want to take part; this I definitely remember. She sat on the porch and smoked. Greta was annoyingly excited, which made my huffing and puffing seem far worse. In the end, Greta, Aunt Wenda, Uncle Yurick, Dad and I took to this puzzle together. My memory says it took hours, but it could have just been thirty minutes.

But what has remained lodged in my memory's throat is this: When we finally got to the end, there was one piece missing. Of course, Greta accused me of stealing it, since I didn't want to do it in the first place. We all just kind of stared at this hole in the landscape.

And then, I remember Aunt Wenda saying, "Well, isn't this just like life. Feels like it's all together, but there is always, always something missing. Something amiss."

I will never, ever forget her saying that.

These months make me realize I've been missing something too. And maybe it's many pieces—but I'm starting to feel like I'm getting warmer. Like where I need to look to find this missing bit is closer to me than I realize.

Like that finger I found at the beach! Decrepit and almost unrecognizable, but I knew what it was. I knew it was from someone. I knew I couldn't just pretend it away.

Wait.

Am I . . . what am *I* pretending away?

Dear Elinore,

When I was six no eight, I got chicken pox. You ever get them? That was the last time my dad was nice to me. My mom filled the bathtub with some sort of oatmeal stuff to stop my skin from itching so much. I remember I kept asking what chicken did this to me. I hadn't touched any so how'd I get their pox? Stupid. But after, I would pretend to be sick, so my dad would let up on me. I feel like I am always looking for his approval, but he never really sees me. And of course, I've made it worse. There is no one I can talk to about this. There is no one I can tell that my dad found a dirty magazine in my bedroom because I am an ~~idot~~ idiot and didn't hide it well enough and now he knows. He knows. I'm sure he's told my mom, but she hasn't said anything. The worst part is I'm sure he wouldn't care if it were a girly mag like the dicks in our grade pass around in the locker room after gym class. But why'd I want to look at that?

Who knew there were so many bad words for being gay? Shit, I never wrote that down before. When my dad whips me, he reads off scripture. I want to tell him that by doing that he's conditioning me to hate religion. Mr. Heraldo taught us that in social studies. How history has conditioned us to treat others or something like that. I want to know what the big deal is that I happen to like other guys. Who decided that was something we couldn't allow? I look at you and wonder if maybe you're like me. Maybe that's why I say what I say to you. I don't know. That's too much to think about. Maybe I'll just take a walk and find a door that leads to ~~knowwhere~~ nowhere. If the earth is round, then there must be a way to fall off it somehow, right? Is that dumb to say? You know, like a diving board. Just find the edge and jump off into space. Float or die or whatever.

Tuesday, December 7

Dear James,

What about me made you think I was gay too?

～

Wednesday, December 8

Dear James,

So I guess Shirley is dating now.

She invited some guy from her therapy group to eat with us.

As I walked down the stairs, I noticed a strange man with a brown sweater vest and comb-over sitting at our kitchen table. He got up as I peeked into the kitchen.

"I'm Ted." He reached out his hand and I just kind of stared at it. It was doughy, like those Pillsbury rolls that start out in a cylinder, and then you pop the paper flap, and it all just combusts.

"I'm Eleanor, but you probably know that."

Was I supposed to make it easy for this guy?

"Well, yes, your mom has talked much about you. And Greta too." I watched his eyes glance over at Shirley in this gross way. Gross to me, because it's a man looking at my mom like she's a *woman*. And not *my mom*. Like he's picturing her giving birth to me or something.

I let my lips curl into themselves. This was code for uh-huh.

"Thanks for letting me join in on your dinner. Smells delicious."

Ted had a pen clipped to the inside of his pant pocket, which I only noticed because it was leaking, leaving a puddle of blue by his thigh. I'm not sure he knew about it and I wasn't about to tell him. It's not my place to tell him this. He smelled like mouthwash and talcum powder, which reminded me of dad and he also smelled like *sour* sour cream. He told me about his cat named Fiona, which he had a picture of in his wallet and didn't hesitate to show me and he has a grown daughter named Sally who lives in Florida. She's got cats too.

I didn't talk much during dinner, which was a casserole with chicken, string beans, corn, cream of mushroom soup, basically a dish of everything in our fridge. Oh, and fried onions on top, my favorite from the can. Ted had three helpings.

Okay, I will admit that it was nice to see Shirley smiling so much. Ted doesn't seem so bad. And maybe it's a good thing to date someone who understands what it's like to be sad. It's not like I'm waiting for her and Dad to get back together. I much prefer how it is now to when they fought so much. It's just weird to see her put her hand on someone else and to googley-eye him so much.

Wednesday, December 8

Dear James,

In school, I spent five extra minutes trying to unlock my locker. I hate these stupid locks. 31-28-14. I spun and paused. 31-28-14. But it wouldn't open. I felt my body get sweaty. This is what happens when I feel rushed or stressed or angry. Finally, it popped open and I noticed a neatly folded piece of torn loose-leaf in handwriting I didn't recognize.

> Elenor,
>
> I don't really know what to say except that yeah, it's me. Can we talk after school?
>
> Brian

Okay, so I wasn't going to mention it in my letters to you, James. Not like you are reading this. But there is something about writing things down that make it real. I just figured I'd put a note in Brian's locker, the Brian I assumed you were talking about in your notebook. I actually didn't expect him to write back, even though I mentioned my locker number just in case.

After school, Brian and I sat in the back of the auditorium while the drama people practiced for the school play. I think they are doing *Flowers for Algernon*. It was definitely awkward at first because I never spoke to this Brian before. I've talked to Brian C. a bunch of times because he was my lab partner last year in Science class. Brian Z. and I used to be acquaintances. Brian M. and I live on the same block, so Dara and I used to go to his house to play board games until he bored us. But Brian S. and I somehow never crossed paths.

"So, James told you? I didn't realize you guys were friends," Brian said as we ended our uncomfortable bout of silence and realized that someone would have to make the first move with words.

"Not exactly. His mom . . . I got his notebook. And I guess he was sort of writing to me for some reason. He mentioned you a bunch of times and . . . I slowly started to figure out which Brian he was talking about."

"Who'd you tell?"

"What do you mean?"

"I mean who's gonna call me a fag now?"

James, I immediately felt uncomfortable, worried that I made a mistake.

"I didn't. I . . . " I didn't really know what to say.

"We were friends and then we weren't. That's pretty much it," he said.

James, here is what I wanted. What I wanted was for Brian to tell me all about you. Tell me he loved you but didn't know how to show it. I think I wanted him to apologize even though it was too late. Even though none of it mattered now. But it's like he was all carved out. A hollow tree.

"He really cared about you," I said.

"Yeah, well, he's gone now. Not much matters about that. Just . . . don't tell anyone alright? I'm not gay, if that's what you're thinking. And even if I was, I can't be. Not here. Definitely not here."

"I don't care if you are, Brian. But *I* am."

"You're what?"

"Gay. And you know what? I don't care who you tell. James killed himself because he was tired of not being allowed to be himself. Always feeling like he was wrong. Do what you need to do. Pretend or whatever. That's on you. Just know that you meant a lot to him. I guess that's all I wanted to say."

James, I am starting to realize that how we imagine things in our head is often far different from how life actually goes. I thought we'd hug, leave as friends, maybe even start a movement of coming out, ripping out all the nails, tearing down the door to our closet—you know, what we come out of?—and start a revolution. Too far? Probably. Anyway, I left feeling like life is far more complicated than that.

⌇

Thursday, December 9

Dear James,

Tonight, at group, my mind was elsewhere. It's like my brain was packed and ready, traveling through various conversations and distracted by everything that has happened in these past few months. It traveled from Aggie to you to Reigh and T'nea to Brian and even Dara. Your mom mentioned something about counseling and separation, and that's when I dumped out my brain's suitcases and tried to focus.

" . . . and it just hasn't gotten better. I'm realizing that I have been very dormant. I should have stood up for James. Should have encouraged him to be whoever and however he wanted to . . . "

James, your mom and dad are separating. This isn't new, I mean, this happens a lot. Peter has mentioned several times the difficulty for parents to remain together after the loss of a child. A bunch of people at group have gotten divorces. I wasn't going to tell you. I wasn't going to write it down, but I am trying to be free in here. Ms. Raimondo said that the moment we edit, we are stopping the natural flow. Like placing a giant boulder in the middle of a stream. The direction changes. No rocks allowed.

I talked to Helaine after group, as I often do. She always asks me for an Eleanor report. How things are at school, home, in life. I told her about T'nea and she smiled. I also mentioned my interaction with Brian.

"Eleanor, we all aren't ready to be who we are at the moment others want us to be. And the other way around, which is . . . which was James's cross. All we have control over is how we live and lead our lives."

"I'm really sorry about you and Burt," I said.

"It was coming. You know, I grew up with parents who absolutely hated one another. I used to stare at their wedding photo and wonder how they were able to smile that long for the camera, standing closer than I'd ever seen them. I carried some of that into my marriage with Burt. I didn't want to give up, but I know it harmed James to see us. To see me not stick up for him when he needed me most."

A few nights ago, I was talking to Reigh on the phone. She's staying in Red Bank with a friend. She said that we are disco balls. Some of us turn real fast, illuminating our mirrored edges, showing off all the sides we ~~encompress~~ encompass. While others have turned ourselves off. They don't rotate, staying still, refusing to open themselves up to new opportunities or ways of thinking. James, I'd like to think I have begun to spin. I'd like to think that this is my disco ball moment.

Friday, December 10

Dear James,

This year is almost over. Soon, I will be sixteen. Today in English class, Aggie's braid was starring in a silent film against her back and I just watched it. I stared at her glistening black strands, while thinking of T'nea. Is that strange?

This time last year I had no idea what was ahead. So what waits for me now?

Saturday, December 11

Dear James,

My parents had me late in life. Most of my friends' parents are younger. Even Helaine looks super young to be a mom. I wonder what it's going to be like when *I'm* old and my parents are so old that I have to sew post-its to their clothes to remind them what to do and how to do it. Hopefully, it won't come down to that. Shirley is dating Ted—it's official. But Dad is still alone. I hope he finds someone who knows how to sew. Greta came home yesterday. Her friend was having some sort of birthday celebration, so she went to that last night. She's still sleeping, amidst a pile of dirty laundry that she brought home because she is too lazy to collect quarters and do it herself. She surprised me by leaving a note on my desk that she was going to join me at Dad's for the weekend. It's been awhile since it's been the three of us.

Downstairs, I could hear Shirley cooking breakfast. French toast with cornflakes on top: Greta's favorite. After breakfast, Shirley is driving us to Dad's. This is the weekend I practice my coming out skills once again.

Aggie reminded me about what we read in class from Audre Lorde. All about breaking our silence. And what happens. Doors open.

A few nights ago, Flor was over for supper and while Shirley was cleaning up, I shared with Flor my nervousness about telling Dad about my sexuality.

"I guess I just wish this was like one giant game of telephone where one person whispers to the next and *they* whisper what they hear to the one beside them and it all just gets carried away."

"But you know, Eleanor, in that game it never ends up the way it started. It's best to always hear news from the newsmaker."

I thought about this for a moment. "Okay. So, what do I do? I mean, do you think Shirley told Dad already?"

"She's in the kitchen. Go ask her."

I screamed out an exasperated sigh. "I almost don't even want to know. Knowing he knows and hasn't said anything would make it worse!"

"Then how about you head into your weekend. Enjoy this time with Greta and allow it to just come out in the way you need it to. I will say one more thing about it, Eleanor. It really doesn't matter if he knows or not. *You* telling him is less about him knowing and more about you getting more and more comfortable with speaking your truth."

~

Sunday, December 12

Dear James,

It's interesting what one notices. Whenever I go over to Dad's house, I am reminded of how different his house smells compared to Shirley's. This makes me wonder if our house's smell changed after he left.

Yesterday, Dad marinated spareribs while Greta and I worked on the dim sum. She sat across from me with a large, metal bowl between us filled with freshly ground pork—so deeply mashed up that it became a paste, various spices, scallions, soy sauce and freshly ground ginger. We each scooped a heaping tablespoon full of filling onto a thin wrapper, pinched the tops closed, then placed on a plate for Dad to steam because Greta is on a diet and nothing can ever be fried anymore.

Making dim sum together has become a ritual at Dad's, even before he moved out. Oftentimes, it would be a full day affair of steaming or frying up the dim sum, while pork spare ribs sizzled in the oven and Dad would stand by the stove with a giant wok full of fried rice.

The rice is always best when it is already a bit old and even hard or stale. He always has leftover chopped pork pieces in the freezer just for this occasion. Peas. Scallions. Fresh bean sprouts from the Asian supermarket where I have a difficult time remaining because the smells are so strong. Not quite rotting fish, but stale, unwashed, smelling of sour salt water fish. Dead fish. Gutted fish. And roasted ducks, with their faces still on. But I never miss a chance to go with Dad because he always buys me my favorite: a pork bun.

Sometimes Dad will make a new recipe like shrimp toast. Once, he attempted egg rolls, which came out kind of bendy like slinkys. Food always brings us together and solves things in this family, or at least tries to. So many hours have been spent creating this Chinese feast, eating in stages, all throughout the day.

After we ate, Greta went into the other room to watch television. I let her know that this was the weekend I had been planning to come out to Dad and she wanted to give us some alone time.

Dad was mixing Uno cards. I kept thinking about all the times we've made our many announcements during games. Now, it was my turn.

As he dealt, I noticed his beard looked like it was bleeding from some leftover sparerib sauce. I pointed to his chin and leaned over to swab away the stain.

"Hey, Dad, can we talk about something?"

He put his cards down and took a deep breath. Did he know?

Suddenly, there was a collision of words like a twelve-car pile-up in my head and I was completely silent.

"I, uh . . . I feel like a lot has changed recently. Greta going to college and Mom getting sick again and—"

"She's doing better, your mom, no?"

"No. I mean, yeah. Yeah, she's doing better. Going to group and meeting people. It's just that I feel like this year has been kind of stressful but also . . . "

Dad's face tightened like the sun was in his way. I know he holds a lot of guilt for Shirley getting sick again. He blamed himself, even though it had nothing to do with him. With any of us. Maybe it's a Jewish thing, this guilt. This sense of when bad things happen, it's because of someone doing something, rather than sometimes, bad things just happen.

"I'm so sorry, Eleanor."

"Dad, why are you apologizing?"

"I made a promise when I married your mom. I never wanted to let you or Greta down."

I watched Dad watch me. There were more than enough sounds to fill our uncomfortable silence: the hum of the refrigerator; the odd birthing of cracks arriving in the walls—yes, I could actually *hear* that; Dad's belly grumbling from over-eating.

"Eleanor," Dad took a deep breath. "Even though I'm not where you are all the time, I'm always here for you. I don't care where I am, even if I'm traveling or working."

"Yeah. I know. Thanks."

"Is there something that you want to tell me?"

My chest jumped out of my body and into my lap. I watched it beat between my thighs.

"Yeah. Umm." Deep breath, Eleanor. C'mon. Don't be a wuss.

"Dad, the thing is . . . I've been thinking about a lot of things and well, I'm still actually figuring them out. So, I mean, you know, it's not like I *get* all of it. Something still feels a bit off and so I'm reading some books and maybe there are movies? I'm not sure. Actually, I've been able to talk to some friends about it. Aggie. She's so great. I really want you to meet her. Actually, maybe she can come with me next time and you can teach her how to make dim sum too. Oh, she's vegetarian, actually. Vegetable dim sum? And it's not why I cut my hair, either. Well, I mean, that isn't what I was thinking about. Or maybe . . . maybe I was. Oh, I guess I could have been . . . "

It's like I was a character in a movie who had forgotten all their lines. I knew the gist of what I was supposed to be saying or wanted to say, but when I put my tongue against my teeth and pushed the sounds out, all sorts of other ones came out. Maybe I already said it? No. I had actually said *nothing*. Dad looked at me, patiently waiting.

"I'm a . . . " For a brief moment, I was going to utter *lesbian*. I thought that that would make it clear, but I couldn't even sound it out. It already felt wrong in my head. For some reason that I couldn't yet quite explain, that word wasn't right.

" . . . gay. I'm gay, Dad."

I couldn't look up. My eyelids were one hundred pound weights, forcing me to look down. Oh no, was he crying? Maybe he left the room. Maybe he collapsed. He wasn't saying anything. I looked up. Scrunched my forehead. Aggie calls my furrow *skin waves*.

"Umm . . . do you want to say anything or . . . ask . . . anything?"

"Eleanor, there really isn't much you can say to me that would make me stop loving you. Nothing has changed. Does your mom know?"

"Yeah, actually, I thought maybe she'd told you."

"No. And I'm glad she didn't. She probably felt that I should hear it from you."

I realized I hadn't been breathing, so I took a giant breath in.

"Dad, I . . . I've been so nervous to tell you. I mean, I knew you'd be supportive. I hoped so at least, and I guess it just feels like . . . it feels weird to have to announce, but . . . "

My hands rested on the table, wrapped in themselves as though my fingers were going to fly away or something, completely detached from my knuckles. He grabbed them and squeezed. His skin was so much rougher than mine. Like gravel to my sanded-down wood. As a kid, I was always mesmerized by how much darker his skin was compared to the paleness of Greta's and mine. He would always respond with, *it's just dirt.*

"So tell me more about Aggie," he inquired.

Dear Elinore,

Even though I don't believe in God, sometimes I pray that my dad and mom will break up and my mom and I will move somewhere much ~~coller~~ cooler than New Jersey like California or Canada. I read that Drew Barrymore divorced her parents when she was like our age which I didn't know kids could do. I don't know how to get a lawyer or anything like that, but what would happen if I just ran away? I could join the circus. I pretty much know how to juggle. Or I could cook for rich people. My mom taught me how to make chicken cachatorry. I feel like I know enough to get by. School is awful and I'd rather just ~~hichike~~ hitchhike to different places across the country.

Monday, December 13

Dear James,

Down the street from my house is Lyle's, which is a little
outdoor farmer's market where we get our tomatoes and basil
and potatoes and other stuff when the season is right. During
Christmastime, Lyle lights up the giant tree outside his house
and market with blinking lights. Growing up, Dad called it the
seizure tree. Lyle no longer grows in New Jersey. He died before
we ever started going there. Now it's run by Lyle's son who is also
named Lyle, so it's almost as though Lyle number 1 never existed
until you ask. But as suburban as this area is, there are punk
rockers and Jehovah's Witnesses and some urban legend about a
farm further upstate where all the animals have two heads. Have
you heard that? I write all this to say that a part of me is missing
out on something. Longing for something else. I know I'm not
supposed to figure it all out right now or even when I'm eighteen
or gosh, will I ever figure it out??! But I just feel like New Jersey
is keeping me from understanding all this. I want to travel and
see what lives and breathes on the other side of the turnpike.

Last night, Reigh and I talked on the phone. She's heading to
Minneapolis. Her visit with her mom didn't go so well. I found
myself talking about you. I asked her if she ever tried to kill herself.

"I tried a bunch of times," she said. "Never good at it. And I
remember my best friend growing up named Kyle always told me
that we fail at the things that we aren't supposed to be trying in
the first place."

"When was the last time?" I asked.

"Actually, about a year before I transitioned. I just couldn't be in
this body anymore. It's like losing your luggage and having to wear
someone else's clothes and use someone else's toothbrush and just
borrowing all these things that are not yours. I had run out of
borrow time. I was ready to give it up."

"And then you just decided to stop trying?"

"Well, a friend of mine called Tito sat me down and urged me to face my fears."

"Like fear of living?"

"Fear of being the human sleeping inside me."

I think about getting my period last month. Feeling like my insides were being battered and like I had no control over what was coming out of me. I didn't mind the hair sprouting beneath my armpits and on my legs. Even my pubic hair felt good to me because it became like a curtain, hiding the parts I didn't care to see in the first place.

"I started seeing someone and got diagnosed—"

"Diagnosed?" I ask.

"Gender dysphoria and transsexualism. There is a giant book put together by a bunch of crotchety white men—that's how I imagine it anyway—alphabetizing all the various disorders and diagnoses. The DSM."

"Reigh, um, can I ask you . . . "

"Sweetie, you can ask me anything."

"After you transitioned, did you stop trying?"

"Yeah, I did."

"And did you ever have any regrets? I mean, do you ever miss your old body? Sorry, I don't mean to . . . "

"It's okay. You know, in the beginning, I felt . . . let me think on what words I want to use here . . . it's kinda like searching for the perfect pair of shoes. You finally find them, and they look exactly as you'd dreamed they would on you, but they're tight because they're new. I used to dress up in my mother's clothing all the time. As a kid, I'd just parade around in my bedroom when I was alone. But after committing to living the way I knew I needed to exist, there was that initial moment of just feeling like I needed to stretch it out, you know? Walk around. And not soon after, I completely forgot what it was like to *not* be like this. Because *this* was how I was all along."

I smiled. I smiled because something in me understood. The missing puzzle piece at Aunt Wenda's. The missing finger floating up at the beach.

"Before I transitioned, I was always looking for my tribe. When I finally lived as the woman swallowed inside me, I knew I had found it."

"James was gay," I blurted. "He wrote about it in his notebook. His dad found out. Made him feel awful about it. James never . . . he never got to find his tribe."

"Oh sweetie, don't you understand? *You* were his tribe."

I felt a rush of tears just fall from my eyes.

"But he didn't even talk to me," I said. "He just wrote everything in a notebook. And the one person he really cared about—maybe even loved—completely stopped talking to him. This kid, Brian, in my grade. I wish he had said something to me. Other than making fun of . . . "

"Eler, he probably saw a lot of himself in you. And didn't know how to articulate it. But you have his words now. That means something."

"It's strange, you know?" I said. "Because people who aren't gay just use one word. Straight. Or heterosexual, I guess too. My mom's friend Flor has been giving me lots of books to read, and I'm learning all this vocabulary that they definitely don't teach in school. It's not just gay for boys and lesbian for girls. Or bisexual for both. You know, T'nea is bise—" I stopped myself and took a deep breath. "I called myself lesbian because I thought that was my word. The word I'm supposed to call myself because I'm a . . . a girl, but . . . "

"Eler, you can call yourself anything you want. Hell, you can make up a word. This is *your* existence. Your words are free; you get to use whichever ones you want."

"I like gay. But also, I don't know, I like *boy* too."

I felt the impact of that last sentence pound against my chest. It made me think of Dara. When she was really young, way before we met, her and her family were in a car accident. No one was too hurt, though she said the car looked like a crushed accordion. She said her mother was hurt the worst because she was driving. The airbag came out and broke her nose. I still don't understand how a bag of air can hurt someone, but she said something about impact and sharp dust or something. Anyway, that is how I felt in that moment on the phone with Reigh. The impact of a giant bag of air pounding into me. Just from words.

"A word is just a word. *You* get to give it meaning." Reigh interrupted my thoughts. "So, tell me . . . what do you mean?"

"I guess I am realizing that my closet is bigger than I thought."

"You are finding your colors, Eler. Your wings are expanding. Don't be afraid of your butterfly. Your flight is the best part of living."

A crackling of silence filled the air between us.

"I saw my mother yesterday," Reigh said. "Perhaps for the last time. She kept calling me Ernest. Said, 'Ernest, your hair is so long.' I'd correct her and remind her to call me Reigh, but she just couldn't speak it. So, I began to call her by her first name. 'The curtains in the kitchen look lovely, Berta.' As we were eating lunch, I said, 'Berta, are these tomatoes from the farmers market or . . . ?' And then, finally she said, 'Ernest, please call me *Mom*. I don't like you calling me by my name.' To which I replied, 'Then, please call me *Reigh*. I don't like you calling me by any other name either.' Growing up, anytime I did anything wrong, my mother would call me by my entire name: Ernest Raymond. I hated my middle name because I only heard it when I did something wrong. But when I chose to take on a new name, I liked the idea of keeping a part of me but changing it a little with the spelling."

"I like that," I said. "Did it change anything?"

"Oh, my mother is pretty damn set in her ways, but it cut a little of the tension away. She called me Reigh once. And then went right on back to Ernest. Used male pronouns too, which made being out with her really strange."

"Where'd you go?"

"Just to the pharmacy to pick up her prescription. I was going to stay at home, but she asked me to come along. I figured she'd want to keep me hidden. She even . . . oh my goodness . . . she even introduced me as her son when we ran into a friend of hers. That was awkward."

Reigh laughed, but even in her laughter, I could sense sadness.

"Listen, some people you can't change," Reigh said. "But that's not going to change how *I* exist. So, I just smiled at her friend and in my softest voice said, 'Hi, darlin', I'm Reigh.' Then I kind of tossed my hair and complimented her on her outfit. Told her I had a dress just like it at home."

"Will I ever see you again?"

"Honey, I will always be a stamp away. Maybe two, depending on how much paper you stuff in there." She laughed.

"I just...I feel so . . . "

"And you better give me all the details when you have your first date with Prince."

I smiled. Oh, yeah, *T'nea.*

~

Tuesday, December 14

Dear James,

I walked in on Shirley and Ted kissing on the couch when I got home from school. All I want to say is that it was ~~simulttanisly~~ simultaneously gross, but also neat to see her happy again. And Flor's got Theresa, who I still haven't met yet, but she seems super happy too. Maybe it's my turn now.

Actually, T'nea and I were on the phone for almost two hours last night. I thought we'd run out of things to talk about, but she's really easy to talk to. I spent most of the conversation trying to build up my nerve to ask her out on a date. I was secretly hoping she'd ask me first. Maybe we were both too nervous. We've already been to first base. Why is the thought of going on a date so scary?

~

Wednesday, December 15

Dear James,

During class today, Ms. Raimondo asked us to write down three goals for the new year. Here is what I wrote:

Work on being unafraid of myself and the butterfly I am becoming

Ask T'nea out on a date

Read more books about people like me

~

Dear Elinore,

Here is when I knew. It was way before Brian and dirty magazines.

I was in the grocery store with my mom. Maybe I was six? There was another boy with his mom or aunt and he looked to be about my age. We caught each other's eyes, not like anything dramatic. Just something that we both recognized in each other that we weren't ready to ~~reoconize~~ recognize in ourselves. I didn't have the words or whatever to say, oh yeah, he's a fag or I am. And I never thought about this until after my first kiss with Brian. Memory vomit. Yeah, see that's the thing. No one says, hey how do you know you're straight. You just are. Or it's assumed you are. And I have a feeling you're like me, Elinore. It's like that boy in the grocery store. I just kinda knew. Probably why I pushed you and called you names and spit on you. Look, I'm sorry. And apologizing in this notebook is just easier than saying it to your face. But I don't know. Maybe you will read this. One day. And you can decide if you accept my apology. Hopefully you will find a way to be free that I just couldn't.

Thursday, December 16

Dear James,

Aggie is going away for winter break to stay at her aunt's house in North Carolina.

She told me this while we were eating lunch together. I promised I'd write her letters. I'm not going anywhere, except my dad's. Greta isn't even coming home. She decided to take a winter class to make up for one of the classes she dropped. I guess that's a good thing, though I'm definitely going to miss her.

Tonight was our last group of the year. Nothing too exciting to report. During chair fold-up time, as people were putting away cups and leftover cookies in plastic containers, I talked with your mom.

"I want life to be like it is in the movies. But I guess people just don't know the lines to the script we write in our head," I said.

I also told her about trying to build the nerve to ask T'nea out.

"This may be shocking, but I asked Burt out. He barely noticed me. Afterward, he told me that he was taken aback that I asked him. He's always been rather traditional. He wanted to know if I was one of those 'bra-burning feminists'." Helaine laughed and her cheeks puffed up. "Maybe that should have been a sign that we weren't quite on the same page. But then we wouldn't have had James and . . . "

When I asked her about how things were with Burt, she just said, "He is living in the basement right now, but searching for an apartment close to the church. I'm not angry at him. I just want to grieve James without having to edit who he was."

Friday, December 17

Dear James,

In school, we raise our hands every time we want to say something. Even if it's just to announce we need to go to the bathroom. And once we are called on, everyone looks and listens to hear what we have to say, as though every time is going to be this newsworthy moment. Usually, it's the wrong answer.

Mr. Lenox will ask, "Who can tell me the answer for 'x' after plugging in the quadratic equation?"

Then, someone will raise their hand, stretch it high, and hold it up with their other hand as though their arm is too heavy to wave.

He'll look around the room and call on someone. Maybe his favorite (Penny, who totally sucks up to him) or someone who rarely ever participates. This is their moment of stardom. Of saying the right thing. Of being celebrated for having actually answered a question. The right answer for the right question. Right?

"X equals seven."

"Wrong," Mr. Lenox announces.

James, the thing is, I feel like I am in the process of still figuring out 'x', which is me, by the way. I've told all the important people in my life that I'm gay and I should feel relief, right? And yet, there is something still itching in me, trying to get out. I was going to write clawing, but actually it's a bit less desperate. Or maybe I've got the right answer, but the question is wrong.

I remember when I was in seventh grade, I was finally allowed to go to the mall and movies without supervision. At that time, Dara and I were still best friends and we'd get dropped off and go crazy in the mall. We played a game called "Charge It" where we'd go from store to store pretending to shop for things for our pretend home and anytime we saw something we liked, we'd say, "Charge it!" like on our pretend credit cards.

Once, we planned to meet at the mall and Dara never showed up. I can't remember what happened. She forgot or changed her mind, I can't even remember now. I think I was mad for about five minutes and then I realized I had the whole mall to myself. I mean, I was able to just wander and eat whatever and whenever I wanted. Dara always liked trying on dresses, which I secretly hated. With her not there, I could try on whatever I wanted. So, that one time—and I think I was maybe in eighth grade by then—I went to the boy's department and tried on a bunch of pants and shirts. I'm not even sure what propelled me there. I remember being in the junior's section—girl's side—just out of habit. Then realized I didn't have to be there. I could be *anywhere*. I peered across the way and saw a cool blue shirt in the boy's section. I remember this because I had seen someone at school wear it and loved the way it looked.

I was petrified someone was going to stop me or say something. But no one cared. I felt so slick in a button-down shirt and jeans, terribly baggy yet fitting me in a way that felt right. Boys' pants had a longer zipper and it puffed by the crotch. I pulled at it; this I remember as though it were yesterday. Gathered it like a ponytail. Puffed it even more.

When I looked at my reflection, I recognized myself in a way I hadn't before. I never told anyone this—not Dara or Flor or even Aggie— and just saw it as a one-time thing. Dress up. No big deal.

And there were a few other instances like that. Trying on Dad's ties a bunch of times. Once, stealing one of his cigars and smoking it because I liked that it felt . . . manly. Heavier than a cigarette, which I took from Shirley only once before realizing how gross it was. But a cigar, you don't inhale—mistake made only once—and it smells thicker. Kind of sweeter.

Sometimes, I feel like a giant road map. These memories are like rest stops, which I actually used to love to go to when I was a kid. I'd always pick out postcards of the places we stopped in to empty our bladders. I wanted to remember that I was there. I guess to remind myself to go back again sometime. Some rest stops we'd stay in longer. We'd eat a meal, if they had food beyond just the fast kind. Greta and I would be allowed to choose a snack or, if Shirley was in a really good mood, *Mad Magazine*, my favorite.

"You're only fifteen," Flor said to me recently. "You've got lots of time to learn all your twists and turns. Don't be in a rush to understand all of yourself right away. I'm still figuring it out and look how old *I* am."

What's my rush? Could it be that remembering all this past reminds me that my present is not the way it's meant to be?

Dear Elinore,

Here is what I'd say if I ever met Kurt Cobaine. Yo. Hi. I don't play the guitar but if my parents ever let me learn an instrument (it's not my parents, it's my dad) I'd want to play drums. No one could ever replace you. And Dave Grohl is cool and everything, but I'd do almost anything to get splinters from banging to "Negative Creep." What is it like to be on stage in front of so many people who know you enough to sing along? What is it like to have fans? To be in a poster on someone's wall (including mine). Kurt, sometimes I think about killing myself. If you were next to me and we were friends or something close to it, what would you say? Would you tell me to hold on, that I'm losing my grip? Would you tell me to just do what I need to do would you tell me how? Would you sing to me enough times to make me forget? You get to be however you want in front of millions of people. No one tells you you're too feminine or not strong enough. You can wear eyeliner and people think it's cool. My dad would beat me into another planet. I'll never really be able to be me. I'll never really be able to even figure what that means, who I am, who I could be.

Saturday, December 18

Dear James,

Shirley and Ted are at the Englishtown flea market, bundled up and probably wrapping themselves up in hot chocolate and each other. Aggie is on her way over to study for a science test. We're not in the same class, but we have the same boring teacher, Mr. Phlemmens. People call him Mr. ~~Phlem Plegm~~ Phlegm, but obviously not to his face. I wonder if he knows, though. Late last night when everyone was sleeping, it snowed. How cool to wake up and see everything covered in freezing white. Stillness. Quiet. I like that snow doesn't make noise like rain does. It sneaks up and rewards you with something beautiful. The only annoying thing is it's much better when it snows on a weekday, because I bet we would have had off from school but whatever. Aggie is coming over and that's enough for me.

We ate grilled cheese sandwiches—Aggie makes them all buttery and overstuffed with cheese. She left about an hour ago, but I can still feel the greasy sweetness coat my tongue.

Aggie wanted to know if I'd asked T'nea out on a date yet and I confessed that I was still too nervous.

"I've been on a few dates," she confessed.

"You have? Tell me everything."

"I had a boyfriend in seventh grade. Lenny. We dated for a few months. Nothing too serious, but . . . "

"What?"

"Well, we almost had sex. I'm sure he'd tell the story differently, but I think what stopped us is we weren't really sure what to do."

I laughed, almost choking on my sandwich.

"Are you serious?"

"I mean, we knew what was *involved* . . . " Aggie's face was now the color of her sweater, two different shades of red. It's easy to tell when Aggie blushes because her face is the color of skim milk.

"Maybe he was afraid he'd be bad at it or something. But we did everything else," Aggie winked at me.

"This all feels so new. I mean, this whole year feels like ten. Like a lifetime, actually. Shirley trying to kill herself. James . . . ," my voice lost track of itself. " . . . Greta going away, Shirley starting to date!!! Meeting you. Meeting Reigh! Oh my gosh, kissing T'nea. Coming out. It's too much. I was thinking of Ms. Raimondo the other day and what she said about stories."

"Which part?"

"Just that there is always some crescendo. A moment of conflict that keeps the reader reading. Involved. I like that Ms. Raimondo says that we are part of everything we read."

"Yeah, she's so cool. I love that too," Aggie said.

"I'm writing to James—"

"I'm still writing to Richard!"

"I guess it's become part of my routine or whatever. I thought about stopping, but I feel like I'm talking to him. Anyway, in these letters, I wonder what the story is. I mean, like is James the conflict? Is his death the . . . trampoline moment?"

"Trampoline moment?"

"Don't you remember? Ms. Raimondo said there is a moment in every story that becomes the trampoline moment . . . what propels you toward something else. An answer or a realization of some—"

"Or they're just letters. And writing to him is about you getting your thoughts out and having someone who will never write back listen somehow. Wasn't that kinda the point all along?"

"Yeah, yeah, I guess."

Dear James, are you my trampoline? Your death. Reading your words, which were meant for me all along. Is all that the point? The propeller?

Sunday, December 19

Dear James,

When my grandmother was young, she was really sick and they really didn't think she was going to make it. When she got better, her parents renamed her. I guess that happens sometimes, or at least that's how my dad tells it. Something about superstition and bad energy. Anyway, I felt this when Reigh called me Eler for the first time. Like something lifted in me.

I wrote something to you in the back of my notebook, but then I scribbled it out. Ms. Raimondo is right: writing something down gives it breath, gives it bones. I think when I wrote it down and saw its skeleton, it scared me. Anyway, I am pasting it below.

I've been staring at crotches. Is that weird? This guy, Sam, in my math class said something about penis envy and I wonder if I have crotch envy. I know I have one. A crotch. But obviously mine is different. More triangular than rectangular and I'm not very good at geometry, but I know that shapes just don't exchange angles and proportions. They are born with the same dimensions as when they die, right? Or do they start getting looser like Shirley's skin? Droopy? Anyway, last night, after dinner, Shirley and Flor watched *Wheel of Fortune* and I went upstairs and took off my shirt. I take my clothes off a lot lately and just stare. I guess it's kind of like reading the same book twice. You know the way it ends, but always hope for something different because time has passed since the last look. Nope. Same story. Boring and predictable ending. I widened my hands, the skin over my palms stretching as far as they could, and pressed them against my boobs.

My nipples (why does that word look so weird when I write it down?) peeked between my two fingers. I pushed hard, trying to flatten them like grilled cheese sandwiches. I always love to watch the cheese burst out from the weight of the spatula against the bread. Maybe my breast innards will seep out and I won't have to wear a stupid bra anymore. I may have to do this routine nightly

~~to see a change. Then I did something kind of weird, James. Oh gosh, I can't believe I'm even writing this. I bent down and took my sock off my foot. Then I kind of bunched it up and stuffed it in my underpants. The cotton felt weird against my vagina, but when I looked back in the mirror, my shape changed. No more triangle. I turned to the side. I grabbed it like the boys do when they think no one is looking. I walked around my bedroom like it was heavy, like it meant something. What does this mean, James? What am I?~~

Monday, December 20

Dear James,

Do you remember when we were in second grade and Allen Danube died? Were you friends with him? It was during recess. Well, he didn't die during recess, but that is when the incident happened. A bunch of people were playing tag. I wasn't. I was probably off in the corner by the aluminum tunnel, which I liked to hide in. Anyway, they were running along the length of the playground behind school. Then, Allen fell and hit his head on a large rock that was on the pavement. No one knew where that rock had come from. I remember people saying that. *Our rocks are small. How did that one get in?*

After he fell, everyone around stopped. They stopped because a river of Allen's blood immediately started seeping out of his head. And nose. And mouth too, according to some. I didn't see any of this. We all got ushered back into school, while the ambulance was called. Allen died soon after arriving at the hospital. Brain hemorrhage or something scary like that.

Allen wasn't exactly my friend, but I did go to his birthday party that year. He pretty much invited everyone in class. I can't remember if you were there. I only went because a few other friends were going, and I heard Allen had a swimming pool. This was the summer before he died.

I was grabbing a piece of pizza from the long table on his deck. Allen walked up beside me. He had been swimming, so his skin was dripping chlorine, and some fell onto the cheese. He smiled at me.

Then, he said—and I remember this so clearly—"I didn't want this party, you know. All I wanted was pizza and to swim some. But . . . but I'm glad I had this because . . . *you're* here."

Then, he walked away with his waterlogged pizza and just continued swimming. Would you believe that that was the only thing he ever said to me? Ever?

Allen is in my mind because I feel like there were parts of him that were still forming. Well, of course, I mean we were only ten years old back then. But more than that, there was a sense that he was going to *be* something. He was obscenely good at math. Perhaps Allen would have gone on to invent something really big and useful. It's impossible to not feel this way about *you,* James. What would you have become? What would you have given to the world? To another? To me?

Dear Elinore,

I saw you stare at Aggie today the way I try to pretend not to stare at Brian. I knew it. Maybe it's because I can't be with Brian or anyone really that I notice these things. We see what we can't allow in ourselves. I've never seen my folks look at each other like that. I don't think I've ever seen them kiss or hold hands. My mom hugs me, but my dad never does. It's like he's afraid to kiss me, doesn't want to catch what I am, what he won't allow me to be. I don't get the feeling Aggie is gay, but at least she seems to like you enough that it probably won't matter. I see the way she looks at you too. Not like in love or anything, but like she thinks you're special. Like maybe you are her best friend. I had one of those once. But not anymore.

Tuesday, December 21

Dear James,

Everyone has vacation brain. That's what Ms. Raimondo calls it. Thursday is our last day of class before winter break and I guess we are all a little restless. I've decided to call T'nea after school today and ask her out. I tried calling her last night, but her mom said she wasn't home. I left a message, but she didn't call back. Did I wait too long?

In math class, same boring stuff. I've gotten used to pretending like Dara and I were never friends. She doesn't even look at me anymore. It was so upsetting at first, but I guess I have gotten used to it. However, I couldn't not notice that she looked really upset today. So, I became the bigger person, James, and approached her after class.

"Hey," I said, tapping her on the shoulder.

"Hi," she said, looking at me as though we hadn't shared our deep dark secrets with each other like our weird crushes on Milli Vanilli and Leonardo of the Teenage Mutant Ninja Turtles. We used to trade Garbage Pail Kids until Shirley threw all mine away because she thought they were gruesome. I know that Dara used to keep her scabs in her dad's cigar box that he initially gave to her for her hair clips. She knows that I picked my nose up until a few years ago. And ate my findings. It was a hard habit to break for some reason. But here we were after months of not talking. Strangers.

"You . . . you looked upset in class and I . . . I know we're not talking but . . . are you—"

She looked at me as though I hadn't showered in weeks. "Why do you even care, Eleanor?"

"I don't know. Because we used to be best friends? It's not my fault that we're not anymore."

"Actually, it kinda is. And if you must know, Damian and I broke up."

"What do you mean it's *my* fault? And I'm sorry you guys broke up. But he was kind of a dick, you know?"

Dara smiled. "Yeah."

"Listen, you're the one who helped me to realize that I'm . . . I mean, I knew before you said, but . . . and since our fight, I've told Shirley and Flor and Gret and my dad. It's not a bad thing. They get that it's just part of me. Nothing needs to change. I don't expect you to understand, though I really wish you would. You know, there are people who die before they ever have the chance to really be themselves. I don't want to wait for that."

Dara didn't say anything for a long time and then the bell went off. I had Science class.

That stupid test.

"Yeah, well, we better get to class, Eleanor," was all she said.

"Oh, okay. Yeah, sure. I've got a test anyway. Sorry about your heart."

⌐

Wednesday, December 22

Dear James,

I did it. I asked T'nea on a date and she said yes and we are going out tomorrow night because winter break officially starts after school tomorrow and Shirley said it was okay (though I asked her afterwards and I have no idea what I would have done if she'd have said no). That's one thing off my winter break list already done!

After enough rings to make me think I'd called the wrong number, I heard a voice.

"Hello?" It was her!

"Hi. T'nea. What's up? It's Eler." Act casual, Eleanor.

"Not much. Just chillin', you know? How about yourself?"

"Just relaxing on my bed, actually." Relaxing on my bed?

I felt like I could hear T'nea smile.

"You know, I told my friend about you."

She's talking about me to her friend?! Stay cool. "Uh huh?"

"And she told me not to call you. To wait for *you* to call *me* and make the next move. But I was definitely starting to feel super impatient." I could hear her smile.

"Well, actually, I'm calling because I wanted to know if maybe you might want to . . . go on a . . . date . . . with . . . me?" I immediately started to panic. What if we ran out of things to talk about? What if T'nea wanted to do more than just kiss? What comes next? What if I don't know what to do?

"Yeah. That'd be cool."

"Cool, cool." James, I did my best impression of John Travolta in *Saturday Night Fever*. He was so slick in that. "How about tomorrow night? Want to see a movie?"

"Sure, how about *Addams Family Values*? That looks good. I think it's playing by Jamesway."

We chatted a little more and it got easier the longer we stayed on the phone. I learned that T'nea's mom is remarried and she thinks her stepdad is even better than her *real* dad. I learned that she loves to paint and wants to be famous one day like Alice Neel (who I hadn't heard of) or Georgia O'Keefe. She said she dreams of moving to New Mexico, even though she's never even been there, because she loves that that is where Georgia painted. I also learned that T'nea is not *out*, though feels like maybe her mom won't be too uncool about it. T'nea calls herself bisexual because she has also dated boys and likes them too, but right now she likes *me* and that's all I really care about.

After we hung up, I felt a mixture of excitement and extreme nervousness. When I looked out my window, it was like the moon was bigger or someone had changed its light bulbs (an astronaut, maybe?) and it was brighter than it had ever been before. I stared at it for a really long time and tried to pretend I didn't know what it was called. That this big bright circle, which was completely full, just sat in the sky without a name. So I called it yellow. And I called it light fixture. And I called it a planet. And I called it the real earth and I called it my girlfriend in the sky and I called it beautiful. I said: Hey, look at that *beautiful* up there. Look at the *yellow*. Look at the *light fixture*. I thought about what language might be spoken on the moon. Would it be English? Or maybe Spanish? Or probably just something no one has ever heard before. Would there be a moon president or one universal religion? Or maybe everyone on the moon would be an ~~athest~~ atheist or a Jehovah's Witness like Michael Jackson. Will we run out of space on this earth and move there one day? I'll probably be dead by then but maybe my kids or kid's kids? No, I don't want any of those. I mean, kids are okay, but I don't really want one. The thought of having a baby inside me kind of grosses me out. I remember when my cousin Jessica was pregnant, and everything got big on her. Big stomach (OBVIOUSLY!) and big boobs (GROSS . . . I mean, to imagine that on ME). Every time I think about being more into my 'womanhood' as Shirley and Flor say, I feel less and less comfortable. Maybe life on the moon would be better than earth. Maybe there would be no words that separate people's male or female. Just humans. Wait. There's *man* in that. Person. No. There's *son* in that. HU-PER! Huper. Huper. Huper. If I lived on the moon, I'd call myself a huper. Or maybe I can call myself this now?

Dear Elinore,

Once upon a time or something cheesy like that, there was a boy. Let's call him ~~Chester William~~ Kurt. His whole life was viewed through the same window. His backyard was big enough to get two bee stings and some kind of spider bite that made his ankle swell long enough for his mom to worry and his dad to actually look at him with concern. There were a bunch of trees and he always hoped there could be a house built into it just for him, just for his ~~drems~~ dreams. His bedroom was his but not really. He knew his dad snooped and maybe his mom too, but she didn't hold things against Kurt like his dad did. Kurt just wanted to be in love. And feel it back. One day, Kurt met someone. Oh, man, this someone was funny and liked the same music. Actually, they would listen to it loud enough to make the walls shake and even feel it in their bones. This someone liked ~~me~~ Kurt even though they looked alike. When they were alone, this someone held Kurt's hand. Traced his veins like words. This someone knew how to read Kurt like he was the most interesting story. This someone promised never to leave. When this someone kissed Kurt, all of the darkness and sadness and death died. Kurt grew. Nothing could be better. And nothing else mattered. Kurt was happy for the first time because he had never been seen like this before. Kurt was finally loved. But see, nothing remains like that. The sun falls. The clouds grow dark. Thunder. Blood. Static. This someone decided Kurt was too much. So this someone stopped holding Kurt's hand and this someone stopped kissing Kurt and this someone stopped. Kurt was alone again. Kurt was dark again. Kurt was no longer happy. Everything that ever mattered no longer did. ~~Then Kurt died.~~

Thursday, December 23

Dear James,

I want to write all of this down before I forget. Before I start to question if it even happened. Flor dropped me off in the Jamesway shopping center and I waited in front for T'nea. My nervousness chilled me. I wasn't wearing a watch, but it felt like I'd been waiting for a while. I was starting to think that maybe I was being stood up. Stood up for my very first date—not a good sign.

And then, just like that, T'nea appeared. She was bundled as well, but so beautiful. Her hair collapsed into various twists like tiny tornadoes. Even though it was dark, her skin glowed.

"Hey, you," she breathed into the air.

"Where'd you come from? I didn't even see you get out of a car or anything."

"I came from my mom's snatch," she laughed. "Just kidding. No, my bro dropped me off."

"Cool," I smiled. "Should we head over to the movies? I'm actually not sure why we didn't just meet there. I was thinking of that on the ride over."

"I thought maybe we could walk around Jamesway. That way we can actually talk to each other before sitting in a dark room, staring at a screen. Maybe grab some candy that's not like a million bucks."

Jamesway was fourteen-thousand-suns-bright. I could see all of T'nea. Her almost hazel eyes and long, painted fingernails, slightly chipped. Her ripped jeans, the kind that you buy that way. Her bright red Doc Martens.

"What do you think?" T'nea put on a wide-brimmed hat with a ribbon of dark purple wrapped around. It was the ugliest hat I'd ever seen, yet she looked even more beautiful.

"Not as beautiful as you," I said.

She blushed, and I blushed from *her* blush.

T'nea took off the hat and laughed.

"Maybe we should grab our candy and—"

T'nea didn't let me finish my sentence. Instead, she leaned in close and pressed her lip-glossed watermelon-flavored lips against my plain ones. She tasted like a meal. Like every sugary candy I ever wanted but Shirley always forbid because she's convinced it will rot our teeth.

T'nea's hands were wrapped around my neck, so I placed mine around her waist. Being so close to her like this made me feel so excited and—

"Ew, lesbians." We gave each other back our tongues and looked up. A guy around our age was beside us, making terrible faces. He called his friend over to stare at us as though we were zoo animals about to do our designated trick.

"Do that again. That's fucking hot," the other one said.

"Why don't you both fuck off," T'nea yelled back. "It's dicks like you who remind us why we don't fuck men."

I stood still, panicked and paralyzed, not wanting to cause any more attention to ourselves. I had forgotten that what we were doing—kissing—wasn't *normal*. I forgot we were two *girls*. In my mind, she was just a girl and I was just a—

"How about I change your mind, *bitch*?"

My chest grew tall and heavy all at once. I hadn't felt this fear since . . . since you pushed me, James.

"Gross. Just walk away, boys," T'nea said, looking at me as though I was supposed to say something, speak up or stand up for lesbians everywhere.

"T'nea," I finally muttered. "Let's just . . . let's just go, okay?"

"I'm not letting them push us out. We can do whatever we want." She grabbed my shoulders, bringing me into her and kissed me even harder. Her tongue went all the way down my throat (or it felt that way) and I was afraid I'd accidentally swallow it.

I could feel the two boys digging their stares into us, and I pulled away.

"Then, *I'm* gonna go," I said. I started walking away, crushed that our date was ending before it had barely even begun.

The boys just stood there in silence.

"Eler, hey . . . sorry. Wait up, please."

T'nea grabbed my shoulder and pulled me into her. She hugged me by the shoe department and I melted into her arms.

"I'm really not looking for that kind of attention," I whispered into her ear. "I'm not trying to put on a show. I just . . . I just want to be next to you without an audience."

"I know. I mean, I'm not either. I just never want them to win, you know? Like why should we have to hide our kissing if they can just mack on their girls all over the place?"

"Because that's just how it is," I said.

"Hey, let's just head out, okay? Please forgive me."

I smiled, weaving my fingers in with hers. My fingertips felt like they could fall asleep against her knuckles. Like tiny, soft hills.

"Let's head to the movies. Then, I can kiss you some more. It'll be dark. No audience."

"Sounds like a much better plan," I said.

We walked toward the movie theater. We'd missed the first half hour, but neither of us seemed to mind. I bought a box of milk duds for her and twizzlers for me. We remained in the back row, interrupted only by the armrest between our seats. The theater wasn't too crowded, and there wasn't really anyone near us.

It was dark, but I could feel all of T'nea beside me. All I could think about was kissing her again and she must have read my mind, because she turned toward me and leaned in.

Her lips pushed against mine and I could taste everything she had eaten all day. Bubblegum. Peanut butter sandwich. The sweet caramel from the milk duds. I wondered what I tasted like to her. A few times, our teeth clinked together like glasses, but we just continued. It's like we were desperate. As though our mouths had been waiting for this moment. And I forgot to breathe or maybe I was breathing inside her. We were inhaling each other's exhales. This was what I've been reading about in Judy Blume books and watching on Shirley's soap operas. The rage of tongues. It felt amazing.

And then. T'nea, with tongue in my mouth, took her hands and began sliding them up my shirt. I jumped, unprepared for this dive from first base to second. Second, right? Yeah, this is definitely second. French kiss, up the shirt, then down the pants, then home run. What would even *be* our home run?

She slowly parted her lips from mine and said, "You alright?"

"Yeah, yeah," I muttered. "I just . . . I wasn't expecting that."

"Your breasts feel so good to me. Want to feel mine?"

Suddenly, I couldn't breathe. Maybe I gave too much breath away to her while we were kissing. I pulled my shirt down and fixed my bra, which I hate hate hate.

"Uh, yeah, but . . . I don't like that."

"What don't you—"

"Sshhh!" Someone from a few rows up turned around to scold us.

"Sorry," I whispered back.

"I just . . . I kinda hate my breasts," I said, in the thinnest whisper I could possibly make.

"But they're so nice. Damn, I wish mine were small like yours. Mine are so heavy. They hurt my back."

"Oh, well, yeah," I clumsily said. I never thought about the weight of breasts and how they could affect the rest of you.

"I just really want to touch you," T'nea said.

I smiled, though she couldn't see this, feeling such pleasure from being wanted. From her wanting to explore me.

"Well, you can touch me. Anywhere," she added.

And so I did, with her permission. We smacked our lips back together and I headed to second base. Her breasts were large, rolling around in my hands. I wanted it to be bright enough to see them, to understand what I was touching. But maybe it was the dark that encouraged our boldness.

In the dark, she moaned. And I worried we would be shushed again, but no one seemed to pay any mind to us. I had no idea what was happening on screen even though I could hear the characters speak. But all of it just became background music to us.

At some point in my second base exploration, she took my hand and placed it between her legs. I froze, completely unsure of what to do.

"Unzip me," she whispered.

What?

She had stolen all of my saliva and I couldn't believe that we were doing what we were doing in the movie theater where my last kind-of-but-not really date was in sixth grade and I saw "The Little Mermaid" with Ryan Gregory. He asked me out, but I was too nervous to be alone with him, so I invited Dara along too. I sat between them and the next week in school, he asked Dara out on a date and they wound up being a couple for one whole month! I remember being so mad at Dara for taking Ryan from me, but also forgiving her since I didn't really like him in the first place.

T'nea was wearing lacey underwear. I couldn't tell you the color because of the darkness, but I could feel with my fingers, the stitching and scratch of it. If blushing made a sound, the whole movie theater would have scolded me because I just know I was covered in head to toe skin flush.

James, I had no idea what to do next. None of this was talked about during health class where we had an abbreviated sex ed. I placed my hand against her underwear, which was peeking through her open zipper.

"I give you permission," she said.

Permission to do *what*?

"I really want you inside me, Eler."

The awkwardness of the arm rest and the movie projected in

front of us and these strangers and my complete lack of knowledge on sex and *this* kind of sex and—

T'nea grabbed my finger and slipped it beneath the elastic of her underwear and then and then pushed my finger into her.

What? Oh my gosh oh my gosh.

I couldn't believe I was inside her. This person who I still barely knew. Were we having sex? Was my finger clean enough? Maybe it was sticky from the Twizzlers. I moved around and felt her get bigger on the inside. Like she was expanding. She was so wet and when I moved around I could actually feel the textures inside her. I was amazed at how turned on I was just from moving around inside her.

James, to be one hundred percent honest, I thought it would be Aggie. When I first started to understand my feelings about her, I hoped she would be my first time. If this was even it. I mean, was this sex? Just thinking that made me feel so utterly dumb, but all I knew was what they taught in health class and that was just about a penis entering a vagina. But if there was no penis, what counts as sex? I couldn't dare ask anyone about this. This is what I was thinking about when I was fingering T'nea.

I called Shirley from the payphone at the movie theater to let her know that T'nea's brother would drive me home. She didn't seem to mind, which I was relieved about. In the car, I sat in the back with T'nea in the front and her brother, Weston, driving. We sat in silence as Weston played his music really loudly. At one point, he asked us how the movie was and we both nervously giggled.

"Really enjoyable," T'nea uttered.

"Yup," I said.

When we pulled up to my house, T'nea casually said goodbye to me. I was relieved because I didn't exactly want to kiss her in front of her brother. And I'm sure she wouldn't have wanted that anyway, since he didn't even know this was a date.

"Call me," she yelled out the window as I walked toward the front door.

I turned around and smiled, but it was dark, so once again the lack of light hid my emotions.

"I will," I yelled back.

~

Friday, December 24

Dear James,

In the ~~midt~~ midst of my excitement over my date with T'nea, I forgot about the last assignment Ms. Raimondo gave us before Winter break, which I am now officially on! In class, we were talking about all of the stories and poems we've read so far.

"I've got one task for all of you to start on during break," Ms. Raimondo said. "And before your groans and moans, I think you might like this one. I want you to craft a reading list for someone. Someone you know, someone you've never met, someone who no longer exists. But keep in mind that this someone you choose has been chosen for a reason. What I mean by that is, choose books they could benefit from. Books they may not have known about but should. Maybe books or poems we've read or discussed here and even ones you've read independently. This is your opportunity to curate someone's literary intake."

Of course I thought of you, James. I knew my list would be for you.

~

Saturday, December 25

Dear James,

In the Fromme household, we don't exactly celebrate today. We don't even celebrate Hanukkah anymore, which was earlier this month. Although I do remember the days we used to. When Shirley and Dad still loved each other, we got presents on all eight days. Mostly books. Earrings for Greta because she got excited over that sort of thing. Usually a tape single or sometimes a whole album. Little things for the first seven nights and then on the last night of Hannukah, we'd get our big present. Fifth grade, I got the best gift ever (though my opinion on this has since changed) when they got me concert tickets to see Milli Vanilli. That was my first concert ever. Dad came with me. Of course, it wasn't until later that we learned it was all a sham and they weren't even singing. Do you remember that, James? I took down all my pictures of them that I'd hung up on my walls from magazines.

Anyway, houses around us are all decorated, bright lights and candles in the windows. Blow-up Santa Clauses and even a Winnie the Pooh dressed as Santa on the Deffino's lawn down the block. We used to drive around and look at the dressed-up houses. There is a neighborhood on the way to school that is full of mansions and they do like a crazy light show with projection on the houses. They play music too. I wonder if you ever went there. Did you decorate your house? I'll have to ask Helaine.

Since Flor has come into our life, we celebrate a little. She doesn't really have family to be festive with. She has a few brothers and a sister, but they are scattered—Oregon, Texas, Michigan—so we do something at our house. Flor makes a ham (yum), Shirley usually makes a roast and then lots of sides. Basically, like a second Thanksgiving. This will be the first one without Greta, but she promised to call. And it will be the first one with Helaine. I asked her in group last week if she'd like to come over. Her first Christmas without you. And without Bert too.

Lately, I've been wondering how different things would be if you were still here. Helaine wouldn't be coming over, I wouldn't be writing these letters. But you'd still be writing to me. Were you ever going to say anything? Maybe senior year, if we both made it there, you'd have let down your guard. Maybe we would have even applied to the same college. Peter says that *maybes* are dead ends. They lead us nowhere. We can only work with what we've got.

Okay, I'm back. Full. Very full. I ate too much ham, but you probably don't care about that. Even though Greta wasn't there, we had a crowded table. Shirley, *Ted*, Flor and Theresa—who I finally got to meet and really like, and Helaine. It's been awhile since we had so many people over.

Today reminded me of the end of Passover. Dad would pick up every kind of bagel imaginable, lox, pickled herring (yuck), all sorts of spreads, and cheeses. He'd cut onions and tomatoes, and the aunts and uncles and cousins would bring cookie platters and babka. So many people that we wouldn't all fit in the dining room, so kids sat in the kitchen.

Helaine shared news that she has decided to take some classes at the community college. Maybe learn bookkeeping.

It didn't take long for Flor to bring up last night.

"Our Eleanor went on a date last night," she said, proudly. I was annoyed because I definitely didn't want to talk about it, but it also meant a lot that she ~~aknowlege~~ acknowledged it.

Helaine was sitting beside me. "That's so wonderful, Eleanor. You mentioned that you met someone. Did you enjoy yourself?"

I could feel my organs blush. How do I describe a date where we went to the movies, but I didn't see anything because we were having sex (I think).

"Yeah," was all I could say.

"You think you'll have a second?" Flor asked. For some reason, Shirley was remaining silent on the matter.

"Maybe. Yeah, I guess. I hope so. Sure." I think I was still digesting everything that happened. It was like swallowing a giant piece of cake without chewing. I love cake and I always want more of it. But if you eat it too fast, you get a stomach-ache.

"I'm so . . . I'm so proud of you, Eleanor," Shirley finally said.

"For going on a date?" I asked.

"You've just . . . grown so much in these months. I'm amazed everyday by you."

James, it was less than a year ago that Shirley tried to kill herself. Less than a year ago that my world felt like it had been pushed into one of those souvenir snow globes, turned upside down and all shook up. Nothing is the same, I'm not the same, you're not here, you were barely even in my thoughts then. Now, I think about you every day.

—

Sunday, December 26

Dear James,

I talked to Reigh today! She's staying in Minneapolis with a friend who is about to have a baby.

"Her belly is darker," she told me. "She's got this bruised color around her belly button from the stretching and I know I'll never get to push one of 'em out of me, but me oh my, what a miraculous thing to have a little human inside you."

I felt like I could hear Reigh's face stretch from her illuminating smile.

"Well, I know I never want one inside *me*. It's bad enough I bleed now," I said.

"So . . . did you go on your date with Prince?"

"Yes, yes!" I said, excited to finally be able to give away some of the details. I had spoken to Aggie on the phone earlier and I felt a little bad that I kept some of the specifics to myself. I guess I felt weird talking about sex with the one person I thought I'd have it with. Does that make any sense, James?

"Tell me everything. Of course, everything you feel comfortable with. I don't want to pry."

I spent the next twenty minutes telling Reigh everything. Those stupid Jamesway boys. Getting mad at T'nea because I didn't want to call extra attention to ourselves. And of course, the best part of all: what happened at the movie theater.

"So, needless to say, you won't be writing up a review of *The Addams Family* movie any time soon, eh?"

I laughed. "I guess not. Hey, um, Reigh, can I ask you something?"

"Of course, doll, anything."

"I'm so embarrassed to ask this but what counts as . . . sex when it's between two . . . of the same bodies?"

"A great question, because we all know our schools aren't talking about *that*, are they? From what you shared, it sounds like you popped your—pardon me, changed your status from virgin to not. If I may be a bit more clinical, some—and I include myself in this group—believe it's anytime you are penetrated."

James, I've blushed plenty in my life but what happened during this conversation was way beyond blushing. I was on fire. I was like what Smokey the Bear warned us about. My wildfire was spreading, and I could smell the melting of my skin. I was—

"You okay out there?" Reigh interrupted my panic.

"Yeah, yeah, sorry."

"Honey, it was consensual, right?"

"Yes, I mean, I definitely wasn't expecting anything like that happening. I barely thought we'd get past first base."

"Oh, first base. My favorite one."

"Really? Why?"

"Because it's the best instrument on your body—beside your brain, of course. Where your words get all noisy and beautiful is touching someone else's. I think it's the most intimate we can ever get with another. But listen, and I don't mean to get all parenty on you or anything like that, but just because you had sex doesn't mean you need to keep at it. Take your time. You get to go at any pace you want. You can slow down, you can stop, or you can keep going. But keep checking in with yourself, okay? Can you promise me that?"

"Yeah, definitely. Thanks, Reigh."

"Oh, honey, of course. How's your mama?"

"Actually a lot better. She's dating, and Flor is too. There's love all around, I guess."

"I guess," Reigh said. "Not for me yet. But . . . "

"Hey, Reigh, can I ask you one more thing?"

"There's no limit. Ask away."

"What if I'm not done? I mean, what if like there is more I am supposed to know about myself, but—"

"Of course there's more! But that's the most delicious part of it all. It will never, ever get boring."

"But like maybe I'm not supposed to be in this . . . in this body?"

"Are you asking? Because only *you* can answer that. Can I offer some aged words? Listen, these bodies we're in? They are mega mysteries. We are Nancy Drew. Or *I* am Nancy and you are one of those sweet Hardy Boys. And we need to just keep on living in order to figure out these clues we're given. And the clues? They are hidden in every breath and behind our rib cages and when we sleep and when we kiss and when we eat and when we cry. Just keep on collecting them. Put 'em in your pocket or drawer that only *you* can access and when you're ready, you'll figure it out. Not *all* of it, of course, because the mysteries keep regenerating."

"Wow," I took a deep breath. Maybe the deepest one of my entire life. "Okay. That's . . . that's a lot to take in. But yeah, you're right."

"I am?"

"Yeah," I said. "And Reigh? I'd definitely be one of the Hardy Boys."

Monday, December 27

Dear James,

Last week in group, Peter talked about intentions for the new year. Since some of us are, as he put it, "walking into a new year with one less beside us," he focused on the need to make open-ended maps. We never do stuff like this in group, but he gave all of us a piece of construction paper. Different colors were passed around—I got blue—and he asked us to draw places we'd like to venture on our map. Not ~~nessarly~~ necessarily physical places, he said, maybe just states of mind. I didn't quite understand. I was sitting between Maeve and Helaine. Maeve started just writing down emotions. Helaine kept staring at her blank piece of paper. I watched her close her eyes, and when she opened them, I watched her slowly draw a flower. The flower was really big. It took up the whole paper.

When I asked her about it after group, she said, "The flower is *me*, Eleanor. I want to be the best person I can for James. For the past few months, I've watched my petals fall. Just deaden. I need to find my way back. Grow again."

She showed me her picture. I hadn't noticed before that she had drawn circles of different sizes beside the flowers. I asked her what the circles represented.

"Each rock is James," she told me. "He is with me every day, leading me on this path."

"Helaine, that is so beautiful." I hugged her and inhaled her lavender scent.

"What does your map look like?" she asked me.

My map was full of drawers. Except I am a terrible artist, so it just looked like random rectangles. I explained to her that I am sorting through the drawers where I've been collecting things. I told her about what Reigh said to me. Maybe Helaine couldn't completely understand what I've been feeling in my body—but I don't really either—and I know the more that I talk about it, the closer I will get to figuring out my clues.

Tuesday, December 28

Dear James,

I wonder if there is a language inside me that isn't English or Spanish (which I am totally failing by the way). Something else. What if I can't translate my body's dialect and we are unable to communicate with each other? This is madness, I am sure. But it is the only way I can fully understand why everything feels off.

I woke up with my period. Blech!!! This is month two of it and yet, it still comes like a surprise that I didn't ask for or want, like a scar or mosquito bite. Shirley insists I start keeping track of it. I wasn't ready and I ruined a pair of my underpants. My vagina hurts (*"Not your vagina, Eleanor. Your uterus."*) and I cannot do anything but wish my body away. I talked to Flor about it. She told me to look at myself like a Jackson ~~Polak~~ Pollack painting. I always thought it was kind of silly that people thought he was such a genius when really, his paintings were just blobs of splattered paint. But Flor told me that it was more than that. She said that he knew where each drop of paint was going to fall and that even when he didn't, he understood why it dripped the way it did. He was a genius, she said, because he created a relationship with the paint which became an illustration of his mind, swollen on each canvas. She said that I needed to develop a relationship with my body. Understand it, I guess. I don't know. I want to be excited. But having my period just becomes another reminder that I've got mixed signals in my body.

Wrong number, I want to say. Dial again.

Wednesday, December 29

Dear James,

I feel bad because I guess I should have called T'nea after our date,
but I didn't. She called me a few times and left a message with Shirley,
but I was nervous about what I should say. Is she my girlfriend? Should
I ask her about what we did in the movie theater and what it means?
Should we pretend it didn't happen? Did I do everything right?
Ahhhhh! James, I've read so many books about boys and girls in
relationships, but where are the books which talk about *this*? I guess
Audre Lorde wrote about her girlfriends in Zami, but I wonder if
there were more books and movies about us, would we feel less alone?

Thursday, December 30

Dear James,

Maybe it's silly, but I like to make a list at the end of every year.
Resolutions, I guess.

But I like to call them my Missions.

ELEANOR'S MISSIONS FOR 1994

1. Be bolder. I'm not really sure what that means, but I've got
   365 days to figure it out!
2. Do better in math and Spanish. ~~Dara used to help me with math, but~~
3. Go to that open mic again that I went to with Reigh. Take
   Aggie. I bet she'd love it.
4. Continue writing and exploring my map
5. Try ~~capars~~ capers. Aggie told me about them and they
   sound really strange, but maybe delicious.
6. Go back to NYC. Maybe Helaine and I can go together
7. Read more books
8. Forgive ~~Shirley~~ Mom

Friday, December 31

Dear James,

I kept something from you, from these letters. Last week, I was heading to the bus after school and saw Ms. Raimondo walking toward her car. I don't think I've ever seen her out of the classroom, so at first, I just waved, and then I started to walk toward her.

"Ms. Raimondo," I said. "Can I . . . can I talk to you about something?"

"Sure, Eleanor. How's everything going? I really enjoyed your most recent essay that you turned in. You're really im—"

"Thanks, but actually it's about James."

I watched as Ms. Raimondo's face turned a different color.

"Remember how you had us start journaling after . . . after James . . . "

"Yes, of course. I was really hoping students could get in touch with how they were feeling. When you free-write, there is less internalized editing and—"

"Yeah, sorry, I don't mean to interrupt, but I've been writing to James since the beginning and I feel like maybe I want to stop, like I want to . . . I don't know, move on, but I'm afraid to stop writing his name. I don't want him to disappear."

"Oh, I . . . I didn't realize you two were so close."

"We weren't. He hated me, and I pretty much felt the same way about him. He bullied me. Actually, there was a part of me that was scared of him, but I've learned some things. I guess . . . well, the thing is I'm gay and my family is cool with it and every time I say it out loud it creates a new shape, feels more solid or something. And I guess I realize that it's not like that for everyone. We're often more scared of ourselves than of each other."

"That is extremely introspective and wise, Eleanor. I'm double your age and I still find myself walking through new doors to who I am. But you don't want all those doors to open at once, right?

They're meant to be walked through one at a time. Carefully. When you're ready."

"Ms. Raimondo, James never got to open his doors."

"No, I guess he didn't. But that should be a reminder of how important it is to give *yourself* time to do so. Is this what you wanted to talk about, dear?"

"Yeah, no. I don't know. I feel like I have so many questions and . . . "

"And eventually, the answers will come. Be patient."

James, I thought about telling her about your notebook. Actually, that is exactly what I wanted to talk to her about, but I didn't want to crack that open. Your words were for me and I have them now. Always. I don't have to write you letters just to communicate with you. I don't know what I believe in, but I want to believe that there is a part of you swirling around. Flor would say it's your energy. Yeah, I like that. So if I want to tell you something, I can just speak it out loud to you. Or think it. And maybe you're watching, watching as my map grows.

~

1994

IT IS DIFFICULT TO KNOW HOW to start a sentence sometimes. I know what constitutes (vocab word from last year) as a run-on and a fragment. I know all of that, but sometimes it is difficult to get it out. I want to feel like the words are properly saying exactly what I intend them to say. But this so rarely happens.

THE WEEKS WEAR RUNNING SHOES AS they speed past and I wonder where these months went. I am sixteen now. I have tried capers. They are actually quite delicious. In fact, Mom made them with chicken and lemons and wow, my mouth was super happy. I went on two more dates with T'nea. I told her that I wasn't quite ready to have sex again, though I definitely enjoyed first and second base. We're sorta friends now, chatting on the phone every so often. Reigh is still in Minneapolis, staying until her friend gives birth which should be sometime next month. I write Reigh letters and she always sends me one back. Helaine and Burt are officially divorced. She still comes to group every Thursday. Now, she picks me up and we drive to group together. Sometimes we meet for dinner before-hand. I give her the Eleanor report and she shares with me what she's learned in community college. Mom and Ted are still dating. Dad met him and called him a stand-up guy. I'm not really sure what that means, but they get along okay. Unfortunately, Flor and Theresa broke up. Flor was heartbroken but has since gone on a few dates. No one special yet. Greta is doing better in school. She's pur-posely not dating, she told me. But she said, "That doesn't stop me from kissing lots of boys, of course."

Suddenly it is April and Winter is behind us, though the days still confuse me on how to dress. Winter is like the uncle you have that always overstays his welcome. Comes early and leaves late. Drinks all the beer or alcohol. Eats the last slice of cake. Doesn't help to clean up. Just leaves his mess wherever he goes. I mentioned this to Aggie the other day. She just smiled at me. That Aggie-smirk-with-tightened lips.

Then, she said, "You know, Eleanor, Winter is actually my favorite season."

"Why?" I said, flabbergasted (not vocab word, but heard it on a television show the other day.)

"I don't know. It's cold and icy, but the white is so beautiful. It's like this magical bleached shell covering the world. Or New Jersey. Or the east coast. Or wherever it hits." She laughed, and her shoulders shook a little.

"I definitely don't mind the layering, but I just hate always shivering and being so cold," I said. "I love to be outside and climb trees."

Even though it's April and springtime, we are still many weeks away from short sleeves and the comfortable settling in of heat and sun. So I still have my layers, though there are moments I can walk without a jacket; these are the moments I savor.

On Tuesday, the fifth day of April, it happened again. I heard whispers in the hallway that Kurt Cobain had committed suicide.

"Yo, he was the only one making music actually not suck!"

"They have to be wrong. It can't be him."

"He did always seem depressed."

"It's totally because of Courtney."

"I think it's a hoax."

Everyone was talking about it, far more than when James died. Maybe it's easier to openly talk about someone who didn't exist in these hallways, who just lived inside of radios and illustrated our walls. Maybe it's easier to mourn strangers than one of us.

In the days which followed, the school was a sea of flannel. Forget ribbons and grief counselors. It seemed everyone had taken on the grunge garb of Kurt. People were sharing lyrics of their favorite songs, humming them between classes and making trips to the local music stores to pick up any albums, cassette singles, and Nirvana paraphernalia they could find.

I had a few flannels in my closet, but I couldn't convince myself to wear them. Aggie was distraught. Nirvana wasn't her favorite band, but she said Kurt was a true poet who never got his due. So, we wore black and we wrote our favorite lines on each other's' notebooks. She told me that Kurt was too much for this world.

"But isn't *he* the one who chose to be famous?" I asked.

"He didn't choose fame, Eleanor. It flooded him. He just wanted to make music. And share it with people. I don't think he ever really liked what came with being famous."

Of course, it was impossible not to think of James. He wrote about Kurt all over his notebook. How would James have responded? Would this have been James's trampoline moment? To remind him how fleeting life can be? I guess I'll never know.

There was a letter James wrote to me in his notebook. He had written it after listening to the Bleach album on repeat. I think he said he stopped at five times, only because his dad had come home, and he hated any kind of rock music. James wrote about the drums digging into his eardrums as he listened to "Negative Creep." And this was before Dave Grohl joined. He said Kurt's constant repetition created something new each time. He said that each time he sang, "I am a negative creep," it was like it grew wings. It became a different animal, he said.

"People are creating vigils all over the country for Kurt," Aggie said. "Want to do something? He's played here before. I mean, not *here*, but Asbury Park for sure."

"Stone Pony, right?"

"Yeah. I mean, we don't have to go there. We can just do something to honor him. Like read a bunch of his lyrics somewhere. I wish we could just get on the loud speaker and repeat his words so everyone in school could hear them."

"Why do you . . . why do you think he did it?" I asked.

Aggie looked at me and crinkled her forehead like the most delicious potato chip.

"I don't know, El. I mean, I think that sometimes it just gets to be too much."

"What, though? What is too much?"

"*This*." She pointed in all directions. "This air, this school, this state, this country. These laws and these rules. This government. This—"

"Life," I interrupted.

"Yeah, this life," she repeated.

OVER THE WEEKEND, I WENT TO Westfield to stay at my Dad's. When we're together, there's always a lot of cooking and eating involved. Usually, we try to choose new recipes to try out or even make up.

"Do you want more?" Dad asked, taunting me with a bowl full of his delicious homemade fried rice. "And there's still some chow mein left in the wok. Did you eat enough?"

I patted my belly. "Yeah, I'm full. I think I ate too fast probably."

"Well, you know it's just as good the next day, so . . . "

"Hey, Dad, can I ask you something?"

"Of course, sweetheart."

"Do you ever wonder why more of us don't do it?"

"Do it?"

"Yeah, umm . . . commit suicide. Sorry, I know this is really dark for after-dinner talk, but it's on my mind and I can just leave it there or—"

"Eleanor, it's fine. We can talk about this. Did someone else . . . "

"Kurt," I said.

"Kurt? Is that another person in your school?"

"*Cobain*, Dad. From Nirvana! Didn't you know he killed himself?"

"I didn't. You liked him?

"Yeah, I mean, Nirvana was awesome and James really liked them. Aggie too. She's been pretty sad about it."

"Well, to answer your question, I think more people don't *do it* because of the impact. It's more than just ending things. There's a lot that one leaves behind. And thinking about that . . . about abandoning family members and loved ones, that is often what keeps people here. And," Dad paused, "hoping it will improve."

"But does it? I mean, all these things that overwhelm us, they may go away, but then they get replaced by other things. Bigger things."

"Quite possibly they do. But Eleanor, as you get older, you learn ways to get through them."

"Then what about Mom?"

"Sometimes people forget. Going into the hospital, getting on medication and having time to work on remembering can help."

"I wish James had asked for help. I wish he had waited. He never got to be himself." I felt the heft of my tears push through my eyes and fall down my cheeks in a slow-motion spectacle.

"Eleanor . . . "

"I don't want to put myself on hold," I blurted. "I'm sixteen now. And I know there are things that I'm not saying. That I'm feeling but—"

"Are you having thoughts of suicide, Eleanor?"

"No, no. Not like that at all. If anything, I want to live even louder because I know I haven't been doing it right."

"What do you mean?"

"Like . . . umm . . . I haven't been *feeling* right. Ever since I . . . came out, you know? It got louder."

"What did?"

"I guess I thought it would pass. But actually, it was the finger—"

"The finger?"

"I never told you guys, but a bunch of years ago, I was at the beach with Mom and I found a . . . finger. Actually, it probably sounds grosser than it actually was. I mean, I wasn't scared or anything. Though I'm not sure why. But it did make me . . . well, maybe not then, but now . . . makes me wonder if maybe *I* lost something? Like you guys didn't want to tell me because you didn't want me to worry? Or, I don't know—"

Dad grabbed one of my hands and touched my fingers. "Yup, five. And . . . I see five on your right."

"Not a finger, Dad. Uh, this isn't . . . this isn't coming out right. Just forget it."

"Eleanor, I'm sorry. I'm trying to understand."

"No, no, it's okay. You know what? I'm . . . I'm gonna grab some more food from the kitchen. Do you want?"

Dad shook his head, and then said, "Well, if *you're* having . . . "

AGGIE CAME HOME AFTER SCHOOL WITH me on Monday and shared an idea she had about honoring Kurt.

"I thought about gathering a whole bunch of flannel shirts, cutting them up, and making a quilt. Just like the AIDS quilt. Everyone can take a square and sew in a memory of Kurt."

"But none of us even knew him. How well do we know anyone?"

"Hey, what's going on with you?"

Aggie put down her notebook, which was apparently full of notes about ways in which to memorialize Kurt, and put her hands on my knees. We were sitting on my bed. I hadn't mentioned my complete failure to utter the right words to Dad this weekend.

"I'm restless. Then I feel guilt about being restless. *Then* I feel guilt about *feeling* guilty."

"How was your dad's house?"

"Always good, you know? But I was trying to tell him about something that's been on my mind. And I couldn't even get it out."

"That doesn't mean you never will."

"Yeah, but . . . I don't know. It's like having to sneeze but it won't come out. You do everything to push it. Gulp a giant fistful of air and swallow it. Anything to not feel that lump of sneeze in my throat."

"I know that feeling. Have you tried writing it down? Remember you said you always felt better after writing to James."

"I've . . . I don't know I could try, I guess. Also, I got my love letter back."

"From *who*? T'nea?"

"What? No. The ones we wrote in Ms. Raimondo's class. At the beginning. Don't you remember?"

"Oh wow, I forgot! What was it like to get it back?"

"Weird. I forgot I even wrote any of it. I guess you haven't gotten yours yet?"

"No, but now I'm excited to."

I told Aggie that I needed to be free for an afternoon. Lose myself in something else. I made the suggestion to go to the open mic on Friday, the one I went to with Reigh.

"And we can check out some of the thrift stores on Main Street," I added. "I haven't been in a while and I bet we can find some old flannels."

"El, I love that idea! I've been wanting to check out that open mic since you mentioned it. Have you been since?"

"Actually, no. But it would be really nice to go back."

On Friday after school, Shirley dropped us off on Main Street in Freehold. The Been to Bean Café open mic was at 7 pm, so we had plenty of time to shop and then grab some food beforehand.

I had no idea what we were going to do with the quilt once it was done or even how we were going to piece everything together because I'm not very good at sewing, but I left these questions behind and hunted the racks.

"I love this one!" Aggie held up a red, yellow and black flannel that looked as if it had been worn up to its expiration date and perhaps several months past that.

"Cool," I said, trying to be encouraging. "I found these too." I showed her the two I picked up which were slung over my shoulder, leaving the hangers behind.

We paid for the shirts and walked outside with our bag full of Kurt. Aggie and I walked arm-in-arm to the next spot as we hunted for more flannels.

After two more thrift stores and a few more purchases, we headed into a burger joint. I ordered a hamburger and she ordered a veggie burger. We decided to share a basket of fries.

After the waiter brought our order, I eyed her plate. "Do you want your pickle?" I asked, knowing that she loves pickles but not as much as I do.

"Yes . . . but . . . how about I give you half. Hey, listen, it means a lot to me that you want to help out with the Kurt quilt. Maybe it's silly and maybe no one will ever see it but us, but I'm glad we are doing it together."

"People will see it!" I said. "I mean, you saw how everyone was at school. They were more bummed than when James . . . " My voice trailed off and I wanted to run along with it. Even though I stopped writing him letters, he has not left my thoughts even once.

"El, it's different. No one knew Kurt—"

"No one knew James."

"No, I mean, no one knew Kurt so it's easier to show sadness."

"Aggie . . . he was writing to me."

"What do you mean?"

"In his notebook. Helaine—his mom—let me have it. Once we met in group, she realized that I was the Eleanor in his letters."

"Wow. Why do you think he wrote to you? You said the only time he ever talked to you was to be mean and bully you."

"Yeah, I don't know. Actually, I *do* know. He felt like I might understand some of the things he needed to say. Ms. Raimondo was right. Writing to someone else, even if you don't give them your words, releases it. Makes space for more thoughts, makes space to understand things."

"What did he say?"

"All sorts of things." I didn't feel right telling James's secrets. They were his to tell. "But what I started to realize was he had so much inside him. He loved Nirvana. He loved music. He wanted to be an astronaut one day. He had emotions and felt pain, but also love. The hardest part about reading his notebook was recognizing that he'd never get to show these parts of himself to anyone. We all missed out."

"It's so much easier on paper, I guess. I used to . . . " Aggie stopped and put down her burger. "I used to write letters to my mom after she died. More like Dear Mom instead of Dear Diary. I never reread them, but they were basically telling her about my day. Who annoyed me or what book I was reading. Probably really stupid stuff that I wouldn't have told her if she were alive, but . . . yeah, it always felt better. Like she was still there."

Aggie took a deep breath and then put the other half of her pickle on my plate and smiled. I put it in my mouth and let the sour sting my tongue.

WHEN MOM WENT TO THE HOSPITAL the first time, she told me that she stopped feeling things and tasting things. Maybe this is why she stopped eating much. Or doing things. All the pleasure had been sucked out. Even with all this sadness wrapped around me, I *want* to feel. I want to taste. I want to be able to enjoy things.

Last year, when she tried again, it was hard in a different way. I knew what was happening. I understood, yet I didn't. I was angrier. Because now we're older—Gret and I—and her trying to kill herself is like her saying, *I don't want to be around you anymore. I don't want to be your mother.*

I'm sure everyone has wished they were dead if even for a moment. But I don't. I don't want to be dead. I'm too hopeful for the something else that exists out there for me. There's more for me to explore. There's so much for me to know. James lost out on his chances for that. We lost out on seeing him do more. I can't let that happen for me.

"Think our waitress would give us more pickles?" I asked.

"I don't know. But let's ask."

WITH OUR BELLIES FULL ON BURGERS and fried potatoes, we headed to Been to Bean Café where I first went with Reigh. Where I met T'nea. Where I had my very first kiss. On the short walk there, Aggie told me a story about how her mom had fallen down a flight of stairs one day, while carrying laundry in her arms. No one else was home, so she just remained at the bottom of the stairs, in agony. Aggie was the first to get home. It was after school, so it had been several hours that her mom had just remained on the floor. By that time, her mom had fallen asleep and when Aggie walked through the door, she thought her mom had died. She screamed, which woke her mom and Aggie just laughed. She laughed out of confusion and discomfort and relief. Her mom explained what happened and Aggie carefully helped her up to the couch. After a few hours, her mom asked why Aggie screamed, but she was too afraid to say why. She didn't want to say it out loud. Then, just a few months later, her mom was diagnosed with cancer.

"It all happened very quickly," she said. "When my mom fell, I remember feeling such relief that it was just a stupid fall. Clumsiness runs in our family, you know. But then . . . when it was real, I feared that moment would happen again. That I'd find her. But my scream wouldn't wake her and . . . .El, I'm sorry. I didn't mean . . . I didn't expect to be so . . . "

"I wish I could have met her. I'm sure she was just as beautiful as you."

Aggie turned toward me and touched my hair, which was growing out and curling a little. I've been so caught up in everything happening at school, that I haven't even thought about cutting it.

"*You're* really beautiful, you know that?"

"Thank you. But I'm not really looking to be . . . "

"And just . . . really amazing," Aggie added.

"Well, I really don't know about all that, but . . . hey, let's go inside. It looks busy; I want to make sure we get a seat."

I held the door open for Aggie and then, we walked arm-in-arm, searching for a spot to sit, taking in the large crowd, which had already gathered. The microphone was set up on the stage with the list on a clipboard beside it on a small table. I pointed at a small table by the window and felt a tap on my back. When I turned around, I saw T'nea.

"Hey, you," she said.

"T'nea, hi!" I said, completely caught off guard. We hadn't seen each other since our third date, which was our last date, which was sometime in January.

"And who is *this*?" she said, referring to Aggie.

"Oh, this is just my friend, Aggie." *Just my friend?*

T'nea laughed and put her arms around me. "I thought she was your date or something."

"Hi," Aggie said to T'nea.

"Hey. I'm T'nea. Cool to meet ya."

"Want to sit with us?" Aggie graciously asked.

"I came with a bunch of my friends, but . . . " She turned toward me and whispered in my ear, "Kiss me like the first time by the bathrooms. Looks like there's a line."

I felt my entire body turn red like an over-boiled lobster. "Uh, I . . . I don't want to be rude and leave Aggie a—"

"El, go right ahead. I'll grab us some drinks. London fogs. I don't mind." She winked at me.

As we walked to the bathroom, T'nea said, "I've missed you. I know you said you weren't looking for anything serious or anything,

I'm not either. But you're totally the coolest person I've ever met. Definitely unique."

I blushed. "Thank you. I like you too, T'nea. I've just . . . I've never done this before. And I'm really just trying to figure out . . . who I am."

"Who you are? Shit, Eler, you're fifteen."

"Sixteen now," I corrected her.

"Anyway, you don't figure it out until you're old, like at least thirty. Now is the time to just be crazy and kiss lots of people and you know, be impulsive."

"Yeah, maybe. I really just . . . I'm unsure of so much these days."

"Ugh. I always pick the complicated ones," T'nea said. She put her long, painted fingernails into my short hair and twirled the little length I had. "Can I still kiss you? I've been daydreaming about your mouth for months."

I smiled, grateful that she didn't press me to explain any further. Grateful that she still wanted to kiss me.

"Definitely," I said, leaning into her, feeling the warmth stored up in her mouth meet mine.

T'nea and I went back to our separate tables, winking, sending flirty glances toward each other. I sipped my London fog and reveled in the excitement in Aggie's face.

"I signed up!" Aggie said.

"Great! What number are you on the list?"

"One."

"Yikes," I said. "Boldly bold. Hey, thanks for getting the teas."

"Thanks for bringing us here. And you were right about T'nea. She is gorgeous."

"Yeah, and a really good kisser," I softly added.

"Eleanor!" Aggie laughed. "That must be the host."

We both noticed a tall redhead walk on stage. I recognized him from last time. His face, sprinkled with tiny hairs, like a beard made of furry freckles. I liked how weird and slightly uncomfortable he seemed on stage, but also really funny. Last time, he started with a poem about being lactose intolerant. I remember Reigh and I cracking up from it.

"Yeah, he's really funny."

"I wish I could have curly hair like that," Aggie said.

"We all want what we don't have, and don't want what we *do* have," I said.

Aggie smiled lightly. She lifted her hands in the air and shook them. "I'm so nervous!"

"You'll be great. Oh, hey, what are you reading?"

"Well, I have my notebook in my bag. I wrote something the other day about Kurt. I guess it could be a poem. I don't know. But I thought I could read that."

"Cool. I'm really excited to hear it."

"Welcome, welcome, all you poets," the host spoke. "All you music makers. All you comedians. All you like-minded creative combustors. Welcome to our weekly open mic. Thanks to Been to Bean Café for housing us each week. I'm Isaac. I'm your host with the most. We got a packed list tonight, so do your best to keep it to under five minutes, if you can, please. Buy drinks. Eat up. All that jazz."

Aggie and I looked at each other and smiled.

"Got an allergy haiku to start us off. Here goes. How'd those bumps get here? Seem to be allergic to everything these days."

Everyone clapped. Aggie grabbed my knee with her hand and squeezed. I looked at her, trying my best to say swarms of good luck words with just my eyes.

"Alright, alright. Please welcome to the stage . . . .Aggie!"

Aggie slowly pushed her chair out, clutching her notebook against her small hips, and walked toward the stage. The sound of hands smacking together filled the room. I hollered my best *wooo* and as she adjusted the microphone, everyone's clapping ceased as we waited for her to speak.

"Dear Kurt," Aggie paused. "What does it feel like to be gone but still able to speak? Even in your death, you make music. We rip up old flannels to remember you, but all we really need to do is press play. Sew thread into each square and knit them together as you scream 'Pennyroyal Tea.' Watch as shirts turn into a blanket to remind us how to stay warm as you call out 'Lithium' and *you* came as *you* are. There is no such thing as a separation of deaths. I believe we all head into the same place, floating and filling up the air with our memories. Say hello to my mother, please. Tell James he had more friends than he ever knew. I'll keep playing your music to keep you down here as you sing along above me."

As Aggie spoke her last word, I felt something on my skin. A tear. It just fell out, effortlessly and without sound. I wiped it as I clapped for her. Mesmerized and blown away.

Isaac, the host, came back on stage and introduced the next person. But I couldn't hear anything but Aggie's words still hovering. I didn't want to hear anything else.

"Let's go," I said to her in the loudest of whispers.

"Huh? It just started. Did I do something wrong?"

"No, no. The opposite. I don't . . . I don't want to hear anyone else. I just want your words to sit in me. I can't believe . . . I can't believe you wrote that."

"It's just notes, really, but . . . thanks, Eleanor. I'm so glad you liked them."

"After this person is done, we can slip out while everyone is clapping."

"Oh," Aggie said, disappointedly. "I really wanted to stay, though."

"I'm sorry, it's just that . . . you made me cry, Aggie. I'm not saying that to make you . . . I think I need to talk right now instead of listen. But if you really want to stay, I can just meet you—"

"Sshhh . . . " Aggie put her fingers on my lips. "After this person, okay?"

I WROTE A TINY NOTE AS the person on stage read a short story about being on a greyhound bus that broke down. On our way out, I handed it to T'nea.

Dear T'nea,
Feeling sad, but seeing you brightened my sight. Have to go, but I will
call you soon. Really. I promise.

Love, Eler

Aggie and I held hands as we walked outside. The early spring air
felt so cool on my skin. Tiny bumps of shiver raised the flesh on my
arms. I felt them beneath my shirt.

"You really think they're just floating?" I asked, still thinking
about Aggie's beautiful letter to Kurt.

"I mean, I *want* to believe that. I don't want to believe that people
get punished even in death. There's got to be a time when we finally
just get to rest, you know?"

"Yeah."

"I know that some people think that people who commit suicide
go directly to hell. But for so many of them—"

"Hell is being alive," I interrupted.

"Yeah. Death is death. And it's no less tragic or forgiving whether
it's by disease or self-inflicted."

"Oh, Aggie . . . "

She squeezed my hand; I squeezed back.

"T'nea said I'm too young to be thinking so much about who I
am. And maybe she's right. Maybe I need to just forget about what's
been haunting my mind."

Aggie turned toward me. "What haunts you, Eleanor?

"My insides."

"What does it feel like?"

"Like . . . I think about something Reigh said to me. She was talking
about her gender. And you know, there is no age to it. I mean, she said
that she knew even when she was little. But it's like . . . we're given these
things to wear and toys to play with. And sometimes it's just easier to go
with the flow. She was putting on her mom's dresses and trying on her
make-up, having all these intense feelings just by putting them on.
Knowing. It's so weird. I feel like I'm not using the right words."

"I'm listening, El. I'll keep listening until they feel . . . until they feel like the right ones."

"Why are you so amazing?"

"Because *you* are. And because I get it. I get feeling like something is wrong and the desire to fix it."

"I'm not sure what to call this . . . this *feeling*. But yeah, it's more than liking girls. It's more than just being gay. I'm . . . " And here is where I paused. Because even in the dark of evening, I noticed what looked exactly like that finger just lying on the sidewalk beside a blue post box. The streetlight illuminated it like a theatrical spotlight, darkening everything else around it.

I felt my words—the ones I let go of and the ones still struggling to be spoken—float above me, as I bent down to see it up close. Aggie stood beside me in silence as I dropped my fingers to the ground to touched it. It was cold or *I* was cold and suddenly I couldn't tell if *I* was touching *it* or *it* was touching me. When I tried picking it up, it just broke away, as though it were made of ash or smoke or my imagination.

"Weird," I said out loud.

"You okay? What was that?"

"It's just . . . I thought it was . . . I thought maybe I dropped something," I said.

"Oh."

"I lost something awhile back . . . I mean, I found something a bunch of years ago and this looked just like . . . it."

Maybe there was no finger. Maybe I never lost anything, and I've just been carrying this *something* around with me. Not lost, just waiting to be discovered. Not lost, just waiting to be named.

⌣

Dear Eleanor,

This could be the year you have waited your whole life for. Maybe you will get all As. Or maybe you will make a new friend or travel to a new place or learn to play an instrument. Who knows? I'm not like Greta, who can stare into the mirror for hours and probably has all sorts of nice things to say about herself. I've never written a love letter and couldn't ever imagine writing one to myself. Do I give myself a compliment? I like my eyes and the way they turn green sometimes. I think I'm nice. I can be smart sometimes. I definitely have a lot of questions about myself.

Anyway, I love you I guess.

Love,
Eleanor

My Book List for James (and some poems too).
Oh, and it's alphabetized because Ms. Raimondo loves that sort of thing.

Baldwin, James: *Giovanni's Room,* "Sonny's Blues," *The Giver*

Barnes, Djuna: "From Third Avenue On"

Blume, Judy: *Are you There, God? It's Me, Margaret, Forever*

Brown, Rita Mae: *Rubyfruit Jungle*

Guy, Rosa: *Ruby*

Kerr, M.E.: *Deliver Us from Evie*

Lorde, Audre: "Movement Song," *Sister Outsider, Zami: A New Spelling of My Name*

Moraga, Cherríe and Gloria Anzaldua: *This Bridge Called My Back: Writings by Radical Women of Color*

Rich, Adrienne: "Dreamwood"

Salinger, J.D.: *The Catcher in the Rye*

White, Edmund: *A Boy's Own Story, The Beautiful Room is Empty*

Whitman, Walt: *Leaves of Grass*

By ~~Eleanor~~ Eler Fromme

acknowledgements

WHEN DOES A STORY BEGIN? PERHAPS all along, we carry these humans, these heartaches, these love stories beneath our skin, cradling our bones. They grow as we grow. Maybe Eleanor was somehow what (barely) got me through high school. Maybe Eleanor is what kept me alive through my own suicide attempts. Maybe Eleanor helped project my voice as I came out as lesbian to my family at nineteen, and then as queer later on.

These stories are never singular. I wrote this through state lines and relationships and break up and between college classes and when I thought I had nothing left to say but somehow found the sounds for.

Thank you to early readers such as Tina Barry, Jessica Hagedorn, Brett Burns, Nicole Smith, and Meagan Brothers. Thank you to Constance Renfrow—an incredible editor who patiently guided me toward this final draft. To my dad who churns out his own novels like breaths. You have traveled hours just to hear me read two poems. To Rebecca Diaz who is a salve to my heart. All these years, you teach me the magnificent richness of friendship. To Daniel Dissinger, my accountability partner and true mentor. To Art Farm's writing residency in Marquette, Nebraska where much of this story was written. More specifically:

Raluca Albu, Lindsay Peyton, Selina Josephs, Laura Rubeck, Ed Dadey, and that family of raccoons. To Max Wolf Valerio: When I first read *The Testosterone Files*, I felt like cupboards in my body opened up. And now, I get to call you friend. Thank you for your openness and wisdom.

To the writers I have never met (beyond the page), yet fuel my own imagination: Audre Lorde, Richard Brautigan, Kathy Acker, Sylvia Plath, Sandra Cisneros, and Joy Harjo.

To The Trevor Project, an incredible suicide prevention resource for LGBTQ youth. Reach out reach out reach out.

Thank you to my ukulele, which has brought music into my life, and helped me to find a little more of my voice. And to my music partner, David Lawton. Hydrogen Junkbox has become my oxygen.

For the ones who could not make it but tried.

For Trae, my pen pal. You me every day how to be a warrior in mind, body, and spirit.

about the author

AIMEE HERMAN IS A TWO-TIME PUSHCART Prize-nominated novelist, poet, and performance artist based in Brooklyn, looking to disembowel the architecture of gender and what it means to queer the body. Aimee is the author of two poetry collections, *to go without blinking* (BlazeVOX books) and *meant to wake up feeling* (great weather for MEDIA). Her work has been widely published in the U.S. and internationally in literary journals including *Lavender Review, EDUCE, Sous Les Pave,* and the Lambda Award-winning anthology *Troubling the Line: Trans and Genderqueer Poetry and Poetics* (Nightboat Books). Aimee currently teaches at Bronx Community College. She sings and plays ukelele in the poetryband Hydrogen Junkbox.

RECENT AND FORTHCOMING BOOKS FROM THREE ROOMS PRESS

FICTION

Meagan Brothers
Weird Girl and What's His Name

Ron Dakron
Hello Devilfish!

Michael T. Fournier
Hidden Wheel
Swing State

William Least Heat-Moon
Celestial Mechanics

Aimee Herman
Everything Grows

Eamon Loingsigh
Light of the Diddicoy
Exile on Bridge Street

John Marshall
The Greenfather

Aram Saroyan
Still Night in L.A.

Richard Vetere
The Writers Afterlife
Champagne and Cocaine

Julia Watts
Quiver

MEMOIR & BIOGRAPHY

Nassrine Azimi and
Michel Wasserman
Last Boat to Yokohama:
The Life and Legacy of
Beate Sirota Gordon

William S. Burroughs & Allen Ginsberg
Don't Hide the Madness:
William S. Burroughs in Conversation
with Allen Ginsberg
edited by Steven Taylor

James Carr
BAD: The Autobiography of
James Carr

Richard Katrovas
Raising Girls in Bohemia:
Meditations of an American Father; A
Memoir in Essays

Judith Malina
Full Moon Stages:
Personal Notes from
50 Years of The Living Theatre

Phil Marcade
Punk Avenue:
Inside the New York City
Underground, 1972-1982

Stephen Spotte
My Watery Self:
Memoirs of a Marine Scientist

PHOTOGRAPHY-MEMOIR

Mike Watt
On & Off Bass

SHORT STORY ANTHOLOGIES

SINGLE AUTHOR

The Alien Archives: Stories
by Robert Silverberg

First-Person Singularities: Stories
by Robert Silverberg
with an introduction by John Scalzi

Tales from the Eternal Café: Stories
by Janet Hamill, with an introduction
by Patti Smith

Time and Time Again:
Sixteen Trips in Time
by Robert Silverberg

MULTI-AUTHOR

Crime + Music: Twenty Stories
of Music-Themed Noir
edited by Jim Fusilli

Dark City Lights: New York Stories
edited by Lawrence Block

Florida Happens:
Bouchercon 2018 Anthology
edited by Greg Herren

Have a NYC I, II & III:
New York Short Stories;
edited by Peter Carlaftes
& Kat Georges

Songs of My Selfie:
An Anthology of Millennial Stories
edited by Constance Renfrow

The Obama Inheritance:
15 Stories of Conspiracy Noir
edited by Gary Phillips

This Way to the End Times:
Classic and New Stories of
the Apocalypse
edited by Robert Silverberg

MIXED MEDIA

John S. Paul
Sign Language: A Painter's Notebook
(photography, poetry and prose)

FILM & PLAYS

Israel Horovitz
My Old Lady: Complete Stage Play
and Screenplay with an Essay on
Adaptation

Peter Carlaftes
Triumph For Rent (3 Plays)
Teatrophy (3 More Plays)

Kat Georges
Three Somebodies: Plays about
Notorious Dissidents

DADA

Maintenant: A Journal of
Contemporary Dada Writing & Art
(Annual, since 2008)

HUMOR

Peter Carlaftes
A Year on Facebook

TRANSLATIONS

Thomas Bernhard
On Earth and in Hell
(poems of Thomas Bernhard
with English translations by
Peter Waugh)

Patrizia Gattaceca
Isula d'Anima / Soul Island
(poems by the author
in Corsican with English
translations)

César Vallejo | Gerard Malanga
Malanga Chasing Vallejo
(selected poems of César Vallejo
with English translations
and additional notes by
Gerard Malanga)

George Wallace
EOS: Abductor of Men
(selected poems in Greek & English)

POETRY COLLECTIONS

Hala Alyan
Atrium

Peter Carlaftes
DrunkYard Dog
I Fold with the Hand I Was Dealt

Thomas Fucaloro
It Starts from the Belly and Blooms

Inheriting Craziness is Like
a Soft Halo of Light

Kat Georges
Our Lady of the Hunger

Robert Gibbons
Close to the Tree

Israel Horovitz
Heaven and Other Poems

David Lawton
Sharp Blue Stream

Jane LeCroy
Signature Play

Philip Meersman
This is Belgian Chocolate

Jane Ormerod
Recreational Vehicles on Fire
Welcome to the Museum of Cattle

Lisa Panepinto
On This Borrowed Bike

George Wallace
Poppin' Johnny

Three Rooms Press | New York, NY | Current Catalog: www.threeroomspress.com
Three Rooms Press books are distributed by PGW/Ingram: www.pgw.com